Shoz-Dijiji, the Black Bear . . .

a white man who believed himself to be a full-blooded Apache, and who had dedicated his life to a feud against the treacherous "white-eyes" who had invaded his country and destroyed his family. . .

To the Pony Soldiers and to white travellers he became known as the Apache Devil, a pitiless scourge who swept in, killed, took his vengeance, and slipped away without a trace. Thus Shoz-Dijiji, the adopted son of Geronimo, was honored in his tribe.

And even among his sworn ⸻ ⸻mies there were those who ⸻⸻ ⸻⸻ ⸻⸻ ⸻ riend. One of these ⸻⸻ ⸻⸻ ⸻⸻ who loved Shoz-Diji⸻ ⸻⸻ ⸻ ⸻ ⸻⸻ mpossible obstacle ⸻ ⸻⸻ ⸻⸻ ⸻ Apache warrior.

So Shoz⸻ ⸻⸻ ⸻ontinued to live his life of hate and loyalty and love, of running fights, of massacre and torture; until at last even the tribe of Geronimo signed a peace treaty with the white men—and Shoz-Dijiji learned that the woman he loved had been stolen by renegade white outlaws. Then Shoz-Dijiji hunted as he had never hunted before.

Apache Devil

EDGAR RICE BURROUGHS

BALLANTINE BOOKS   NEW YORK

Contents

Chapter One

GERONIMO GOES OUT

THE silver light of Klego-na-ay, the full moon, shone down from out the starlit heavens of an Arizona night upon the camp of the Be-don-ko-he Apaches; shone upon sleek copper shoulders; shone upon high cheek bones; softened the cruel lines of swart, savage faces—faces as inscrutable as is the face of Klego-na-ay herself.

Shone the silver moonlight upon Nan-ta-do-tash, the izzenantan of his people, as he led them in the dance, as he prayed for rain to save their parched crops. As he danced, Nan-ta-do-tash twirled his tzi-ditinidi about his head, twirled it rapidly from front to rear, producing the sound of a gust of rain-laden wind; and the warriors and the women, dancing with Nan-ta-do-tash, listened to the tzi-ditinidi, saw the medicine man cast hoddentin to the four winds, and knew that these things would compel the wind and the rain to come to the aid of their crops.

A little to one side, watching the dancers, sat Shoz-Dijiji, the Black Bear, with Gian-nah-tah, friend of boyhood days, companion of the war trail and the raid. Little more than a youth was Shoz-Dijiji, yet already a war chief of the Be-don-ko-he, proven in many battles with the soldiers of the pindah-lickoyee; terror of many a scattered hacienda of Sonora and Chihuahua—the dread Apache Devil.

The old men beat upon the es-a-da-ded, the primitive drum of buckskin stretched across a hoop; and to their cadence Nan-ta-do-tash led the dancers, his naked body painted a greenish brown with a yellow snake upon each arm; upon his breast, in yellow, a bear; and upon his back the zig-zag lines of lightning.

His sacred izze-kloth, passing across his right shoulder, fell over his left hip. Of a potency almost equal to this four strand medicine cord of twisted antelope skin was the buck-

7

skin medicine hat of Nan-ta-do-tash by means of which he was able to peer into the future, to foresee the approach of an enemy, cure the sick, or tell who had stolen ponies from other people.

The downy feathers and black-tipped plumes of the eagle added to the efficacy and decoration of this potent headdress, the value of which was further enhanced by pieces of abalone shell, by duklij, and a snake's rattle which surmounted the apex, while in brownish yellow and dirty blue there were depicted upon the body of the hat clouds, a rainbow, hail, the morning star, the God of Wind, with his lungs, the black Kan, and the great suns.

"You do not dance with the warriors and the women, Shoz-Dijiji," said Gian-nah-tah. "Why is it?"

"Why should I?" demanded the Black Bear. "Usen has forsaken the Shis-Inday. No longer does He hear the prayers of His people. He has gone over to the side of the pindah-lickoyee, who have more warriors and better weapons.

"Many times went Shoz-Dijiji to the high places and made big medicine and prayed to Usen; but He let Juh steal my little Ish-kay-nay, and He let the bullet of the pindah-lickoyee slay her. Why should I dance to the Kans if they are blind and deaf?"

"But did not Usen help you to find Juh and slay him?" urged Gian-nah-tah.

"Usen!" The tone of the Black Bear was contemptuous. "No one helped Shoz-Dijiji find Juh. No one helped Shoz-Dijiji slay him. Alone he found Juh—alone, with his own hands, he killed him. It was Shoz-Dijiji, not Usen, who avenged Ish-kay-nay."

"But Usen healed the wound of your sorrow," persisted Gian-nah-tah. "He placed in your heart a new love to take the place of the old that was become but a sad memory."

"If Usen did that it was but to add to the sorrows of Shoz-Dijiji," said the Black Bear. "I have not told you, Gian-nah-tah."

"You have not spoken of the white girl since you took her from our camp to her home after you had saved her from Tats-ah-das-ay-go and the other Chi-e-a-hen," replied Gian-nah-tah;

"but while she was with us I saw the look in your eyes, Shoz-Dijiji, and it told me what your lips did not tell me."

"Then my eyes must have known what my heart did not know," said Shoz-Dijiji. "It would have been better had my heart not learned, but it did.

"Long time have we been friends, Gian-nah-tah. Our tsochs, swinging from the branches of the trees, swayed to the same breezes, or, bound to the backs of our mothers, we followed the same trails across deserts and mountains; together we learned to use the bow and the arrow and the lance; and together we went upon the war trail the first time. To me you are as a brother. You will not laugh at me, Gian-nah-tah; and so I shall tell you what happened that time that I took the white-eyed girl, Wichita, back to the hogan of her father that you may know why I am unhappy and why I know that Usen no longer cares what becomes of me."

"Gian-nah-tah does not laugh at the sorrow of his best friend," said the other.

"It was not in my heart to love the white-eyed girl," continued the Black Bear. "To Shoz-Dijiji she was as a sister. She was kind to me. When the soldiers of the pindah-lickoyee were all about, she brought me food and water and gave me a horse to carry me back to my people. I knew that she did that because I had once saved her from a white-eyed man who would have harmed her. No thought of love was in my mind. How could it have been? How could I think that Shoz-Dijiji, an Apache, a war chief of the Be-don-ko-he, could love a girl of the pindah-lickoyee!

"But Usen deserted me. He let me look upon the face of the white-eyed girl for many days, and every day He made her more beautiful in my eyes. I tried not to think of love. I put it from my mind. I turned my thoughts to other things, but I could not keep my eyes from the face of the pindah-lickoyee girl.

"At last we came close to the hogan of her father; and there I stopped and told her to go on, but she wanted me to come with her that her father might thank me. I would not go. I dared not go. I, The Apache Devil, was afraid of this white-eyed daughter of the pindah-lickoyee!

"She came close to me and urged me. She laid her two

hands upon my breast. The touch of those soft, white hands, Gian-nah-tah, was more powerful than the will of Shoz-Dijiji; beneath it crumbled all the pride and hate that are of the heritage of the Apaches. A flame burst forth within me—the signal fire of love.

"I seized her and pressed her close; I put my mouth upon her mouth. And then she struck at me and tried to push me away, and I saw fear in her eyes; and something more terrible than fear—loathing—as though I were unclean.

"Then I let her go; and I came away, but I left my heart and happiness behind. Shoz-Dijiji has left to him only his pride and his hate—his hate of the pindah-lickoyee."

"If you hate the white-eyed girl now, it is well," said Gian-nah-tah. "The pindah-lickoyee are low born and fools. They are not fit for an Apache!"

"I do not hate the white-eyed girl, Wichita," said Shoz-Dijiji, sadly. "If I did I should not be unhappy. I love her."

Gian-nah-tah shook his head. "There are many pretty girls of the Shis-Inday," he said presently, "who look with bright eyes upon Shoz-Dijiji."

"I do not love them," replied the Black Bear. "Let us talk no more of these things. Gian-nah-tah is my friend. I have spoken. Let us go and listen to the talk of Geronimo and the other old warriors."

"That is better talk for men," agreed Gian-nah-tah.

Together they strolled over and joined the group of warriors that surrounded the old war chief of the Apaches. White Horse, Geronimo's brother, was speaking.

"There is much talk," he said, "among the Indians at San Carlos that the chiefs of the white-eyed soldiers are going to put Geronimo and many other of our leaders in prison."

"They put me in prison once before and kept me there for four months," said Geronimo. "They never told me why they kept me there or why they let me out."

"They put you in prison to kill you as they did Mangas Colorado," said Na-tanh; "but their hearts turned to water, so that they were afraid."

"They will never get Geronimo in prison again," said the old war chief. "I am getting old; and I should like to have peace, but rather would I take the war trail for the rest of my life than be again chained in the prison of the pindah-lickoyee.

"We do not want to fight any more. We came in as Nan-tan-des-la-par-en* asked us to. We planted crops, but the rain will not come. Usen is angry with us; and The Great White Chief cannot feed us because his agent steals the beef that is meant for us, and lets us starve. He will not let us hunt for food if we live at San Carlos."

"Who is this white-eyed thief that he may say where an Apache warrior may make his kunh-gan-hay or where he shall hunt?" demanded Shoz-Dijiji. "The Black Bear makes his camp where he will, hunts where he will!"

"Those are the big words of a young man, my son," said Geronimo. "It is fine to make big talk; but when we would do these things the soldiers come and kill us; every white-eyed man who meets our hunters upon the trails shoots at them. To them we are as coyotes. Not content with stealing the land that Usen gave to our forefathers, not content with slaughtering the game that Usen put here to feed us, they lie to us, they cheat us, they hunt us down like wild beasts."

"And yet you, Geronimo, War Chief of the Apaches, hesitate to take the war trail against them!" Shoz-Dijiji reproached him. "It is not because you are afraid. No man may say that Geronimo is afraid. Then why is it?"

"The son of Geronimo speaks true words," replied the old chief. "Go-yat-thlay,"** the son of Tah-clish-un, is not afraid to take the war trail against the pindah-lickoyee even though he knows that it is hopeless to fight against their soldiers, who are as many as the needles upon the cedars, because Go-yat-thlay is not afraid to die; but he does not like to see the warriors and the women and the children slain needlessly, and so he waits and hopes—hopes that the pindah-lickoyee will some day keep the words of the treaties they have made with the Shis-Inday—the treaties that they have always been the first to break.

"If that day should come, the Shis-Inday could live in

* "Captain-with-the-brown-clothes"—Major-General George Crook, U. S. A.

** Geronimo.

peace with the pindah-lickoyee; our women and children would have food to eat; we should have land to till and land to hunt upon; we might live as brothers with the white-eyed men, nor ever again go upon the war trail."

"I do not wish to live with the white-eyed men in peace or otherwise," cried the Black Bear. "I am an Apache! I was born to the war trail. From my mother's breasts I drew the strong milk that makes warriors. You, my father, taught me to string a bow, to hurl a lance; from your lips my childish ears heard the proud deeds of my ancestors, the great warriors from whose loins I sprung; you taught me to hate the pindah-lickoyee, you saw me take my first scalp, you have seen me kill many of the warriors of the enemy, and always you approved and were proud. How then may I believe that the words you have just spoken are true words from your heart?"

"Youth speaks from the heart, Shoz-Dijiji, as you speak and as I spoke to you when you were a child; but old age speaks from the head. My heart would go upon the war trail, my son; my heart would kill the white-eyed men wherever it found them, but my head tells me to suffer and be sad a little longer in the hope of peace and justice for my people."

For a time after Geronimo had spoken there was silence, broken only by the beating of the es-a-da-ded and the mumbling of the medicine man, as he led the dancers.

Presently a figure stepped into the outer rim of the circle of firelight from the darkness beyond and halted. He gave the sign and spoke the words of peace, and at the command of Geronimo approached the group of squatting braves.

It was Klo-sen, the Ned-ni. He came and stood before the Be-don-ko-he warriors and looked into the face of Geronimo.

"I bring word from the white-eyed chiefs at San Carlos," he said.

"What message do they send?" asked Geronimo.

"They wish Geronimo and the other chiefs to come to Fort Thomas and hold a council with them," replied Klo-sen.

"Of what matters would they speak?" demanded the old war chief.

"There are many things of which they wish to speak to the chiefs of the Apaches," replied Klosen. "They have heard that we are dissatisfied, and they have promised to listen to our troubles. They say that they want to live in peace with us, and that if we come, they will have a great feast for us, and that together we shall plan how the white-eyes and the Shis-Inday may live together like brothers."

Shoz-Dijiji grunted skeptically.

"They want to make reservation Indians of us forever," said a warrior.

"Tell them we shall hold a council here and send word to them," said Geronimo.

"If you do not come," said Klo-sen, "neither will the Ned-ni —this word De-klu-gie sends to Geronimo and the Be-don-ko-he."

With the coming of the messenger the dance had stopped and the warriors had gathered to listen to his words, forming naturally and in accordance with their rank in a circle about a small fire, so that they were all present when Geronimo suggested that they hold a council to determine what action they should take; and as Chief of the Be-don-ko-he he was the first to speak.

"We, the Shis-Inday, are vanishing from the earth," he said sadly, "yet I cannot think we are useless, or Usen would not have created us. He created all tribes of men, and certainly had a righteous purpose in creating each.

"For each tribe of men Usen created He also made a home. In the land created for any particular tribe He placed whatever would be best for that particular tribe.

"When Usen created the Apaches, He also created their homes in the mountains and the valleys of New Mexico, Arizona, Sonora, and Chihuahua. He gave to them such grain, fruits, and game as they needed to eat. To restore their health when disease attacked them, He made many different herbs to grow. He taught them where to find these herbs and how to prepare them for medicine. He gave them a pleasant climate, and all they needed for clothing and shelter was at hand.

"Usen created, also, the white-eyed men; and for them He created a country where they could live, but they are not satisfied. They want the country that Usen created for them and also the country that He created for the Apaches. They wish to live in the way that Usen intended that they should live, but they are not satisfied that the Apaches should live as Usen wished them to. They want the Apaches to live as the white-eyes live.

"The Apaches cannot live as the white-eyed men live. They would not be happy. They would sicken and die. They must have freedom to roam where they will in their own country; they must be able to obtain the food to which they are accustomed; they must have freedom to search for the herbs that will cure them of sickness.

"These things they cannot do if they live upon the reservations set aside by the white-eyed men for them. They cannot live their own lives if their chiefs must take orders from an Indian Agent who knows little about Indians and cares less.

"As I grow older my mind turns more to peace than to the war trail. I do not wish to fight the pindah-lickoyee, but neither do I wish to be told by the pindah-lickoyee how and where I shall live in my own country." The old man paused and looked around the circle of savage faces.

"I want peace. Perhaps there are wiser men sitting about this council fire who can tell me how the Shis-Inday may have both peace and freedom. Perhaps if we go to this council with the white-eyes they may tell us how we may have peace with freedom.

"Geronimo would like to go; but always there is in his mind the recollection of that day, long ago, when the chiefs of the white-eyed soldiers invited the Be-don-ko-he to a council and a feast at Apache Pass. Mangas Colorado was Chief then, and he went with many of his warriors.

"Just before noon the soldiers invited the Be-don-ko-he into a tent where, they were told, they would be given food to eat. When they were all in the tent the soldiers attacked them. Mangas Colorado and several other warriors, by cutting through the tent, escaped; but most of them were killed or captured.

"I have spoken."

A warrior at Geronimo's right hand arose. "I, too, want peace," he said, "but I hear the spirit voices of Sanza, Kla-de-ta-he, Ni-yo-ka-he, Gopi, and the other warriors who were

killed that day by the soldiers at Apache Pass. They tell me
not to trust the white-eyed men. The spirit of Kla-de-ta-he, my
father, reminds me that the white-eyed men are all liars
and thieves. This they have proved to us many times. They
make treaties and break them; they steal the beef and the
other provisions that are intended for us. That, all men know.
I do not think that we should go to this council. I have
spoken."

Thus, one after the other, all who wished to speak spoke,
some for and some against attending the council; and when
the final vote was taken the majority had spoken against it.

That same night Klo-sen left to carry the word back to the
white men and to De-klu-gie, chief of the Ned-ni, and also
to De-klu-gie an invitation to him and his people to join the
Be-don-ko-he on a hunting trip into Mexico.

"You know," said Geronimo to his warriors, "that this
will mean war! The white-eyed ones will not permit us to
leave the reservation and hunt in peace."

"It is more manly to die on the warpath than to be killed
in prison," replied Shoz-Dijiji.

Two days later the Ned-ni Apaches joined the Be-don-ko-he,
and that all felt that their contemplated move meant war was
evidenced by their hurried preparations for departure and
for the war trail. Disordered hair was shampooed with tallow
and slicked down; war bands were adjusted; smaller, lighter
earrings replaced the heavy pendants of peace times; neck-
laces were discarded down to a single strand; many a bronze
forefinger was stained with color as each brave laid on the
war paint in accordance with his individual taste, ability, and
imagination.

The squaws, with awl and deer sinew, sewed the final
patches to worn war moccasins, gathered together their few
belongings, prepared for the grueling marches, the days of
hunger, of thirst, of battle.

From many an eminence, eagle-eyed scouts watched the
approaches to the camp. In advance of these, other scouts
ranged far in the direction from which troops might be expected to advance. These scouts knew the hour at which the
Be-don-ko-hes and Ned-nis would start their southward march
toward Sonora; and, as the main body of the Apaches broke

camp and moved out along the selected route, the scouts fell
slowly back; but always they watched toward the north, and
the eyes of the marching tribes were turned often in the same
direction.

So it was that, shortly after they had left camp, the Indians
saw little puffs of smoke arising in quick succession from
the summit of a mountain range far to the north. Those
rapidly multiplied and repeated puffs of smoke told them
that a large, well-armed enemy party was approaching; but
it was still a long way off, and Geronimo had little fear that
it could overtake him.

On they moved, well-armed, well mounted, secure in the
belief that all the white-eyed soldiers lay to the north of
them. Shoz-Dijiji, astride his pinto stallion, Nejeunee, rode in
advance leading the way toward Apache Pass.

Suddenly from a hill top close to the pass they were
approaching, a column of smoke rose into the air—it broke
into a puff—was followed by another and another in quick
succession. Another body of the enemy was approaching
Apache Pass from the opposite side!

Shoz-Dijiji reined about and raced Nejeunee back to
Geronimo who, with the balance of the Apaches, had already seen the smoke signal.

"Take ten warriors and ride through the pass," instructed
Geronimo. "If the pindah-lickoyee are too close to permit
us to get through send one back with the word, and we will
turn south through the mountains on this side of the pass.
With the other warriors you will hold them as long as you
can—until dark if possible—and then follow us. With stones
we will tell you which way we have gone.

"If they are not already too close, advance until you find a
good place to hold them. That will give us time to get through
the pass and past them on the trail toward Sonora. Go!"

Shoz-Dijiji asked Gian-nah-tah and nine other braves if
they wished to accompany him; and turned and raced off toward Apache Pass without waiting for a reply, for he knew
that they would all follow him. He had little fear of meeting
the soldiers unexpectedly in the pass, for he knew that the
scout who had sent up the smoke signal would never cease
to watch the enemy and that he would fall back before

them, keeping always between the soldiers and the Apaches.

Shoz-Dijiji and his ten reached the far end of the pass. There were no soldiers in sight yet, but a half mile to the west they saw their scout signaling them to hasten forward, and when they reached him he took Shoz-Dijiji to the hill top and pointed toward the south.

Half a mile away Shoz-Dijiji saw three troopers in dusty blue riding slowly in the direction of the pass. They were the point. Behind them, but hidden by an intervening hill, was the main body, its position well marked by the dust cloud hovering above it. That the soldiers had seen the smoke signal was apparent by the extreme caution with which the point advanced.

Now a small advance party came into view with flankers well out, but Shoz-Dijiji did not wait to see more—the warriors of the pindah-lickoyee were coming, and they were prepared.

The young War Chief of the Be-don-ko-he had fought against the soldiers of the white-eyed men before, and he knew what they would do when attacked. He thought that he could hold them long enough for the main body of the Apaches to get through the pass, and so he sent one messenger racing back to urge Geronimo to hasten; he sent a warrior to the hilltop to fire upon the point, and he sent two warriors with all the ponies upon the new trail toward the south that the tribes would now have to follow. Thus he burned his bridges behind him, but he was confident of the result of his plan.

Counting himself, there were now nine warriors opposing the enemy; and Shoz-Dijiji lost no time in disposing his little force to carry out the strategy of his defense of Apache Pass.

The point, having uncovered the enemy, did what Shoz-Dijiji had known that it would do—turned and raced back toward the advance party, which now deployed. The main body halted and was dismounted to fight on foot, the terrain not justifying mounted action.

This delay, which Shoz-Dijiji had counted on, was utilized by him and six of his warriors in racing through the hills, just out of sight of the enemy, toward a point where they could overlook the main body. Two warriors he left upon the hill top that commanded the approach to the pass.

When the seven painted warriors reached their stations they were spread along the low hills looking down upon the enemy and at intervals of about fifty yards. Shoz-Dijiji was farthest from the pass. It was his rifle that spoke first from above and behind the troopers holding the horses of those who were now slowly advancing in skirmish line on foot.

A struck horse screamed and lunged, breaking away from the trooper that held it. Along the line of hills now the seven rifles were cracking rapidly down upon the unprotected rear and flank of the enemy. Riderless horses, breaking away from those who held them, ran, snorting, among the dismounted troopers, adding to the confusion. The commanding officer, steadying his men by word and example, ordered them to seek shelter and lie down, forming them in a ragged line facing the hills. A lieutenant directed the removal of the remaining horses to a place of safety.

The Apaches did not fire again after the first few disconcerting rounds. Shoz-Dijiji had no wish to precipitate a charge that might reveal his weakness, his sole aim being to delay the advance of the enemy toward the pass until Geronimo should have come through with the two tribes.

The officer commanding the cavalry had no means of knowing that he was not faced by the entire strength of the renegades, and in the lull that followed the first attack he started withdrawing his men to a safer position, and as this withdrawal took them away from the pass Shoz-Dijiji made no effort to embarrass it but waited until the troopers had found shelter. He watched them dig little trenches for their bodies and pile rocks in front of their heads, and when he was sure that they felt more secure, he passed the word along his line to fire an occasional shot and that after each shot the warrior should change his position before he fired again that an impression might be given the enemy that it faced a long line of warriors.

The soldiers had formed their line some hundred yards from where their horses were hidden in a dry wash, and at every effort that was made to cross this space and reach the horses the Apaches concentrated their fire upon this zone, effectually discouraging any considerable enthusiasm in the project, since as long as they remained passive there were no casualties.

The commanding officer was mystified by the tactics of the Apaches. He hoped they were preparing to charge, and in that hope he hesitated to order his own men up the steep hillside in the face of the fire of an unknown number of savages. Then, too, he could afford to wait, as he was suffering no losses and was momentarily expecting the arrival of the infantry that was following with the baggage train.

And so the afternoon wore on. A messenger came to Shoz-Dijiji with word that the two tribes had passed safely through the pass. Shoz-Dijiji fired a shot at the line of dusty blue and sent two of his warriors to join the main body of the Apaches. During the following half hour each of the remaining braves fired once, and then two more left to overtake the renegades. The next half hour was a busy one for the three remaining warriors as each fired two or three rounds, changing his position after each shot and thus giving the impression of undiminished strength. Then two more warriors retired.

Now only Shoz-Dijiji remained. In the north rose a great dust cloud that drew constantly nearer. The infantry was coming!

Shoz-Dijiji fired and scuttled to a new position nearer Apache Pass. The troopers peppered away at the spot from which the smoke of his shot had arisen, as they had all the long hot afternoon. Shoz-Dijiji fired again and moved on.

The infantry was met by a messenger from the cavalry. All afternoon they had heard the firing and had hastened forward. Hot, dusty, tired, they were in bad humor. Spitting dust from swollen tongues, they cursed all Indians in general and Apaches in particular as they deployed and started up the hillside to flank the embattled reds. This time, by God, they would get old Geronimo and all his dirty, sneaking Siwashes!

Simultaneously the dismounted troopers charged straight into the face of the enemy. Fat chance the doughboys had of beating *them* to it!

It was a race now to see which would reach the renegades first—cavalry or infantry. The cavalry, having the advantage of propinquity, arrived first, and they got something, too—when the infantry arrived, they got the laugh. There was not an Indian in sight!

From a hilltop a mile to the south of them a lone warrior watched them, estimating the numbers of the infantry, the size of the wagon train. Satisfied, he turned and trotted along the trail made by his fellows as they moved southward.

Down into Sonora the long trail was leading, down to a camp in the Sierra de Sahuaripa Mountains.

Geronimo had gone out again!

Chapter Two

SPOILS OF WAR

THE camp of Be-don-ko-he and Ned-ni Apaches lay in the Sierra de Sahuaripa not far from Casa Grande, but the activities of the renegades led them far afield in both Sonora and Chihuahua during the ensuing year.

Shoz-Dijiji, restless, unhappy, filled with bitterness against all men who were not Apaches, often brooding over the wrongs and injustices inflicted upon his people, became a living scourge throughout the countryside.

Sometimes alone, again with Gian-nah-tah and other young braves, he raided shops and ranches and isolated cottages, or waylaid travelers upon the road.

He affected a design in face painting that was distinctive and personal, so that all who saw him knew him, even though they never had seen him before. He laid a broad band of white from temple to temple across his eyes—the remainder of his face, above and below the band, was blue.

Entering a small village alone, he would step into the little tienda and stand silently upon the threshold for a moment watching the effect of his presence upon the shopkeeper and his customers. He derived pleasure from seeing the pallor of fear overspread their faces and hearing their mumbled prayers; he loved the terror in their voices as they voiced his name, "The Apache Devil!"

If they ran he let them go, but if they offered resistance he shot them down; then he took what he wanted and left. He did not kill women or children, nor did he ever mutilate the dead or torture the living; but others did—Apaches, Indians of other tribes, Mexicans—and The Apache Devil was held responsible for every outrage that left no eyewitness living to refute the charge.

In the year that they remained in Mexico the Apaches collected a considerable herd of horses and cattle by similar means and according to the same ethics that govern civilized troops in an enemy's country. They considered themselves at war with all mankind, nor was there any sufficient reason why they should feel otherwise. For over three hundred years they had been at war with the white men; for over three hundred years they had been endeavoring to expel the invader from their domain. In the history of the world no more courageous defense of a fatherland against overwhelming odds is recorded, but the only accolade that history will bestow upon them is that which ratifies the titles, thieves and murderers, conferred upon them by those who ravished their land for profit.

It was late summer. The growing herd of the Apaches was becoming unwieldy. Scouts and raiding parties were almost daily reporting to Geronimo the increasing activities of Mexican troops, proof to the old War Chief that the Mexican government was inaugurating a determined campaign against him, which he realized must assuredly result in the eventual loss of their hard-earned flocks, since the tactics of Apache warfare depend, for success, chiefly upon the marvelous mobility of the savages.

From the summit of a mountain in the Sierra de Sahuaripa range rose a tall, thin column of smoke. It scarcely wavered in the still air of early morning. Fed by trained hands, its volume remained almost constant and without break. From a distance it appeared a white pillar topped by a white cloud that drifted, at last, lazily toward the north.

Fifty, a hundred miles away keen eyes might see it through the thin, clear air of Sonora. *Caballero* and peon in little villages, in scattered huts, in many a distant hacienda saw it and, cursing, looked to their weapons, prepared the better to guard their flocks and their women, for it told them that the Apaches were gathering; and when the Apaches gathered, let honest folk beware!

Other eyes saw it, savage eyes, the eyes for which its message was intended; and from plain and mountain painted warriors, scouting, raiding, turned their ponies' heads toward the soft, white beacon; and thus the scattered members of the Be-don-ko-he and the Ned-ni joined forces in the Sierra de Sahuaripa and started north with the spoils of war safely ahead of the converging troops.

"For more than a year," Geronimo had said to them during the council in which they had determined to leave Mexico, "we have been absent from the country of the pindah-lickoyee. In all this time we have not struck a blow against them. We have shown them that we are not at war with them but with the Mexicans. Let us return with our herds to our own country and settle down in peace. With what we have won we can increase our cattle and our horses to such an extent that we shall not have to go upon the war trail again for a long time—possibly never again. Thus we can live in peace beside the pindah-lickoyee. Let us not strike again at them. If our young men must go upon the war trail, there is always Mexico. The Mexicans are our natural enemies. They were our enemies before the pindah-lickoyee came; I do not forget Kas-ki-yeh, where my wife, my mother, and my children were treacherously slain. Let not the young warriors forget Kas-ki-yeh either! Many were the women and the children and the warriors killed there that day while most of the fighting braves were peaceably trading in the nearby village.

"Perhaps now that we have obtained the means to guard against hunger we may live in peace in our own country with the white-eyed men. I have made big medicine and prayed to Usen that this thing may be. I am tired of fighting. I am tired of seeing my people killed in the hopeless struggle against the white-eyes."

And so the two tribes came back to the reservation at San Carlos, bringing their great herd with them, and there was feasting and dancing and much tizwin was consumed.

The White Mountain Apaches, who had not gone out with Geronimo, profited also for they had furnished many of the rifles and much of the ammunition that had aided in the success of the renegades; and they received their reward in the division of the spoils of war.

After the freedom and excitement of the war trail it was difficult for the young braves to settle down to the monotony of reservation life. Herding cattle and horses was far from a thrilling occupation and offered little outlet for active, savage spirits; and it could as well be done by boys as by men.

The result was that they spent much time in gambling and drinking, which more often than not led to quarreling. Shoz-Dijiji suffered in a way, perhaps, more than the majority, for his was naturally a restless spirit which had not even the outlet afforded by strong drink, since Shoz-Dijiji cared nothing for this form of dissipation. Nausea and headaches did not appeal to him as particularly desirable or profitable. He found a certain thrill in gambling, but most of all he enjoyed contests of skill and endurance.

He challenged other braves to wrestle, jump, or run. The stakes were ornaments, ammunition, weapons, ponies; but as Shoz-Dijiji always won it was not long before he was unable to find an antagonist willing to risk a wager against him.

Perhaps his chief diversion was pony racing, and many a round of ammunition, many a necklace of glass beads, magical berries, and roots, bits of the valued duklij came into his possession because of the speed of Nejeunee and other swift ponies of his string.

Shoz-Dijiji, gauged by the standards of Apachedom, was wealthy. He possessed a large herd, fine raiment, the best of weapons and "jewelry" that was the envy of all. Many a scheming mother and lovelorn maiden set a cap for him, but the Black Bear was proof against all their wiles.

Sometimes his father, Geronimo, or his mother, Sons-ee-ah-ray, reproached him, telling him that it was not fitting that a rich and powerful war chief should be without women to wait upon him. They told him that it was a reflection on them, but Shoz-Dijiji only shrugged his shoulders and grunted, saying that he did not want to be bothered with women and children. Only Shoz-Dijiji and Gian-nah-tah knew the truth.

Just off the reservation was a place known locally as the Hog Ranch, though the only swine that frequented it were human; and while a single member of the family Suidæ would have tended to elevate its standing in the community it was innocent of even this slight claim to decency.

Its proprietor was what is still known in the vernacular of the Southwest as a tinhorn. "Dirty" Cheetim had tried prospecting and horse stealing, but either of these vocations were dependent for success upon a more considerable proportion of courage and endurance than existed in his mental and physical endowment.

His profits were derived through the exploitation of the pulchritude of several blondined ladies from the States and about an equal number of dusky señoritas from below the border, from cheating drunken soldiers and cowboys at cards, from selling cheap, adulterated whiskey to his white patrons openly and to Indians surreptitiously. It was whispered that he had other sources of revenue which Washington might have found interesting had it been in any measure interested in the welfare of the Indians, but how can one expect overworked Christian congressmen to neglect their electorate in the interests of benighted savages who have no votes?

However, it seemed strange to those who gave it any thought that such a place as "Dirty" Chee-tim's Hog Ranch should receive even the passive countenance of the Indian Agent.

Tall and straight, silently on moccasined feet, an Apache brave stepped through the doorway of the Hog Ranch. Pausing within he let his quick, keen glance pass rapidly over the faces of the inmates. The place was almost deserted at this hour of the day. Two Mexicans, an American cowboy, and a soldier were playing stud at a table in one corner of the room. Two other soldiers and two girls were standing at the bar, behind which, one of "Dirty" Chee-tim's assistants was officiating. One of the soldiers turned and looked at the Indian.

"Hello, Black Bear!" he called. "Have a drink?"

Shoz-Dijiji looked steadily at the soldier for a moment before replying.

"No sabe," he said, presently, his eyes moving to a closed door that led to a back room.

"He's a damn liar," said the soldier. "I'll bet he savvies English as good as me."

"Gee!" exclaimed one of the girls; "he's sure a good lookin' Siwash." She looked up into Shoz-Dijiji's face and smiled boldly as he approached them on his way across the room toward the closed door; but the face of the Indian remained expressionless, inscrutable.

"They don't none of 'em look good to me," said the other soldier. "This guy was out with Geronimo, and every time I lamp one of their mugs I think maybe it's The Apache Devil. You can't never tell."

The first soldier took hold of Shoz-Dijiji's arm as he was passing and stopped him; then from the bar he picked up a glass filled with whiskey and offered it to the Apache.

Shoz-Dijiji grunted, shook his head and passed on. The girl laughed.

"I reckon he's got more sense than we have," she said; "he knows enough not to drink 'Dirty's' rotgut."

"You must be stuck on the Siwash, Goldie," accused the first soldier.

"I might have a mash on a lot o' worse lookin' hombres than him," she shot back, with a toss of her faded, golden curls.

Shoz-Dijiji heard and understood the entire conversation. He had not for nothing spent the months of Geronimo's imprisonment at San Carlos in the post school, but not even by the quiver of an eyelid did he acknowledge that he understood.

At the closed door, unembarrassed by the restrictions of an etiquette that he would have ignored had he been cognizant of it, he turned the knob and stepped into the room beyond without knocking.

Two men were there—a white man and an Indian. They both looked up as Shoz-Dijiji entered. This was the first time that Shoz-Dijiji had been in "Dirty" Cheetim's Hog Ranch. It was the first time that he had seen the proprietor or known who "Dirty" Cheetim was; but he had met him before, and he recognized him immediately.

Instantly there was projected upon the screen of memory a sun-scorched canyon, boulder strewn, through which wound a dusty wagon road. At the summit of the canyon's western wall a young Apache brave crouched hidden beneath a grey blanket that, from the canyon's bottom, seemed but another boulder. He was watching for the coming of the soldiers of the pindah-lickoyee that he might carry the word of it back to Geronimo.

Presently three bearded men rode into view. The Apache gazed down upon them with contempt. His fingers, resting upon his rifle, twitched, but he was scouting and must forego this Usen-given opportunity. The men were not soldiers, so they were of no concern to Shoz-Dijiji, the scout.

Suddenly the Apache's attention was attracted by a sound coming from the south, a rhythmical sound that announced the approach of a loping horse. Two of the three men drew quickly behind a great boulder, the third behind another upon the opposite side of the road. Silence once more enveloped the seemingly deserted canyon.

The Apache waited, watching. The loping horse drew nearer. It entered the lower end of the canyon and presently came within range of Shoz-Dijiji's vision. Its rider was a girl —a white girl. As she came abreast of the three whites they rode directly into the trail and barred her passage, and as she sought to wheel her horse one of them reached out and seized her bridle rein.

The girl reached for a six-shooter that hung at her hip, but another of the three had slipped from his saddle and run to her side. Now he grasped her wrist, tore the weapon from its holster, and dragged the girl to the ground. It was all done very quickly. Shoz-Dijiji watched. His hatred of the men mounted.

He heard the conversation that passed between the men and the girl and understood it—understood that the men were going to take the girl away by force. He saw one of them —the one that he was facing now in the back room of the Hog Ranch—jerk the girl roughly and order her to remount her horse.

Then the barrel of a rifle slid quietly from beneath the edge of a gray boulder at the top of the canyon's wall, there was a loud report that resounded thunderously, and the man whose hand lay upon Wichita Billings dropped in his tracks.

From that moment to this Shoz-Dijiji had thought "Dirty" Cheetim dead, yet here he was in the flesh, looking him straight in the eye and smiling. Shoz-Dijiji knew that Cheetim would not be smiling if he had recognized Shoz-Dijiji.

"How, John!" exclaimed the white man. "Mebby so you want red-eye, eh?"

In no slightest degree did Shoz-Dijiji register by any changed expression the surprise he felt at seeing this man alive, nor the hatred that he felt for him, nor the terrific urge he experienced to kill him. He looked at him just once, briefly, and then ignored him as he did his greeting and his question. Instead he turned to the Apache standing behind Cheetim.

It was Gian-nah-tah. In one hand he held a glass of whiskey, in the other a bottle. Shoz-Dijiji looked straight into the eyes of his friend for a moment, and those of Gian-nah-tah wavered and dropped beneath the steady, accusing gaze of the Black Bear; then the latter spoke in the language of the Shis-Inday.

"Gian-nah-tah, you are a fool!" said Shoz-Dijiji. "Of all the things that the white-eyed men have to offer the Apache only their weapons and their ammunition are of any value to us— all else is vile. And you, Gian-nah-tah, choose the vilest. You are a fool!

"Our own tizwin and the mescal of the Mexicans is bad medicine, but this firewater of the white-eyed men is poison. To drink it is the madness of a fool, but even worse is the drinking of it in friendship with the white-eyed dogs.

"You are a fool to drink it—you are a traitor to drink with the enemies of your people. Put down the glass and the bottle, and come with me!"

Gian-nah-tah looked up angrily now. Already he had had a couple of drinks of the vile concoction, and they had had their effect upon him.

"Gian-nah-tah is a warrior!" he exclaimed, "Not a child. Who are you to tell Gian-nah-tah to do this, or not to do that, or to come or go?"

"I am his best friend," said Shoz-Dijiji, simply.

"Then go away and mind your own business!" snapped Gian-nah-tah, and he raised the glass to his lips.

With the swift, soft sinuosity of a cat Shoz-Dijiji stepped forward and struck the glass from his friend's hand and almost in the same movement seized the bottle and hurled it to the floor.

"Here, you damn Siwash!" cried Cheetim; "what the hell you think you're doin'?" He advanced belligerently. Shoz-Dijiji turned upon the white man. Towering above him he gave the fellow one look that sent him cowering back. Perhaps it was fortunate for the peace of San Carlos that "Dirty" Cheetim had left his gun behind the bar, for he was the type of badman that shoots an unarmed adversary.

But Gian-nah-tah, Be-don-ko-he warrior, was not thus a coward; and his finer sensibilities were numbed by the effects of the whiskey he had drunk. He did not shrink from Shoz-Dijiji. Instead, he whipped his knife from its scabbard and struck a savage blow at the breast of his best friend.

Shoz-Dijiji had turned away from Cheetim just in time to meet Gian-nah-tah's attack. Quickly he leaped aside as the knife fell and then sprang close again and seized Gian-nah-tah's knife wrist with the fingers of his left hand. Like a steel vise his grip tightened. Gian-nah-tah struck at him with his free hand, but Shoz-Dijiji warded the blow.

"Drop it!" commanded the Black Bear and struck Gian-nah-tah across the face with his open palm. The latter struggled to free himself, striking futilely at the giant that held him.

"Drop it!" repeated Shoz-Dijiji. Again he struck Gian-nah-tah—and again, and again. His grasp tightened upon the other's wrist, stopping the circulation—until Gian-nah-tah thought that his bones were being crushed. His fingers relaxed. The knife clattered to the floor. Shoz-Dijiji stooped quickly and recovered it; then he released his hold upon Gian-nah-tah.

"Go!" commanded the Black Bear, pointing toward the doorway.

For an instant Gian-nah-tah hesitated; then he turned and walked from the room. Without even a glance in the direction of Cheetim, Shoz-Dijiji followed his friend. As they passed the bar the girl called Goldie smiled into the face of Shoz-Dijiji.

"Come down and see me sometime, John," she said.

Without a word or a look the Apache passed out of the building, away from the refining influences of white man's civilization.

Sullenly, Gian-nah-tah walked to where two ponies were tied. From the tie-rail he unfastened the hackamore rope of one of them and vaulted to the animal's back. In silence Shoz-Dijiji handed Gian-nah-tah his knife. In silence the other Apache took it, wheeled his pony, and loped away toward the Be-don-ko-he village. Astride Nejeunee Shoz-Dijiji followed slowly—erect, silent, somber; only his heart was bowed, in sorrow.

As Shoz-Dijiji approached the village he met Geronimo and two warriors riding in the direction of the military post. They were angry and excited. The old War Chief beckoned Shoz-Dijiji to join them.

"What has happened?" asked the Black Bear.

"The soldiers have come and driven away our herd," replied Geronimo.

"Where are you going?"

"I am going to see Nan-tan-des-la-par-en," replied Geronimo, "and ask him why the soldiers have stolen our horses and cattle. It is always thus! When we would live at peace with the white-eyed men they will not let us. Always they do something that arouses the anger of the Shis-Inday and makes the young braves want to go upon the war trail. Now, if they do not give us back our cattle, it will be difficult to keep the young men in peace upon the reservation—or the old men either."

At the post Geronimo rode directly to headquarters and demanded to see General Crook, and a few minutes later the four braves were ushered into the presence of the officer.

"I have been expecting you, Geronimo," said Crook.

"Then you knew that the soldiers were going to steal our herds?" demanded the War Chief.

"They have not stolen them, Geronimo," replied the officer. "It is you who stole them. They do not belong to you. The soldiers have taken them away from you to return them to their rightful owners. Every time you steal horses or cattle they will be taken away from you and returned. You promised me once that you would not steal any more, but yet you went out and killed and stole."

"We did not go upon the war trail against the white-eyed men," replied Geronimo. "We were going down into Mexico, and your soldiers attacked us and tried to stop us."

"It was the Apaches who started the fight at Apache Pass," Crook reminded him.

"It was the Apaches who fired the first shot," corrected Geronimo, "but they did not start the fight. You started it by sending troops to stop us. We are neither fools nor children. We knew why those troops were marching to Apache Pass. Had they seen us first they would have fired the first shot. You cannot say that we started the fight just because our chiefs and our warriors are better soldiers than yours. You would have been glad enough to have surprised us, but you were not wise enough."

Crook smiled. "You say you are not a fool nor a child, Geronimo," he said. "Well, neither am I. You went out with a bad heart to kill innocent people and rob them. It got too hot for you in Mexico, and so you came back here and brought your stolen herds with you. You are no fool, Geronimo, and so I know you were not foolish enough to think that we would let you keep these cattle. I do not know why you did it, unless you just wanted to make more trouble."

"I did not want to make trouble," replied the chief. "We were at war with the Mexicans. We took the horses and cattle as spoils of war. They belong to us. They do not belong to you. They were not taken from your people but from Mexicans. Your own country has been at war with Mexico in the past. Did you return everything that you took from them at that time?"

"But we are not at war with them now. We are friends. You cannot steal from our friends. If we let you they will say that we are not their friends."

"That is not true," replied Geronimo. "The Mexicans are not fools, either. They know the difference between Apaches and white-eyed men. They know that it was the Apaches, with whom they are at war, who took their herds. They do not think that it was you. If you take the herds from us and return them to the Mexicans, both the Mexicans and the Apaches will think that you are fools. If you took them and kept them, that would be different. That is precisely what we did and what we would do again. You say that you do not want to be at war with the Apaches—that we are good friends! How then can you make me believe that it is right to take cattle from your friends?"

Crook shook his head. "It's no use, Geronimo," he said.

"How can we live if you take our herds from us?" demanded the Apache. "With these cattle and horses we were rich. We did not intend to kill them. We were going to breed them and thus become richer, so that we would not have to go out raiding again. It was our chance to live comfortably and in peace with the white-eyed men. Now you have taken this chance from us. We cannot live here and starve."

"You do not have to starve," replied Crook. "The government rations are ample to take care of you."

"We do not get them. You know that we do not get them. The Agent robs us. Every man knows that. Now you rob us. I told you that I wished to live in peace with the white-eyed men, but I cannot control the young men when they learn that you will not return their cattle and horses. If they make trouble do not blame me. I did not do it. You did it. I have spoken!"

"There will be no trouble, Geronimo," said Crook, "if you do not start it. I cannot give you back the cattle. Go back to your camp and tell your people that. Tell them that the next time they go out and kill and steal I shall not be as easy with them. The next time they will be punished, just as any murderers are. Do you hear?"

"Geronimo hears, but he does not understand," replied the War Chief. "Usen seems to have made one set of laws for the Apaches and another for the white-eyed men. It is right for the white-eyed men to come into the country of the Apaches and steal their land and kill their game and shut the Apaches up on reservations and shoot them if they try to go to some other part of their own country; but it is wrong for the Apaches to fight with the Mexicans who have been their natural enemies since long before the white-eyed men came to the country. It is wrong for the Apaches to profit by their victories against their enemies.

"Yes, Geronimo hears; but he does not understand."

Chapter Three

"NO SABE!"

AS Shoz-Dijiji followed Geronimo and the two braves from General Crook's office a white girl chanced to be passing in front of headquarters. Her eyes and the eyes of Shoz-Dijiji met, and into the eyes of the girl leaped the light of recognition and pleasure.

"Shoz-Dijiji!" she exclaimed. "I am so glad to see you again." The brave stopped and looked gravely into her face, listening to her words. "I am visiting with Mrs. Cullis. Won't you come and see me?"

"No sabe," said Shoz-Dijiji and brushed past her to rejoin his fellows.

A flush of mortification colored the face of Wichita Billings; and the fire of anger and resentment lighted her eyes, but the flush quickly faded and, as quickly, an expression of sorrow supplanted that of displeasure. For a moment she stood looking after the tall, straight form of the Apache as he walked toward his pony, and then, with a sigh, she resumed her way.

A white man, coming from the canteen, had witnessed the meeting between Shoz-Dijiji and Wichita Billings. He had recognized the girl immediately and the Indian as the same that had, a short time before, spoiled a sale for him and smashed a bottle of whiskey upon the floor of his back room.

He was surprised to see Wichita Billings at the post, and as she turned again in his direction he stepped quickly behind the corner of a building and waited there until she had passed.

The natural expression that mirrored in the face of "Dirty" Cheetim whatever atrophied thing may have done questionable duty as his soul, was evil; but peculiarly unclean was the look in his eyes as he watched the girl walking briskly along the path that led to the officers' quarters.

Presently his eyes wandered to the figure of the Apache brave riding across the parade on the pinto stallion, and his brows contracted in thought. Where had he seen that buck before?—a long time before. There was something mighty familiar about him—something that Cheetim had not noticed until he saw the Indian talking with Wichita Billings; but even so he failed to connect the associated ideas that had subconsciously aroused the suggestion of previous familiarity, and so, dismissing the matter from his mind, he went on about his affairs.

Geronimo rode back to the camp of the Be-don-ko-he in silence. It was as impossible for him to get the viewpoint of the white man as it was for the white man to get the viewpoint of the Apache. He felt that he had been treated with rank injustice and treachery. Geronimo was furious, yet his stern, inscrutable face gave no evidence of what was passing in his savage brain. He did not rant nor rave, raising his voice in loud oaths, as might a white man under stress of similar circumstance.

Geronimo dismounted before his hogan and turned to Shoz-Dijiji and the others who had accompanied him. "Tell the braves of the Be-don-ko-he that Geronimo is going away from San Carlos," he said. "Perhaps they would like to come and talk with Geronimo before he goes."

As the three braves rode away through the village Geronimo sat down before the entrance to his hogan. "Geronimo cannot live in peace with thieves and liars, Morning Star," he said to his wife. "Therefore we shall go away and live as Usen intended that we should live. He never meant that we should live with the white-eyed men."

"We are going on the war trail again?" asked Sons-ee-ah-ray.

Geronimo shook his head. "No," he replied. "If they will leave Geronimo alone he will not fight the pindah-lickoyee again. Geronimo wishes only to lead his own life in his own way far from any pindah-lickoyee. In that way only lies peace."

"Sons-ee-ah-ray will be glad to leave San Carlos," said the squaw. "She will be glad to go anywhere to get away from the white-eyed men. They are bad. Their women are bad, and they think because their women are bad that the Apache women are bad. The white-eyed men make bad talk to Sons-ee-ah-ray when she passes them on her way to the Agency. She will be glad not to hear this talk any more.

"Geronimo knows that Sons-ee-ah-ray, the mother of his children, is a good woman. Why, then, do the white-eyed men talk thus to her?"

The War Chief shook his head. "I do not know," he said. "I do not understand the white-eyed men."

When the warriors of the Be-don-ko-he gathered, many of the older men appeared apprehensive. They looked sad and worried but the young men were excited and gay. Many of the latter were already painting their faces, but when Geronimo saw this he frowned and shook his head.

"Geronimo is going away," he said, "because he can no longer live under the conditions that the white-eyed men impose and still maintain his self-respect; but he does not mean, as some of the young men seem to think, that he is going to take the war trail against the pindah-lickoyee.

"With his family he is going up somewhere around Fort Apache and live in the mountains where he will not have to see any white-eyes."

"We will go with you!" said many of the Be-don-ko-he.

"No," remonstrated Geronimo. "If you go with me the Agent will say that Geronimo has gone out again with his warriors, but if only Geronimo and his own family go the Agent cannot say that Geronimo has gone upon the war trail.

"If you come with me they will send soldiers after us, and then there will be war, and already there have been enough of us killed. Therefore Geronimo goes alone.

"Shoz-Dijiji, my son, will remain here for a while and learn if the white-eyed men are going to make trouble because Geronimo has left San Carlos. If they do, he will bring the word to me, and then I shall know what next to do; but I shall not return to San Carlos to be treated like a fool and a child —no, not I, Geronimo, War Chief of all the Apaches!"

And so that night Geronimo, with all his family except Shoz-Dijiji, rode silently northward toward Fort Apache, and at San Carlos the Indians, the Agent, and the soldiers slept in peaceful ignorance of this event that was so soon to lead to the writing of one of history's bloodiest pages.

After Geronimo had left, Shoz-Dijiji sought out Gian-nah-tah with whom he had had no opportunity to speak since the moment of their altercation in the Hog Ranch. In the heart of the Black Bear was only love for this friend of his childhood; and while he knew that Gian-nah-tah had been very angry with him at the time, he attributed this mostly to the effect of the whiskey he had drunk, believing that when this had worn off, and Gian-nah-tah had had time to reflect, he would harbor no ill will.

Shoz-Dijiji found his friend sitting alone over a tiny fire and came and squatted down beside him. Neither spoke, but that was nothing unusual. Near by, before her hogan, a squaw was praying to the moon. "Gun-ju-le, klego-na-ay," she chanted.

At a little distance a warrior cast hoddentin into the air and prayed: "Gun-ju-le, chil-jilt, si-chi-zi, gun-ju-le, inzayu, ijanale,"—"Be good, O Night; Twilight, be good; do not let me die." Peace and quiet lay upon the camp of the Bedonkohe.

"Today," said Shoz-Dijiji, "I recognized the white-eyed man who sells firewater to the Apaches. He is the man who tried to steal the white-eyed girl that day that Gian-nah-tah and Shoz-Dijiji were scouting near the hogan of her father.

"I thought that I killed him that day; but today I saw him again, selling firewater to Gian-nah-tah. He is a very bad man. Some day I shall kill him; but I shall do it when no one is around to see, for the white-eyed fools would put me in prison as quickly for killing a bad man as a good."

Gian-nah-tah made no reply. Shoz-Dijiji turned and looked into the face of his friend. "Is Gian-nah-tah still angry?" he asked.

Gian-nah-tah arose, turned around, and squatted down again with his back toward Shoz-Dijiji. The Black Bear shook his head sadly; then he stood up. For a moment he hesitated as though about to speak, but instead he turned, drew his blanket more closely about him, and walked away. His heart was heavy. During his short life he had seen many of his friends killed in battle; he had seen little Ish-kay-nay, his first love, die in his arms, slain by the bullet of a white man; he had seen the look of horror in the eyes of the white girl he had grown to love, when he had avowed that love; he had just seen his father and his mother driven by the injustices of the white conqueror from the society of their own kind; and now he had lost his best friend. The heart of Shoz-Dijiji, the Black Bear, was heavy indeed.

Wichita Billings was visiting in the home of Margaret Cullis at the post. The two were sitting in the modest parlor, the older woman sewing, the younger reading. Presently Wichita closed her book and laid it on the table.

"I can't seem to get interested," she said. "I don't feel very 'literary' tonight."

"You haven't been yourself all day," said Mrs. Cullis. "Aren't you feeling well?"

"I feel all right, physically," replied the girl; "but I'm blue."

"About what?"

"Oh, nothing—I just feel blue. Didn't you ever feel that way when there wasn't any reason for it?"

"There usually is a reason."

"I suppose so. Perhaps it's in the air." There was a silence that lasted a minute or two. "Lieutenant King's calling this evening."

"I'm sure that shouldn't make you blue, my dear girl," exclaimed Margaret Cullis, laughing.

"Well, it doesn't cheer me up much, because I know what he's going to say, and I know what I'm going to answer. It's always the same thing."

"I can't see why you don't love him, Wichita. It would be a wonderful match for you."

"Yes, for me, but not for him. His people would be ashamed of me."

"Don't be silly! There isn't any man or any family too good for you—I doubt if there is any good enough for you."

"You're a dear, but the fact remains that they are stiff-backed Bostonians with more culture than there is in the whole state that I came from and a family tree that started as a seedling in the Garden of Eden, while I got most of my education out of a mail-order catalog; and if I ever had a family tree it must have been blown away by a Kansas cyclone while my folks were fighting Indians.

"And speaking of Indians, whom do you think I saw today?"

"Who?"

"Shoz-Dijiji!"

Margaret Cullis looked up quickly. Was it the intonation of the girl's voice as she spoke the name? The older woman frowned and looked down at her work again. "What did he have to say?" she asked.

"Nothing."

"Oh, you didn't see him to talk with?"

"Yes, but he wouldn't talk to me—just fell back on that maddening 'No sabe' that they use with strangers."

"Why do you suppose he did that?" asked Mrs. Cullis.

"I hurt him—the last time I saw him," replied Wichita.

"Hurt one of Geronimo's renegades! Child, it can't be done."

"They're human," replied the girl. "I learned that in the days that I spent in Geronimo's camp while Chief Loco was out with his hostiles. Among themselves they are entirely different people from those we are accustomed to see on the reservation. No one who has watched them with their children, seen them at their games, heard them praying to Dawn and Twilight, to the Sun, the Moon, and the Stars as they cast their sacred hoddentin to the winds would ever again question their possession of the finer instincts of sentiment and imagination.

"Because they do not wear their hearts upon their sleeves, because they are not blatant in the declaration of their finer emotions, does not mean that they feel no affection or that they are incapable of experiencing spiritual suffering."

"Perhaps," said Margaret Cullis, "but you, who have lived in Indian country all your life, who have seen the heartless cruelties they inflict upon their helpless victims, who know their treachery and their dishonesty, cannot but admit that whatever qualities of goodness they possess are far outweighed by those others which have made them hated and feared the length and breadth of the Southwest."

"For every wrong that they have committed," argued

Wichita, "they can point out a similar crime perpetrated upon them by the whites. Oh, Margaret, it is the old case again of the pot calling the kettle black. We have tortured them and wronged them even more than they have tortured and wronged us.

"We esteem personal comfort and life as our two most sacred possessions. When the Apaches torture and kill us we believe that they have committed against us the most hideous of conceivable crimes.

"On the other hand the Apaches do not esteem personal comfort and life as highly as do we and consequently, by their standards—and we may judge a people justly only by their own standards—we have not suffered as much as they, who esteem more highly than life or personal comfort the sanctity of their ancient rites and customs and the chastity of their women. From the time of the white man's first contact with the Apaches he has ridiculed the one and defiled the other.

"I have talked with Shoz-Dijiji, and Geronimo, with Sons-ee-ah-ray, and many another Be-don-ko-he man and woman; they have laid bare their hearts to me, and never again can anyone convince me that we have not tortured the Apaches with as malignant cruelty as they have tortured us."

"Why you are a regular little Apache yourself, Wichita," cried Margaret Cullis. "I wonder what your father would say if he could hear you."

"He has heard me. Don't think for a minute that I am afraid to express my views to anyone."

"Did he enjoy them and argee with you?"

"He did not. He did everything but tear his hair and take me out to the woodshed. You know Mason was killed about two months ago, and it had all the earmarks of an Apache killing. Mason was one of Dad's best friends. Now, every time he thinks or hears Apache he sees red."

"I don't blame him," said Margaret Cullis.

"It's silly," snapped Wichita, "and I tell him so. It would be just as logical to hate all French-Canadians because Guiteau assassinated President Garfield."

"Well, how in the world, feeling toward the Apaches as

you do, could you have found it in your heart to so wound Shoz-Dijiji that he will not speak to you?"

"I did not mean to," explained the girl. "It—just happened. We had been together for many days after the Chi-e-a-hen attacked the Pringe ranch and Shoz-Dijiji got me away from them. The country was full of hostiles, and so he took me to the safest place he could think of—the Be-don-ko-he camp. They kept me there until they were sure that all the hostiles had crossed the border into Mexico. He was lovely to me—a white man could have been no more considerate—but when he got me home again and was about to leave me he told me that he loved me.

"I don't know what it was, Margaret—inherited instinct, perhaps—but the thought of it revolted me, and he must have seen it in my face. He went away, and I never saw him again until today—three years."

The old woman looked up quickly from her work. There had been a note in the girl's voice as she spoke those last two words that aroused sudden apprehension in the breast of Margaret Cullis.

"Wichita," she demanded, "do you love this—this Apache?"

"Margaret," replied the girl, "you have been like a sister to me, or a mother. No one else could ask me that question. I have not even dared ask myself." She paused. "No, I cannot love him!"

"It would be unthinkable that you would love an Indian, Wichita," said the older woman. "It would cut you off forever from your own kind and would win you only the contempt of the Indians. A white girl had better be dead than married to an Indian."

Wichita nodded. "Yes, I know," she whispered, "and yet he is as fine as any man, white or red, that I have ever known."

"Perhaps, but the fact remains that he is an Apache."

"I wish to God that he were white!" exclaimed the girl.

A knock on the door put an end to their conversation, and Wichita arose from her chair and crossed the room to admit the caller. A tall, good-looking subaltern stood smiling on the threshold as the door swung in.

"You're prompt," said Wichita.

"A good soldier always is," said Mrs. Cullis.

"That is equivalent to a medal of honor, coming from the wife of my troop commander," laughed King as he stepped into the room.

"Give me your cap," said Wichita, "and bring that nice easy chair up here beside the table."

"I was going to suggest that we take a walk," said King, "that is if you ladies would care to. It's a gorgeous night."

"Suits me," agreed Wichita. "How about you, Margaret?"

"I want to finish my sewing. You young folks run along and have your walk, and perhaps Captain Cullis will be here when you get back. If he is we'll have a game of euchre."

"I wish you'd come," said Wichita.

"Yes, do!" begged King, but Mrs. Cullis only smiled and shook her head.

"Run along, now," she cried gaily, "and don't forget the game."

"We'll not be gone long," King assured her. "I wish you'd come with us."

"Sweet boy," thought Margaret Cullis as the door closed behind them leaving her alone. "Sweet boy, but not very truthful."

As Wichita and King stepped out into the crisp, cool air of an Arizona night the voice of the sentry at the guard house rang out clearly against the silence: "Number One, eight o'clock!" They paused to listen as the next sentry passed the call on: "Number Two, eight o'clock. All's well!" Around the chain of sentries it went, fainter in the distance, growing again in volume to the final, "All's well!" of Number One.

"I thought you said it was a gorgeous night," remarked Wichita Billings. "There is no moon, it's cloudy and dark as a pocket."

"But I still insist that it is gorgeous," said King, smiling. "All Arizona nights are."

"I don't like these black ones," said Wichita; "I've lived in Indian country too long. Give me the moon every time."

"They scarcely ever attack at night," King reminded her.

"I know, but there may always be an exception to prove the rule."

"Not much chance that they will attack the post," said King.

"I know that, but the fact remains that a black night always suggests the possibility to me."

"I'll admit that the sentries do suggest a larger assurance of safety on a night like this," said King. "We at least know that we shall have a little advance information before any Apache is among us."

Numbers Three and Four were mounted posts, and at the very instant that King was speaking a shadowy form crept between the two sentries as they rode slowly in opposite directions along their posts. It was Shoz-Dijiji.

Though the Apache had demonstrated conclusively that Wichita Billings' intuitive aversion to dark nights might be fully warranted, yet in this particular instance no danger threatened the white inhabitants of the army post, as Shoz-Dijiji's mission was hostile only in the sense that it was dedicated to espionage.

Geronimo had charged him with the duty of ascertaining the attitude of the white officers toward the departure of the War Chief from the reservation, and with this purpose in view the Black Bear had hit upon the bold scheme of entering the post and reporting Geronimo's departure in person that he might have firsthand knowledge of Nan-tan-des-la-paren's reaction.

He might have come in openly in the light of day without interference, but it pleased him to come as he did as a demonstration of the superiority of Apache cunning and of his contempt for the white man's laws.

He moved silently in the shadows of buildings, making his way toward the adobe shack that was dignified by the title of Headquarters. Once he was compelled to stop for several minutes in the dense shadow at the end of a building as he saw two figures approaching slowly. Nearer and nearer they came. Shoz-Dijiji saw that one was an officer, a war chief of the pindah-lickoyee, and the other was a woman. They were talking earnestly. When they were quite close to Shoz-Dijiji the white officer stopped and laid a hand upon the arm of his companion.

"Wait, Wichita," he said. "Before we go in can't you give

me some hope for the future? I'm willing to wait. Don't you think that some day you might care for me a little?"

The girl walked on, followed by the man. "I care for you a great deal, Ad," Shoz-Dijiji heard her say in a low voice just before the two passed out of his hearing; "but I can never care for you in the way you wish." That, Shoz-Dijiji did not hear.

"You love someone else?" he asked.

In the darkness he did not see the hot flush that overspread her face as she replied. "I am afraid so," she said.

"Afraid so! What do you mean?"

"It is something that I cannot tell you, Ad. It hurts me to talk about it."

"Does he know that you love him?"

"No."

"Is it any one I know?"

"Please, Ad, I don't like to talk about it."

Lieutenant Samuel Adams King walked on in silence at the girl's side until they reached Mrs. Cullis' door. "I'm going to wait—and hope, Chita," he said just before they entered the house.

Captain Cullis had not returned, and the three sat and chatted for a few minutes; but it was evident to Margaret Cullis that something had occurred to dash the spirits of her young guests, nor was she at a loss to guess the truth. Being very fond of them both, believing that they were eminently suited to one another, and, above all, being a natural born matchmaker, Margaret Cullis was determined to leave no stone unturned that might tend toward a happy consummation of her hopes.

"You know that Chita is leaving us in the morning?" she asked King, by way of inaugurating her campaign.

"Why, no," he exclaimed, "she did not tell me."

"I should have told you before you left," said the girl. "I wouldn't go without saying goodbye, you know."

"I should hope not," said King.

"She really should not take that long ride alone," volunteered Mrs. Cullis.

"It is nothing," exclaimed Wichita. "I've been riding alone ever since I can recall."

"Of course she shouldn't," said King. "It's not safe. I'll get leave to ride home with you. May I?"

"I'd love to have you, but really it's not necessary."

"I think it is," said King. "I'll go over to headquarters now and arrange it. I think there'll be no objections raised."

"I'm leaving pretty early," warned Wichita.

"What time?"

"Five o'clock."

"I'll be here!"

Chapter Four

GIAN-NAH-TAH RELENTS

"I CARE for you a great deal, Ad!" Shoz-Dijiji heard these words and recognized the voice of the girl who had spurned his love. Now he recognized her companion also.

Wounded pride, racial hatred, the green-eyed monster jealousy, clamored at the gates of his self-restraint, sought to tear down the barriers and loose the savage warrior upon the authors of his misery. His hand crept to the hunting knife at his hip, the only weapon that he carried; but Shoz-Dijiji was master of his own will; and the two passed on, out of his sight, innocent of any faintest consciousness that they had paused within the shadow of the Apache Devil.

A half hour later a tall, straight figure loomed suddenly before the sentry at Headquarters. The cavalryman, dismounted, snapped his carbine to *port* as he challenged: "Halt! Who is there?"

"I have come to talk with Nan-tan-des-la-par-en," said Shoz-Dijiji in Apache.

"Hell!" muttered the sentry; "if it ain't a damned Siwash," and shouted for the corporal of the guard. "Stay where you are, John," he cautioned the Indian, "until the corporal comes, or I'll have to make a good Indian of you."

"No sabe," said Shoz-Dijiji.

"You'd better savvy," warned the soldier.

The corporal of the guard appeared suddenly out of the darkness. "Wot the hell now?" he demanded. "Who the hell's this?"

"It's a Goddamn Siwash."

"How the hell did he get inside the lines?"

"How the hell should I know? Here he is, and he don't savvy United States."

The corporal addressed Shoz-Dijiji. "Wot the hell you want here, John?" he demanded.

Again the Apache replied in his own tongue.

"Try Mex on him." suggested the sentry. "Some of 'em savvy that lingo all right."

In broken, badly broken, Spanish, the corporal of the guard repeated his questions.

"No sabe," lied Shoz-Dijiji again.

"Hadn't you better shove him in the guard house?" suggested the sentry. "He aint got no business inside the post at night."

"I think he wants to talk to the Old Man—he keeps sayin' that fool Siwash name they got for Crook. You hold him here while I goes and reports to the O.D. And say, if he ain't good don't forget that it costs Uncle Sam less to bury a Injun than to feed him."

It chanced that the Officer of the Day was one of the few white men in the southwest who understood even a little of the language of the Apaches, and when he returned with the corporal he asked Shoz-Dijiji what he wanted.

"I have a message for Nan-tan-des-la-par-en," replied the Apache.

"You may give it to me," said the officer. "I will tell General Crook."

"My message is for General Crook, not for you," replied Shoz-Dijiji.

"General Crook will be angry if you bother him now with some matter that is not important. You had better tell me."

"It is important," replied Shoz-Dijiji.

"Come with me," directed the officer, and led the way into the headquarters building.

"Please inform General Crook," he said to the orderly in the outer office, "that Captain Crawford has an Apache here who says that he brings an important message for the General."

A moment later Shoz-Dijiji and Captain Crawford stepped into General Crook's presence. Captain Cullis was sitting at one end of the table behind which Crook sat, while Lieutenant King stood facing the commanding officer from whom he had just requested leave to escort Wichita Billings to her home.

"Just a moment, King," said Crook. "You needn't leave.

"Well, Crawford," turning to the Officer of the Day, "what does this man want?"

"He says that he has an important message for you, sir. He refuses to deliver it to anyone else; and as he apparently neither speaks nor understands English I came with him to interpret, if you wish, sir."

"Very good! Tell him that I say you are to interpret his message. Ask him who he is and what he wants."

Crawford repeated Crook's words to Shoz-Dijiji.

"Tell Nan-tan-des-la-par-en that I am Shoz-Dijiji, the son of Geronimo. I have come to tell him that my father has left the reservation."

Shoz-Dijiji saw in the faces of the men about him the effect of his words. To announce that Geronimo had gone out again was like casting a bomb into a peace meeting.

"Ask him where Geronimo has gone and how many warriors are with him," snapped Crook.

"Geronimo has not gone on the war trail," replied Shoz-Dijiji after Crawford had put the question to him, waiting always for the interpretation of Crook's words though he understood them perfectly in English. "There are no warriors with Geronimo other than his son. He has taken his wife with him and his small children. He wishes only to go away and live in peace. He cannot live in peace with the white-eyed men. He does not wish to fight the white-eyed soldiers any more."

"Where has he gone?" asked Crook again.

"He has gone toward Sonora," lied Shoz-Dijiji, that being the opposite of the direction taken by Geronimo; but Shoz-Dijiji was working with the cunning of an Apache. He knew well that Geronimo's absence from the reservation might

well come to the attention of the authorities on the morrow,
and he hoped that by announcing it himself and explaining
that it was not the result of warlike intentions they might
pass it over and let the War Chief live where he wished,
but if not, then it would give Geronimo time to make good his
escape if the troops were sent upon a wild goose chase
toward Sonora, while it would also allow Shoz-Dijiji ample
time to overtake his father and report the facts.

Furthermore, by bringing the message himself and by as-
suming ignorance of English, he was in a position where he
might possibly learn the plans of the white-eyed men concerning Geronimo. All in all, Shoz-Dijiji felt that his strategy
was not without merit.

Crook sat in silence for a moment, tugging on his great
beard. Presently he turned to Captain Cullis.

"Hold yourself in readiness to march at daylight, Cullis,
with all the available men of your troop. Proceed by the most
direct route to Apache Pass and try to pick up the trail. Bring
Geronimo back, alive if you can. If he resists, kill him.

"Crawford, I shall have you relieved immediately. You
also will march at dawn. Go directly south. You will each
send out detachments to the east and west. Keep in touch
with one another. Whatever else you do, bring back Geronimo!"

He swung back toward Shoz-Dijiji. "Crawford, give this
man some tobacco for bringing me this information, and see
that he is passed through the sentries and sent back to his
camp. Tell him that Geronimo had no business leaving the
reservation and that he will have to come back, but do not
let him suspect that we are sending troops after him."

The corporal of the guard escorted Shoz-Dijiji through
the line of sentries, and as they were about to part the
Apache handed the soldier the sack of tobacco that Captain
Crawford had given him.

"You're not such a bad Indian, at that," commented the
corporal; "but," he added, scratching his head, "I'd like to
know how in hell you got into the post in the first place."

"Me no sabe," said Shoz-Dijiji.

Mrs. Cullis arose early the following morning and went
directly to Wichita's room, where she found her guest already

dressed in flannel shirt, buckskin skirt, and high-heeled boots, ready for her long ride back to the Billings' ranch.

"I thought I'd catch you before you got dressed," said the older woman.

"Why?"

"You can't go today. Geronimo has gone out again. 'B' Troop and Captain Crawford's scouts have started after him already. Both Captain Cullis and Mister King have gone out with 'B' Troop, but even if there were anyone to go with you, it won't be safe until they have Geronimo back on the reservation again."

"How many went out with him?" asked the girl.

"Only his wife and children. The Indians say he has not gone on the warpath, but I wouldn't take any chances with the bloodthirsty old scoundrel."

"I'm not afraid," said Wichita. "As long as it's only Geronimo I'm in no danger even if I meet him, which I won't. You know we are old friends."

"Yes, I know all about that; but I know you can't trust an Apache."

"I trust them," said Wichita. She stooped and buckled on her spurs.

"You don't mean that you are going anyway!"

"Why of course I am."

Margaret Cullis shook her head. "What am I to do?" she demanded helplessly.

"Give me a cup of coffee before I leave," suggested Wichita.

The business at the Hog Ranch had been good that night. Two miners and a couple of cattlemen, all well staked, had dropped in early in the evening for a couple of drinks and a few rounds of stud. They were still there at daylight, but they were no longer well staked. "Dirty" Cheetim and three or four of his cronies had annexed their bank rolls. The four guests were sleeping off the effects of their pleasant evening on the floor of the back room.

"Dirty" and his pals had come out on the front porch to inhale a breath of fresh air before retiring. An Indian, lithe, straight, expressionless of face, was approaching the building.

"Hello, John!" said "Dirty" Cheetim through a wide yawn. "What for you want?"

"Whiskey," said the Apache.

"Le'me see the color of your dust, John."

A rider coming into view from the direction of the post attracted Cheetim's attention. "Wait till we see who that is," he said. "I don't want none of those damn long hairs catchin' me dishin' red-eye to no Siwash."

They all stood watching the approaching rider.

"Why it's a woman," said one of the men.

"Durned if it ain't," admitted another.

"Hell!" exclaimed Cheetim. "It's Billings' girl—the dirty——!"

"What you got agin' her?" asked one of the party.

"Got against her? Plenty! I offered to marry her, and she turned me down flat. Then her old man run me offen the ranch. It was lucky for him that they was a bunch of his cow-hands hangin' around."

The girl passed, her horse swinging along in an easy, running walk—the gait that eats up the miles. Down the dusty trail they passed while the five white men and the Apache stood on the front porch of the Hog Ranch and watched.

"Neat little heifer," commented one of the former.

"You fellers want to clean up a little dust?" asked Cheetim.

"How?" asked the youngest of the party, a puncher who drank too much to be able to hold a job even in this country of hard-drinking men.

"Help me c'ral that critter—she'd boom business in the Hog Ranch."

"We've helped you put your iron on lots of mavericks, 'Dirty,'" said the young man. "Whatever you says goes with me."

"Bueno! We'll just slap on our saddles and follow along easy like till she gets around Pimos Canyon. They's a old shack up there that some dude built for huntin', but it ain't ben used since the bronchos went out under Juh in '81 —say, that just natch'rly scairt that dude plumb out o' the country. I'll keep her up there a little while in case anyone raises a stink, and after it blows over I'll fetch her down to the Ranch. Now who's this a-comin'?"

From the direction of the post a mounted trooper was approaching at a canter. He drew rein in front of the Hog Ranch.

"Hello, you dirty bums!" he greeted them, with a grin. "You ain't worth it, but orders is orders, and mine is to notify the whites in this neck o' the woods that Geronimo's gone out again. I hope to Christ he gets you," and the messenger spurred on along the trail.

Cheetim turned to the Apache. "Is that straight, John?" he asked. "Has Geronimo gone out?"

The Indian nodded affirmatively.

"Now I reckon we got to hang onto our scalps with both hands for another couple months," wailed the young puncher.

"Geronimo no go on war trail," explained the Apache. "Him just go away reservation. Him no kill."

"Well, if he ain't on the warpath we might as well mosey along after the Billings' heifer," said Cheetim, with a sigh of relief. He turned to the Indian. "I ain't got no time now," he said. "You come round tomorrow—maybe so I fix you up then, eh?"

The Apache nodded. "Mebbe so, mebbe not," he replied, enigmatically; but Cheetim, who had already started for the corral, failed to note any hidden meaning in the words of the Indian. Perhaps none had been intended. One seldom knows what may be in the mind of an Apache.

As the five men saddled and prepared to ride after Wichita Billings the Indian started back toward the reservation. He had not understood every word that the white men had spoken, but he had understood enough, coupled with his knowledge of the sort of men they were, to fully realize their purpose and the grave danger that threatened the white girl.

In the heart of Gian-nah-tah was no love for her. In the breast of Gian-nah-tah burned sullen resentment and anger against Shoz-Dijiji. When Cheetim's purpose with the girl had first dawned upon him it had not occurred to him that he might interfere. The girl had spurned Shoz-Dijiji. Perhaps it would be better if she were out of the way. But he knew that Shoz-Dijiji loved her and that even though she did not love the war chief of the Be-don-ko-he he would protect her from injury if he could.

He recalled how Shoz-Dijiji had struck the whiskey from his hand the previous day; he felt the blows upon his face as Shoz-Dijiji slapped him; he burned at recollection of the indignities that had been put upon him before the eyes of the white-eyed man; but he kept on in the direction of the Be-don-ko-he camp.

They say that an Apache is never moved by chivalry or loyalty—only by self-interest; but this day Gian-nah-tah gave the lie to the author of this calumny.

As Wichita Billings was about to pass the mouth of Pimos Canyon she heard the sound of galloping hoofs behind her. In effete society it is not considered proper for a young lady to turn and scrutinize chance wayfarers upon the same road; but the society of Arizona in the '80's was young and virile —so young and so virile that it behooved one to investigate it before it arrived within shooting distance.

Impelled, therefore, by a deep regard for Nature's first law, Wichita turned in her saddle and examined the approaching horsemen. Instantly she saw that they were five and white. It occurred to her that perhaps they had seen her pass and were coming to warn her that Geronimo was out, for she knew that word of it would have passed quickly throughout the country.

As the riders neared she thought that she recognized something vaguely familiar in the figure and carriage of one of them, for in a country where people go much upon horseback individual idiosyncrasies of seat and form are quickly and easily observable and often serve to identify a rider at considerable distances.

Cheetim rode with an awkward hunch and his right elbow higher than his left. It was by these that Wichita recognized him even before she saw his face, though she was naturally inclined to doubt her own judgment, since she had believed "Dirty" Cheetim dead for several years.

An instant later she discerned his whiskered face. While she did not know that these men were pursuing her, she was quite confident that there would be trouble the instant that Cheetim recognized her, and so she spurred on at a faster gait, intending to keep ahead of the five without actually seeming to be fleeing them.

But that was to be more easily planned than executed, for the instant that she increased her speed they spurred after her at a run, shouting to her to stop. She heard them call that Geronimo was out, but she was more afraid of Cheetim than she was of Geronimo.

So insistent were they upon overtaking her that presently her horse was extended at full speed, but as it is seldom that a horse that excels in one gait is proportionally swift at others it was soon apparent that she would be overhauled.

Leaning forward along her horse's neck, she touched him again with her spurs and spoke encouraging words in his back-laid ears. The incentive of spur and spoken word, the lesser wind resistance of her new position, had their effects, with the result that for a short time she drew away from her pursuers; but presently the young cow-puncher, plying long rowels, wielding pliant, rawhide quirt that fell with stinging blows alternately upon either flank of his wiry mount, edged closer.

"Hold on, Miss!" he called to her. "You gotta come back —Geronimo's out!"

"You go back and tell 'Dirty' Cheetim to lay off," she shouted back over her shoulder. "If I've got to choose between him and Geronimo, I'll take the Apache."

"You better stop and talk to him," he urged. "He ain't goin' to hurt you none."

"You're damn tootin' cowboy," she yelled at him; "he sure ain't if I know it."

The young puncher urged his horse to greater speed. Wichita's mount was weakening. The man drew closer. In a moment he would be able to reach out and seize her bridle rein. The two had far outdistanced the others trailing in the dust behind.

Wichita drew his six-shooter. "Be careful, cowboy!" she warned. "I ain't got nothin' agin you, but I'll shore bore you if you lay ary hand on this bridle."

Easily Wichita lapsed into the vernacular she had spent three years trying to forget, as she always and unconsciously did under stress of excitement.

"Then I'll run that cayuse o' yourn ragged," threatened the man. "He's just about all in now."

"Yours is!" snapped Wichita, levelling her six-shooter at the horse of her pursuer and pulling the trigger.

The man uttered an oath and tried to rein in to avoid the shot. Wichita's hammer fell with a futile click. She pulled the trigger again and again with the same result. The man voiced a loud guffaw and closed up again. The girl turned her horse to one side to avoid him. Again he came on in the new direction; and when he was almost upon her she brought her mount to its haunches, wheeled suddenly and spurred across the trail to the rear of the man and rode on again at right angles to her former direction, but she had widened the distance between them.

Once more the chase began, but now the man had taken down his rope and was shaking out the noose. He drew closer. Standing in his stirrups, swinging the great noose, he waited for the right instant. Wichita tried to turn away from him, but she saw that he would win that way as easily, since she was turning back toward the other four who were already preparing to intercept her.

Her horse was heavier than the pony ridden by the young puncher and that fact gave Wichita a forlorn hope. Wheeling, she spurred straight toward the man with the mad intention of riding him down. If her own horse did not fall too, she might still have a chance.

The puncher sensed instantly the thing that was in her mind, and just before the impact he drove his spurs deep into his pony's sides, and as Wichita's horse passed behind him he dropped his noose deftly to the rear over his left shoulder, and an instant later had drawn it tight about the neck of the girl's mount.

She reached forward and tried to throw off the rope, but the puncher backed away, keeping it taut, and then "Dirty" Cheetim and the three others closed in about her.

Chapter Five

THE SNAKE LOOK

GIAN-NAH-TAH entered the hogan of Shoz-Dijiji. The young war chief, awakening instantly, sprang to his feet when he saw who it was standing in the opening.

"Does Gian-nah-tah come to the hogan of Shoz-Dijiji as friend or enemy?" he asked.

"Listen, Shoz-Dijiji, and you will know," replied Gian-nah-tah. "Yesterday my heart was bad. Perhaps the firewater of the white-eyed man made it so, but it is not of that that Gian-nah-tah has come to speak with Shoz-Dijiji. It is of the girl, Wichita."

"Shoz-Dijiji does not wish to speak of her," replied the war chief.

"But he will listen while Gian-nah-tah speaks," said the other, peremptorily. "The white-eyed skunk that sells poisoned water has ridden with four of his braves to capture the white-eyed girl that Shoz-Dijiji loves," continued Gian-nah-tah. "They follow her to Pimos Canyon, and there they will keep her in the hogan that the white fool with the strange clothing built there six summers ago. Shoz-Dijiji knows the place?"

The Black Bear did not reply. Instead he seized the cartridge belt to which his six-shooter hung and buckled it about his slim hips, took his rifle, his hackamore, ran quickly out in search of his hobbled pony.

Gian-nah-tah hastened to his own hogan for weapons. Warriors, eating their breakfasts, noted the haste of the two and questioned them. Nervous, restless, apprehensive of the results that might follow Geronimo's departure from the reservation, smarting under the injustice of the white-eyed men in taking their herds from them, many of the braves welcomed any diversion, especially one that might offer an outlet to their pent wrath against the enemy; and so it was that by the

53

time Shoz-Dijiji had found and bridled Nejeunee he discovered that instead of riding alone to the rescue of the white
girl he was one of a dozen savage warriors.

Wrapped in blankets they rode slowly, decorously, until
they had passed beyond the ken of captious white eyes, six-
shooters and rifles hidden beneath the folds of their blankets;
then the blankets fell away, folded lengthways across the
withers of their ponies, and a dozen warriors, naked but for
G strings, quirted their ponies into swinging lope.

Knowing that the troops were out, the Indians followed
no beaten road but rode south across the Gila and then
turned southeast through the hills toward Pimos Canyon.

"Dirty" Cheetim, with a lead rope on Wichita's horse,
rode beside the girl.

"Thought you was too high-toned for 'Dirty' Cheetim, eh?"
he sneered. "You was too damn good to be Mrs. Cheetim,
eh? Well, you ain't a-goin' to be Mrs. Cheetim. You're just
a-goin' to be one o' 'Dirty' Cheetim's girls down at the Hog
Ranch. Nobody don't marry them."

Wichita Billings made no reply. She rode in silence,
her eyes straight to the front. Hicks, the young puncher who
had roped the girl's horse, rode a few paces to the rear. In
his drink muddled brain doubts were forming as to the pro-
priety of the venture into which Cheetim had led him.
Perhaps he was more fool than knave; perhaps, sober, he
might have balked at the undertaking. After all he was but
half conscious of vaguely annoying questionings that might
eventually have crystallized into regrets had time sufficed,
but it did not.

They were winding up Pimos Canyon toward the deserted shack. "Your old man kicked me out," Cheetim was
saying to the girl. "I reckon you're thinking that he'll get me
for this, but he won't. After you ben to the Ranch a spell
you won't be advertising to your old man, nor nobody else,
where you be. They's other girls there as good as you be,
an' they ain't none of 'em sendin' out invites to their folks
to come an' see 'em. You—Hell! Look! Injuns!"

Over the western rim of Pimos Canyon a dozen yelling
Apaches were charging down the steep hillside.

"Geronimo!" screamed Cheetim and, dropping the lead

rope, wheeled about and bolted down the canyon as fast as spur and quirt and horse flesh could carry him.

The four remaining men opened fire on the Apaches, and in the first exchange of shots two had their horses shot from under them. Hicks' horse, grazed by a bullet, became unmanageable and started off down the canyon after Cheetim's animal, pitching and squealing, while a third man, realizing the futility of resistance and unhampered by sentiments of chivalry, put spur and followed.

One of the dismounted men ran to the side of Wichita's horse, seized her arm and dragged her from the saddle before she realized the thing that was in his mind; then, vaulting to the horse's back, he started after his fellows while the girl ran to the shelter of a boulder behind which the sole remaining white man had taken up a position from which he might momentarily, at least, wage a hopeless defense against the enemy.

Shoz-Dijiji and Gian-nah-tah, racing toward the girl, saw her dragged from her horse, saw her take refuge behind the boulder, and the latter, knowing that the girl was safe, raced after the white man who had stolen her horse and left her, as he thought, to the merciless attentions of a savage enemy.

Shoz-Dijiji, calling his warriors together, circled away from the boulder behind which the two were crouching. The white man looked from behind the boulder. Slowly he raised his rifle to take aim. The girl raised her eyes above the level of the boulder's top. She saw the Apache warriors gathered a hundred yards away, she saw the rifle of the white man leveled upon them, and then she recognized Shoz-Dijiji.

"Don't shoot!" she cried to her companion. "Wait!"

"Wait, hell!" scoffed the man. "We ain't got no more chance than a snowball in Hell. W'y should I wait?"

"One of those Indians is friendly," replied the girl. "I don't think he'll hurt us or let the others hurt us when he knows I'm here."

Gian-nah-tah, riding fast, had pulled alongside his quarry. With clubbed rifle he knocked the white man from the saddle and in a dozen more strides had seized the bridle rein of the riderless horse.

The man behind the boulder drew a fine sight on the buck

who appeared to be the leader of the renegades. It was Shoz-Dijiji. Wichita Billings snatched the white man's six-shooter from its holster and shoved the muzzle against his side.

"Drop that gun!" she cautioned, "or I'll bore you."

The man lowered his rifle to the accompaniment of lurid profanity.

"Shut up," admonished Wichita, "and look there!"

Shoz-Dijiji had tied a white rag to the muzzle of his rifle and was waving it to and fro above his head. Wichita stood up and waved a hand above her head. "Stand up!" she commanded, addressing the white man behind the boulder. The fellow did as he was bid and, again at her command, accompanied her as she advanced to meet Shoz-Dijiji, who was walking toward them alone.

As they met, the Black Bear seized the white man's rifle and wrenched it from his grasp. "Now I kill him," he announced.

"No! Oh, no!" cried Wichita, stepping between them.

"Why not?" demanded Shoz-Dijiji. "He steal you, eh?"

"Yes, but you mustn't kill him," replied the girl. "He came forward under the protection of your white flag."

"White flag for you—not for dirty coyote," the Black Bear assured her. "I give him his rifle, then. Him go back. Then I get him."

"No, Shoz-Dijiji, you must let him go. He doesn't deserve it, I'll admit; but it would only bring trouble to you and your people. The troops are already out after Geronimo. If there is a killing here there is no telling what it will lead to."

"No sabe white-eyed men," said Shoz-Dijiji disgustedly. "Kill good Indian, yes; kill bad white-eye, no." He shrugged. "Well, you say no kill, no kill." He turned to the white man. "Get out, pronto! You sabe? Get out San Carlos. Shoz-Dijiji see you San Carlos again, kill. Get!"

"Gimme my rifle and six-gun," growled the white, sullenly.

Shoz-Dijiji laid his hand on Wichita's arm as she was about to return the man's six-shooter. "Shut up, and hit the trail, white man," he snapped.

The other hesitated a moment, as though about to speak, looked into the savage face of the Apache, and then started down Pimos Canyon toward the main trail just as Gian-nah-tah rode up leading the girl's horse.

"Gian-nah-tah," said the Black Bear, "Shoz-Dijiji, the Be-don-ko-he Apache, rides with the white-eyed girl to the hogan of her father to see that she is not harmed by white-eyed men upon the way." There was the trace of a smile in the eyes of the Indian as he spoke. "Perhaps," he continued, "Gian-nah-tah will ride to the camp of my father and tell him that Nan-tan-des-la-par-en has sent troops *toward the south* to bring Geronimo in, dead or alive.

"When the white-eyed girl is safe Shoz-Dijiji will join his father. Perhaps other Apache warriors will join him. Who knows, Gian-nah-tah?"

"I shall join him," said Gian-nah-tah.

The other warriors, who had slowly drawn near, had overheard the conversation and now, without exception, each assured Shoz-Dijiji that he would join Geronimo at once or later.

As Wichita mounted her horse and looked about her at the half circle of savage warriors partially surrounding her it seemed incredible that yesterday these men were, and perhaps again tomorrow would be, the cruel, relentless devils of the Apache war trail.

Now they were laughing among themselves and poking fun at the white man plodding down the canyon and at the other whom Gian-nah-tah had knocked from Wichita's horse and who was already regaining consciousness and looking about him in a dazed and foolish manner.

It seemed incredible that she should be safe among them when she had been in such danger but a moment before among men of her own race. Many of them smiled pleasantly at her as she tried to thank them for what they had done for her; and they waved friendly hands in adieu as they rode off with Gian-nah-tah toward the north, leaving her alone with Shoz-Dijiji.

"How can I ever thank you, Shoz-Dijiji?" she said. "You are the most wonderful friend that a girl could have."

The war chief of the Be-don-ko-he looked her straight in the eyes and grunted.

"Me no sabe," he said, and wheeled his pinto down toward the main trail, beckoning her to follow.

Wichita Billings looked at the man at her side in astonishment. She opened her lips to speak again but thought better of it and remained silent. They passed the two habitués of the Hog Ranch trudging disgustedly through the dust. The Apache did not even deign to look at them. They came to the main trail, and here Shoz-Dijiji turned southeast in the direction of the Billings' ranch. San Carlos lay to the northwest. Wichita drew rein.

"You may go back to the reservation," she said. "I shall be safe now the rest of the way home."

Shoz-Dijiji looked at her. "Come!" he said, and rode on toward the southeast.

Wichita did not move. "I shall not let you ride with me," she said. "I appreciate what you have done for me, but I cannot permit myself to be put under further obligations to you."

"Come!" said Shoz-Dijiji, peremptorily.

Wichita felt a slow flush mounting her cheek, and it embarrassed and angered her.

"I'll sit here forever," she said, "before I'll let you ride home with me."

Shoz-Dijiji reined Nejeunee about and rode back to her side. He took hold of her bridle rein and started leading her horse in the directon he wished it to go.

For an instant Wichita Billings was furious. Very seldom in her life had she been crossed. Being an only child in a motherless home she had had her own way more often than not. People had a habit of doing the things that Wichita Billings wanted done. In a way she was spoiled; and, too, she had a bit of a temper. Shoz-Dijiji had humiliated her and now he was attempting to coerce her. Her eyes flashed fire as she swung her heavy quirt above her head and brought it down across the man's naked shoulders.

"Let go of my bridle, you—" but there she stopped, horrified at what she had done. "Oh, Shoz-Dijiji! How could I?" she cried, and burst into tears.

The Apache gave no sign that he had felt the stinging blow,

but the ugly welt that rose across his back testified to the force with which the lash had fallen.

As though realizing that she had capitulated the Apache dropped her bridle rein; and Wichita rode on docilely at his side, dabbing at her eyes and nose with her handkerchief and struggling to smother an occasional sob.

Thus in silence they rode as mile after mile of the dusty trail unrolled behind them. Often the girl glanced at the rugged, granitic profile of the savage warrior at her side and wondered what was passing through the brain behind that inscrutable mask. Sometimes she looked at the welt across his shoulders and caught her breath to stifle a new sob.

They were approaching the Billings' ranch now. In a few minutes Wichita would be home. She knew what Shoz-Dijiji would do. He would turn and ride away without a word. Battling with her pride, which was doubly strong because it was composed of both the pride of the white and the pride of the woman, she gave in at last and spoke to him again.

"Can you forgive me, Shoz-Dijiji?" she asked. "It was my ugly temper that did it, not my heart."

"You only think that," he said, presently. "The thing that is deep down in your heart, deep in the heart of every white, came out when you lost control of yourself through anger. If Shoz-Dijiji had been white you would not have struck him!"

"Oh, Shoz-Dijiji, how can you say such a thing?" she cried. "There is no white man in the world that I respect more than I do you."

"That is a lie," said the Apache quite simply. "It is not possible for a white-eyes to respect an Apache. Sometimes they think they do, perhaps, but let something happen to make them lose their tempers and the truth rises sure and straight, like a smoke signal after a storm."

"I do not lie to you—you should not say such a thing to me," the girl reproached.

"You lie to yourself, not to me, for you only try to deceive yourself. In that, perhaps, you succeed; but you do not deceive me. Shoz-Dijiji knows—you tell him yourself, though you do not mean to. Shoz-Dijiji will finish the words you started when you struck him with your quirt, and then you will understand what Shoz-Dijiji understands: 'Let go of my bridle. you—' dirty Siwash!"

Wichita gasped. "Oh, I didn't say that!" she cried.

"It was in your heart. The Apache knows." There was no rancor in his voice.

"Oh, Shoz-Dijiji, I *couldn't* say that to you—I couldn't mean it. Can't you see that I couldn't?"

They had reached the ranch gate and stopped. "Listen," said the Apache. "Shoz-Dijiji saw the look in the white girl's eyes when he kissed her. Shoz-Dijiji has seen that look in the eyes of white women when a snake touched them. Shoz-Dijiji understands."

"You do not understand!" cried the girl. "God! You do not understand anything."

"Shoz-Dijiji understands that white girl is for white man— Apache for Apache. If not, you would not have looked that way when Shoz-Dijiji took you in his arms. Cheetim wanted you. He is a white man." There was a trace of bitterness in his tone. "Why did not you go with him? He is no Apache to bring the snake-look to your eyes."

The girl was about to reply when they were interrupted by the sound of a gruff voice and looking up saw Billings striding angrily toward them.

"Get in here, Chita!" he ordered, roughly, and then turned to Shoz-Dijiji. "What the hell do you want?" he demanded.

"Father!" exclaimed the girl. "This is my friend. You have no right——"

"No dirty, sneaking, murdering Siwash can hang around my ranch," shouted Billings angrily. "Now get the hell out of here and stay out!"

Shoz-Dijiji, apparently unmoved, looked the white man in the eyes. "She my friend," he said. "I come when I please."

Billings fairly danced about in rage. "If I catch you around here again," he spluttered, "I'll put a bullet in you where it'll do the most good."

"Pindah-lickoyee," said the Apache, "you make big talk to a war chief of the Be-don-ko-he. When Shoz-Dijiji comes again, then maybe so you not talk so big about bullets any more," and wheeling his little pinto stallion about he rode away.

Attracted by the loud voice of Billings a cowhand, loitering near the bunkhouse, had walked down to the gate, arriving just as Shoz-Dijiji left.

"Say," he drawled, "why that there's the Injun that give me water that time an' tol' me how to git here."

"So he's the damn skunk wot stole the ewe-neck roan!" exclaimed Billings.

"Yes," snapped Wichita, angrily, "and he's the 'damn skunk' that kept 'Dirty' Cheetim from gettin' me three years ago. He's the 'damn skunk' that saved me from Tats-ah-das-ay-go down at the Pringe ranch. He's the 'damn skunk' that heard this mornin' that Cheetim was after me again with a bunch of his bums and rode down to Pimos Canyon from San Carlos and took me away from them and brought me home. You ought to be damn proud o' yourself, Dad!"

Billings looked suddenly crestfallen and Luke Jensen very much embarrassed. He had never heard the boss talked to like this before, and he wished he had stayed at the bunkhouse where he belonged.

"I'm damned sorry," said Billings after a moment of silence. "If I see that Apache again I'll tell him so, but ever since they got poor Mason I see red every time I drops my eyes on one of 'em. I'm shore sorry, Chita."

"He won't ever know it," said the girl. "Shoz-Dijiji won't ever come back again."

Chapter Six

THE WAR TRAIL

SHOZ-DIJIJI, riding cross country, picked up the trail of Geronimo where it lay revealed to Apache eyes like a printed message across the open pages of Nature's book of hieroglyphs, and in the evening of the second day he came to the camp of the War Chief.

Giannahtah and several of the warriors who had accompanied Shoz-Dijiji in the pursuit of Cheetim and his unsavory company were already with Geronimo, and during the next two days other warriors and many women came silent footed into the camp of the Be-don-ko-he.

The Apaches were nervous and irritable. They knew that troops were out after them, and though the cunning of Shoz-Dijiji had sent the first contingent upon a wild goose chase toward Sonora the Indians were well aware that it could be but a matter of days before their whereabouts might be discovered and other troops sent to arrest them.

Among those that urged upon them the necessity of immediately taking the war trail was Mangas, son of the great dead chief, Mangas Colorado; but Geronimo held back. He did not wish to fight the white men again, for he realized, perhaps better than any of them, the futility of continued resistance; but there were two forces opposing him that were to prove more potent than the conservatism of mature deliberation. They were Sago-zhu-ni, the wife of Mangas, and the tizwin she was brewing.

It was in the early evening of May 16, 1885 that Shoz-Dijiji rode into the camp of Geronimo. The sacred hoddentin had been offered up with the prayers to Evening, and already the Bedonkohe had gathered about the council fire. Tizwin was flowing freely as was evidenced by the increasing volubility of the orators.

Mangas spoke forcefully and definitely for war, urging it upon Na-chi-ta, son of old Cochise and chief of the Chihuicahui Apaches and ranking chief of all those gathered in the camp of Geronimo; but Na-chi-ta, good-natured, fonder of tizwin and pretty squaws than he was of the war trail and its hardships, argued, though half-heartedly, for peace.

Chihuahua, his fine head bowed in thought, nodded his approval of the moderate counsel of Na-chi-ta; and when it was his turn to speak he reminded them of the waste of war, of the uselessness and hopelessness of fighting against the soldiers of the white men; and old Nanáy sided with him; but Ulzanna, respected for his ferocity and his intelligence, spoke for war, as did Kutle, the bravest of them all.

Stinging from the insults of the father of Wichita Billings, Shoz-Dijiji was filled with bitterness against all whites; and when Kut-le had spoken, the young war chief of the Be-don-ko-he arose.

"Geronimo, my father," he said, "speaks with great wisdom and out of years filled with experience, but perhaps he has forgotten many things that have happened during the long years that the Shis-Inday have been fighting to drive the enemy from the country that Usen made for them. Shoz-Dijiji, the son of Geronimo, has not forgotten the things that he has seen, nor those of which his father has told him; they are burned into his memory.

"Geronimo is right when he says that peace is better than war for those who may no longer hope to win, and I too would speak against the war trail if the pindah-lickoyee would leave us in peace to live our own lives as Usen taught us to live them. But they will not. They wish us to live in their way which is not a good way for Apaches to live. If we do not wish to they send soldiers and arrest us. Thus we are prisoners and slaves. Shoz-Dijiji cannot be happy either as a prisoner or as a slave, and so he prefers the war trail and death to these things.

Na-chi-ta speaks against the war trail because there will be no tizwin there but, instead, many hardships. Shoz-Dijiji knew well the great Cochise, father of Na-chi-ta. Cochise would be angry and ashamed if he could have heard his son speak at the council fire tonight.

"Chihuahua speaks against war. Chihuahua thinks only of the little farm that the pindah-lickoyee are permitting him to use and forgets all the wide expanse of country that the pindah-lickoyee have stolen from him. Chihuahua is a brave warrior. I do not think that Chihuahua will long be happy working like a slave for the Indian Agent who will rob him of the sweat of his brow as he robs us all.

Nanáy is old and lives in memories of past war trails when he fought with glory at the side of Victorio and Loco. His day is done, his life has been lived. Why should we young men, who have our own lives to live, be content to live upon the memories of old men. We want memories of our own and freedom, if only for a short time, to enjoy them as our fathers did before us.

"Ulzanna and Kut-le are brave men. They do honor to the proud race from which we all spring. They know that it would be better to die in freedom upon the war trail against the hated pindah-lickoyee than to live like cattle, herded upon a reservation by the white-eyes.

"They think of the great warriors, of the women, of the little children who have been murdered by the lies and treachery of the pindah-lickoyee. They recall the ridicule that is heaped upon all those things which we hold most sacred. They do not forget the insults that every white-eyed man hurls at the Shis-Inday upon every occasion except when the Shis-Inday are on the war trail. Then they respect us.

"Shall we wait here until they come and arrest and kill our chiefs, as Nan-tan-des-la-par-en has ordered them to do, or shall we take to the war trail and teach them once more to respect us? I, Shoz-Dijiji, war chief of the Be-don-ko-he, speak for the war trail. I have spoken."

An old man arose. "Let us wait," he said. "Perhaps the soldiers of the pindah-lickoyee will not come. Perhaps they will let us live in peace if we do not go upon the war trail. Let us wait."

The tizwin had not as yet spoken its final word, and there were more who spoke against the war trail than for it, and before the council was concluded many had spoken. Among the last was Sago-zhu-ni—Pretty Mouth—the wife of Mangas, for the voice of women was not unknown about the council fires of the Apaches. And why should it be? Did not they share all the hardships of the war trail with their lords and masters? Did they not often fight, and as fiercely and terribly as the men? Were they not as often the targets for the rifles of the pindah-lickoyee? Who, then, had better right to speak at the councils of the Apaches than the wives and mothers of their warriors.

Sago-zhu-ni spoke briefly, but to the point. "Are you men, old women, or children?" she cried fiercely. "If you are old women and children, you will stay here and wait to receive your punishment, but if you are warriors, you will take the war trail, and then Nan-tan-des-la-par-en must catch you before he can punish you. Maybeso, you go to Sonora, he no catch you. I have spoken."

Now Na-chi-ta, encouraged by tizwin and goaded by the reproaches of Shoz-Dijiji spoke for war. Geronimo, his savage brain inflamed by the fumes of the drink, applauded Sago-zhu-ni and demanded the blood of every pindah-lickoyee.

With fiery eloquence he ranged back through the history of the Shis-Inday for more than three hundred years and reminded them of every wrong that white men had committed against them in all that time. He spoke for more than an hour, and while he spoke Sago-zhu-ni saw that no warrior suffered from lack of tizwin. Of all who spoke vehemently for the war trail Shoz-Dijiji alone spoke out of a clear mind, or at least a mind unclouded by the fumes of drink, though it was dark with bitter hatred and prejudice.

When Geronimo sat down they voted unanimously for the war trail; and the next morning they broke camp and headed south—thirty-four warriors, eight boys, and ninety-one women. Hair was slicked down with tallow, swart faces streaked with war paint, weapons looked to. Hoddentin was sprinkled on many a tzi-daltai of lightning riven pine or cedar or fir as copper warriors prayed to these amulets for protection against the bullets of the pindah-lickoyee, for success upon the war trail.

Shoz-Dijiji, with Gian-nah-tah and two other warriors, rode in advance of the main party, scouting far afield, scanning the distances from every eminence. No creature stirred in the broad landscape before them that was not marked by those eagle eyes, no faintest spoor beneath their feet was passed unnoted.

The young war chief of the Be-don-ko-he was again the Apache Devil. His face was painted blue but for the broad band of white across his eyes from temple to temple; around his head was wound a vivid yellow bandanna upon the front of which was fastened a silver disc in the center of which was mounted a single turquoise; small rings of silver, from each of which depended another of these valued gems, swung from the lobes of his ears; other bits of this prized duklij were strung in the yard-long necklace of glass beads and magical berries and roots that fell across the front of his brown print shirt, which, with his heavy buckskin war moccasins and his G-string, completed his apparel.

About his waist and across one shoulder were belts filled with ammunition for the revolver at his hip and the rifle lying across the withers of Nejeunee, and at his left side hung a pair of powerful field glasses that he had taken in battle from a cavalry officer several years before. From below the skirts of his shirt to the tops of his moccasins the Apache Devil's bronzed legs were naked, as he seldom if ever wore the cotton drawers affected by many of his fellows. The bracelets of silver and brass that adorned his muscular arms were hidden by the sleeves of his shirt, a shirt that he probably soon would discard, being ever impatient of the confining sensation that clothing imparted.

Down into the mountains of southwestern New Mexico the Apaches marched, following trails known only to themselves, passing silently through danger zones by night, and established themselves among caves and canyons inaccessible to mounted troops.

Striking swiftly, raiding parties descended upon many an isolated ranch house both in Arizona and New Mexico, leaving behind horrid evidence of their ferocity as they rode away upon stolen horses from the blazing funeral pyres that had once been homes.

Scouts kept Geronimo informed of the location of the troops in the field against him; and the shrewd old war chief successfully avoided encounters with any considerable body of enemy forces, but scouting parties and supply trains often felt the full force of the strategy and courage of this master general of guerilla warfare and his able lieutenants.

It was during these days that the blue and white face of the Apache Devil became as well known and as feared in the mountains as it was in Sonora and Chihuahua, for, though relentless in his war against the men of the pindah-lickoyee, Shoz-Dijiji killed neither women nor children, with the result that there were often survivors to describe the boldness and ferocity of his attacks.

Scouting far north for information relative to the movement of troops, Shoz-Dijiji one day came upon an Indian scout in the employ of the enemy; and having recognized him as an old friend he hailed him.

"Where are the soldiers of the pindah-lickoyee?" demanded Shoz-Dijiji.

"They cannot catch you," replied the scout, grinning, "and

so they are sending Apaches after you. Behind me are a hundred White Mountain and Cho-kon-en braves. They are led by one white-eyed officer, Captain Crawford. Tell Geronimo that he had better come in, for he cannot escape the Shis-Inday as he has escaped the pindah-lickoyee."

"Why do you and the others go upon the war trail against your own people?" demanded Shoz-Dijiji. "Why do you fight as brothers at the side of the enemy?"

"We take the war trail against you because you are fools and we are not," replied the scout. "We have learned that it is useless to fight against the pindah-lickoyee. We do not love them more than you; and if we could kill them all we would, but we cannot kill them all—they are as many as the weeds that grow among our corn and beans and pumpkins—for though we cut them down they come again in greater numbers than before, flourishing best in soil that is wet with blood.

"When you go upon the war trail against the white-eyed men it only makes more trouble for us. Geronimo is a great troublemaker. Therefore we fight against him that we may live in peace."

"Either your mouth is full of lies or your heart has turned to water," said Shoz-Dijiji. "No Apache wants peace at the price of slavery, unless he has become a coward and is afraid of the pindah-lickoyee. Shoz-Dijiji has the guts of a man. He would rather die on the war trail than be a reservation Indian. You have not even the guts of a coyote, which snarls and snaps at the hand of his captor and risks death to regain his freedom."

"Be a coyote then," sneered the scout, "and I will put your pelt on the floor of my hogan."

"Here it is, reservation Indian," replied the Black Bear. "Take it."

Both men had dismounted when they met and were standing close and face to face. The scout reached quickly for his six-shooter, but the Apache Devil was even quicker. His left hand shot out and seized the other's wrist, and with his right he drew from its scabbard the great butcher knife that hung at his hip.

The scout warded the first blow and grasped Shoz-Dijiji's

arm, and at the same instant tore his right arm free; but as he did so the renegade snatched the other's gun from its holster and tossed it aside, while the scout, profiting by the momentary freedom of his right hand, drew his own knife, and the two closed in a clinch, each striving to drive his blade home in the body of his adversary.

At the time that their altercation had reached the point of physical encounter each of the men had dropped his hackamore rope with the result that Shoz-Dijiji's horse, recently stolen from a raided ranch, took advantage of this God-Given opportunity to make a break for freedom and home, while the scout's pony, lured by the call of consanguinity, trotted off with the deserter.

Each of the combatants now held the knife arm of the other and the struggle had resolved itself into one of strength and endurance, since he who could hold his grip the longer stood the greater chance for victory, the other the almost certain assurance of death.

They struggled to and fro, pushing one another here and there about the sandy dust of a parched canyon bottom. The painted face of the Apache Devil remained almost expressionless, so well schooled in inscrutability were his features, nor did that of the scout indicate that he was engaged in a duel to the death.

Two miles to the north a detachment of twenty White Mountain Apaches from Crawford's Indian Scouts were following leisurely along the trail of their comrade. In twenty minutes, perhaps, they would come within sight of the scene of the duel.

It is possible that the scout engaged with Shoz-Dijiji held this hope in mind, for when it became obvious to him that he was no match in physical strength for his adversary he dropped his own knife and grasped the knife arm of his foe in both hands.

It was a foolish move, for no sooner did the Apache Devil regain the freedom of his left hand than he transferred his weapon to it and before his unfortunate antagonist realized his danger Shoz-Dijiji plunged the blade between his ribs, deep into his heart.

Stooping over the body of his dead foe Shoz-Dijiji tore

the red band that proclaimed the government scout from his brow and with a deft movement of his knife removed a patch of scalp. Then he appropriated the ammunition and weapons of his late adversary and turned to look for the two ponies. Now, for the first time, he realized that they were gone and that he was afoot far from the camp of Geronimo, probably the sole possessor of the information that a hundred scouts were moving upon the stronghold of the War Chief.

A white man might doubtless have been deeply chagrined had he found himself in a similar position, but to the Apache it meant only a little physical exertion to which he was already inured by a lifetime of training. The country through which he might pass on foot by the most direct route to Geronimo's camp was practically impassable to horses but might be covered by an Apache in less time than it would have required to make the necessary detours on horseback. However, Shoz-Dijiji would have preferred the easier method of transportation, and so he regretted that he had ridden the new pony instead of Nejeunee, who would not have run away from him.

Knowing that other scouts might be near at hand, Shoz-Dijiji placed an ear to the ground and was rewarded by information that sent him quickly toward the south. Clambering up the side of the canyon, he adjusted the red band of the dead scout about his own head as he climbed, for he knew that eyes fully as keen as his own were doubtless scanning the horizon through powerful field glasses at no great distance and that if they glimpsed the red band they would not hasten in pursuit.

He grinned as he envisaged the anger of the scouts when they came upon the dead body of their scalped comrade, and the vision lightened the dreary hours as he trotted southward beneath the pitiless sun of New Mexico.

Late in the afternoon Shoz-Dijiji approached a main trail that led west to Fort Bowie and which he must cross, but with the caution of the Apache he reconnoitered first. From the top of a low hill the trail was in sight for a mile or two in each direction and to this vantage point the Black Bear crept. Only his eyes and the top of his head were raised above the summit of the hill, and these were screened by a small bush that he had torn from the ground and which he held just in front of him as he wormed his way to the hilltop.

Below him the trail led through a defile in which lay scattered huge fragments of rock among which the feed grew thick and rank, suggesting water close beneath the surface; but it was not these things that caught the eyes and interest of the Apache Devil, who was already as familiar with them as he was with countless other square miles of New Mexico, Arizona, Chihuahua, and Sonora, or with the wrinkles upon the face of his mother, Sons-ee-ah-ray.

That which galvanized his instant attention and interest was a cavalryman sitting upon a small rock fragment while his horse, at the end of a long riata, cropped the green feed. Shoz-Dijiji guessed that here was a military messenger riding to or from Fort Bowie. Here, too, was a horse, and Shoz-Dijiji was perfectly willing to ride the rest of the way to the camp of Geronimo.

A shot would dispose of the white-eyed soldier, but it would, doubtless, also frighten the horse and send him galloping far out of the reach of Apache hands; but Shoz-Dijiji was resourceful.

He quickly cached the rifle of the scout, for the possession of two rifles might raise doubts that two six-shooters would not; he adjusted the red scout band and with a bandanna carefully wiped from his face the telltale war paint of the Apache Devil. Then he arose and walked slowly down the hillside toward the soldier, who sat with his back toward him. So silently he moved that he was within four or five feet of the man when he halted and spoke.

The soldier wheeled about as he sprang to his feet and drew his pistol, but the sight of the smiling face of the Indian, the extended hand and the red band of the government scout removed his fears instantly.

"Nejeunee, nejeunee," Shoz-Dijiji assured him, using the Apache word meaning friend, and stepping forward grasped the soldier's hand.

Smiling pleasantly, Shoz-Dijiji looked at the horse and then at the riata approvingly.

"You belong Crawford's outfit?" inquired the soldier.

"Me no sabe," said Shoz-Dijiji. He picked up the riata and examined it. "Mucho bueno!" he exclaimed.

"You bet," agreed the cavalryman. "Damn fine rope."

The Apache examined the riata minutely, passing it through his hands, and at the same time walking toward the horse slowly. The riata, a braided hair "macarthy," was indeed a fine specimen, some sixty feet in length, of which the soldier was pardonably proud, a fact which threw him off his guard in the face of the Indian's clever simulation of interest and approval.

When Shoz-Dijiji reached the end of the rope which was about the horse's neck he patted the animal admiringly and turned to the soldier, smiling enthusiastically. "Mucho bueno," he said, nodding toward the horse.

"You bet," said the trooper. "Damn fine horse."

With his back toward the white man, Shoz-Dijiji drew his knife and quickly severed the rope, holding the two ends concealed in his left hand. "Mucho bueno," he repeated, turning again toward the soldier, and then, suddenly and with seeming excitement, he pointed up the hill back of the trooper. "Apache on dahl!" he shouted—"The Apaches are coming!"

Quite naturally, under the circumstances, the soldier turned away to look in the direction from which the savage enemy was supposed to be swooping upon him, and as he did so the Apache Devil vaulted into the saddle and was away.

The great boulders strewing the floor of the canyon afforded him an instant screen and though the soldier was soon firing at him with his pistol he offered but a momentary and fleeting target before he was out of range, carrying away with him the cavalryman's carbine, which swung in its boot beneath the off stirrup of the trooper's McClellan.

Shoz-Dijiji was greatly elated. He knew that he might have knifed the unsuspecting pindah-lickoyee had he preferred to; but a victory of wits and cunning gave him an even greater thrill of satisfaction, for, Apache to the core though he was, the Black Bear killed not for the love of it but from a sense of duty to his people and loyalty to the same cause that inspired such men as Washington and Lincoln—freedom.

Chapter Seven

HARD PRESSED

REMOUNTED, and richer by a carbine, a six-shooter and many rounds of ammunition, Shoz-Dijiji rode into the camp of Geronimo late at night. When he had awakened the War Chief and reported the approach of the hundred scouts under Crawford, preparations were immediately started to break camp; and within an hour the renegades were moving silently southward.

Down into Sonora they went, raiding and killing as they passed through the terror-stricken country, but moving swiftly and avoiding contact with the enemy. In the mountains west of Casa Grande Geronimo went into camp again, and from this base raiding parties took relentless toll throughout the surrounding country.

In the mountains above Casa Grande, Pedro Mariel, the woodchopper, felled trees, cut them into proper lengths which he split and loaded upon the backs of his patient burros. This he did today as he had done for many years. With him now was Luis, his nineteen-year-old son. Other woodchoppers, joining with the Mariels for company and mutual protection, camped and worked with them. In all there were a dozen men—hardy, courageous descendants of that ancient race that built temples to their gods upon the soil of the Western Hemisphere long before the first showboat stranded on Ararat.

As the sound of their axes rang in the mountains, a pair of savage eyes set in a painted face looked down upon them from the rim of the canyon in which they labored. The eyes were the eyes of Gian-nah-tah, the Be-don-ko-he Apache. They counted the number of the men below, they took in every detail of the nearby camp, of the disposal of the men engaged in felling new trees or cutting those that had been felled. For a half hour they watched, then Gian-nah-tah withdrew, silently as a shadow. The Mexicans, unsuspecting, continued at their work, stopping occasionally to roll a cigarette or pass some laughing remark. Luis Mariel often sang snatches of songs which usually concerned señoritas with large, dark eyes and red lips, for Luis was young and lighthearted.

An hour passed. Gian-nah-tah returned, but not alone. With him, this time, were a dozen painted warriors, moving like pumas—silently, stealthily. Among them was Shoz-Dijiji, the Apache Devil. Down the canyon side they crept and into the bottom below the woodchoppers. Spreading out into a thin line that crossed the canyon's floor and extended up either side they advanced slowly, silently, hiding behind trees, crawling across open spaces upon their bellies. They were patient, for they were Apaches—the personification of infinite patience.

Luis Mariel sang of a castle in Spain, which he thought of vaguely as a place of many castles and beautiful señoritas somewhere across a sea that was also "somewhere." Close beside him worked his father, Pedro, thinking proudly of this fine son of his.

Close to them, cruel eyes looked through a band of white out of a blue face. The Apache Devil, closest to them, watched the pair intently. Suddenly a shot rang above the ringing axes. Manuel Farias clutched his breast and crumpled to the ground. Other shots came in quick succession, and then the air was rent by wild Apache war-whoops as the savages charged the almost defenseless woodchoppers.

Luis Mariel ran to his father's side. Grasping their axes they stood shoulder to shoulder, for between them and whatever weapons they had left in camp were whooping Apaches. Some of the other men tried to break through and reach their rifles, but they were shot down. Three surrendered. A huge warrior confronted Pedro and Luis.

"Pray," said Pedro, "for we are about to die." He was looking at the face of the warrior. "It is the Apache Devil!"

"Who is that?" demanded the Indian, pointing to the lad.

"He is my oldest son," replied Pedro, wondering.

"Put down your axes and come here," ordered the Apache. "You will not be harmed."

Pedro was not surprised to hear the Indian speak in broken Spanish, as most Apaches understood much and spoke a little of the language of their ancient enemies; but he was surprised at the meaning of the words he heard, surprised and skeptical. He hesitated. Luis looked up at him, questioningly.

"If we lay down our axes we shall be wholly unarmed," said Pedro.

"What difference does it make?" asked Luis. "He can kill us whether we have axes in our hands or not—they will not stop his bullets."

"You are right," said Pedro and threw down his axe. Luis did likewise and together they approached the Apache Devil. "May the Holy Mary protect us!" whispered the father.

The other Mexicans, having been killed or captured, Giannah-tah and the balance of the braves came running toward Pedro and Luis; but Shoz-Dijiji stepped in front of them and raised his hand.

"These are my friends," he said. "Do not harm them."

"They are enemies," cried one of the warriors, excited by blood and anticipation of torture. "Kill them!"

"Very well," said Shoz-Dijiji quietly. "You may kill them, but first you must kill Shoz-Dijiji. He has told you that they are his friends."

"Why does Shoz-Dijiji protect the enemy?" demanded Giannahtah.

"Listen," said Shoz-Dijiji. "Many years ago Shoz-Dijiji was hunting in these mountains. He was alone. He often saw this man felling trees, but he did not harm him because the Apaches were not upon the war trail at that time. A tree fell upon the man in such a way that he could not free himself. He must have died if no one came to help him. There was no one to come but Shoz-Dijiji.

"Shoz-Dijiji lifted the tree from him. The man's leg was broken. Shoz-Dijiji placed him upon one of his burros and took him to Casa Grande, where he lived.

"You all remember the time when we made the treaty of peace with the people of Casa Grande and while we were celebrating it the Mexican soldiers came and attacked us. They made us prisoners and were going to shoot us.

"This man came to look at the captives and recognized

Shoz-Dijiji. He begged the war chief of the Mexicans to let
me go, and he took me to his home and gave me food and set
me free. It was Shoz-Dijiji who was able to release all the
other Apache prisoners because of what this man did. The
other here is his son.

"Because of what his father did for Shoz-Dijiji neither of
them shall be killed. We shall let them take their burros and
their wood and go back in safety to their home. I have
spoken."

"Shoz-Dijiji speaks true words when he says that these two
shall not be harmed," said Gian-nah-tah. "Let them go in
peace."

"And look at them well," added Shoz-Dijiji, "that you may
know them and spare them if again you meet them." He
turned to Pedro. "Get your burros and your wood and go
home quickly with your son. Do not come again to the
mountains while the Apaches are on the war trail, for
Shoz-Dijiji may not be always near to protect you. Go!"

Bewildered, stammering their thanks, Pedro and Luis hastened to obey the welcome mandate of the savage while
Shoz-Dijiji's companions fell to with savage ardor upon the
hideous business that is the aftermath of an Apache victory.

Uninterested, Shoz-Dijiji stood idly by until the Mariels
had hastily packed their few belongings and departed, leaving
their wood behind them. No longer did his fellows ridicule or
taunt Shoz-Dijiji for his refusal to join them in the torture
of their captives or the mutilation of the dead. His courage
had been proved upon too many fields of battle, his hatred of
the enemy was too well known to leave any opening for
charges of cowardice or disloyalty. They thought him peculiar and let it go at that. Perhaps some of the older
braves recalled the accusation of the dead Juh that Shoz-Dijiji
was no Apache but a white-eyed man by birth; but no one
ever mentioned that now since Juh was dead, and it was well
known that he had died partly because he had made this
charge against the Black Bear.

Back in the camp of the renegades Gian-nah-tah and the
others boasted loudly of their victory, exhibited the poor
spoils that they had taken from the camp of the woodchoppers, while the squaws cooked the flesh of one of the burros

for a feast in celebration. Perhaps they were off their guard, but then, even Homer is charged with carelessness.

Just as a bullet had surprised the camp of the woodchoppers earlier in the day, so a bullet surprised the camp of the renegades. A little Indian boy clutched his breast and crumpled to the ground. Other shots came in quick succession, and then the air was rent by wild Apache war-whoops. Apache had surprised Apache. Perhaps no other could have done it so well.

As Crawford's Scouts charged the camp of Geronimo, the renegades, taken completely off their guard, scattered in all directions. Pursued by a part of the attacking force, Geronimo's warriors kept up a running fight until all the fighting men and a few of the women and children had escaped; but a majority of the latter were rounded up by the scouts and taken back to Crawford's camp, prisoners of war. Only the dead body of a little boy remained to mark the scene of happy camp, of swift, fierce battle. In the blue sky, above the silent pines, a vulture circled upon static wings.

That night the renegades gathered in a hidden mountain fastness, and when the last far flung scout had come they compared notes and took account of their losses. They found that nearly all of their women and children had been captured. Of Geronimo's family only Shoz-Dijiji remained to the old War Chief. Sons-ee-ah-ray was a captive.

When their brief council was concluded, Geronimo arose. "Above the water that falls over the red cliff in the mountains south of Casa Grande there is a place that even the traitors who hunt us for the pindah-lickoyee may find difficult to attack. If you start now you will be almost there before the rays of chigo-na-ay light the eastern sky and reveal you to the scouts of the enemy. If Geronimo has not returned to you by the second darkness he will come no more. Pray to Usen that he may guide and protect you. I have spoken." The War Chief turned and strode away into the darkness.

Shoz-Dijiji sprang to his feet and ran after him. "Where do you go, Geronimo?" he demanded.

"To fetch Sons-ee-ah-ray from the camp of the enemy," replied Geronimo.

Two other braves who had followed Shoz-Dijiji overheard. One of them was Gian-nah-tah.

"Shoz-Dijiji goes with Geronimo to the camp of the enemy," announced the Black Bear.

Gian-nah-tah and the other warrior also announced their intention of accompanying the War Chief, and in silence the four started off single file down the rugged mountains with Geronimo in the lead. There was no trail where they went; and the night was dark, yet they skirted the edge of precipice, descended steep escarpment, crossed mountain stream on slippery boulders as surely as man trods a wide road by the light of day.

They knew where Crawford's camp lay, for Giannahtah had been one of the scouts who had followed the victorious enemy, and they came to it while there were yet two hours before dawn.

Crawford had made his camp beside that of a troop of United States Cavalry that had been scouting futilely for Geronimo for some time, and in addition to the Indian Scouts and the cavalry men in the combined camps there were a number of refugees who had sought the protection of the troops. Among them being several Mexican women and one American woman, the wife of a freighter.

Never quite positive of the loyalty of the Indian Scouts, Crawford and the troop commander had thought it advisable to post cavalrymen as sentries; and as these rode their posts about the camp the four Apaches crept forward through the darkness.

On their bellies, now, they wormed themselves forward, holding small bushes in front of their heads. When a sentry's face was turned toward them they lay motionless; when he passed on they moved forward.

They had circled the camp that they might approach it up wind, knowing that were their scent to be carried to the nostrils of a sentry's horse he might reveal by his nervousness the presence of something that would warrant investigation.

Now they lay within a few paces of the post toward which they had been creeping. The sentry was coming toward them. There was no moon, and it was very dark. There were bushes upon either side of him, low sage and greasewood. That there were four more now upon his left than there had been before he did not note, and anyway in ten minutes he was to be relieved. It was this of which he was thinking—not bushes.

He passed. Four shadowy patches moved slowly across his post. A moment later he turned to retrace his monotonous beat. This time the four bushes which should now have been upon his right were again upon his left. His horse pricked up his ears and looked in the direction of the camp. The horse had become accustomed to the scent of Indians coming from the captives within the camp, but he knew that they were closer now. However, he was not startled, as he would have been had the scent come from a new direction. The man looked casually where the horse looked—that is second nature to a horseman—then he rode on; and the four bushes merged with the shadows among the tents.

The American woman, the wife of the freighter, had been given a tent to herself. She was sleeping soundly, secure in the knowledge of absolute safety, for the first time in many weeks. As she had dozed off to sleep the night before she had hoped that her husband was as comfortable as she; but, knowing him as she had, her mind had been assailed by doubts. He had been killed by Apaches a week previously.

She was awakened by a gentle shaking. When she opened her eyes she saw nothing as it was dark in the tent; but she felt a hand upon her arm, and when she started to speak a palm was slapped across her mouth.

"Make noise, gettum killed," whispered a deep voice. "Shut up, no gettum killed."

The hand was removed. "What do you want?" whispered the woman. "I'll keep shet up."

"Where is the wife of Geronimo?" pursued the questioner.

"I dunno," replied the woman, sullenly. "Who are you— one o' them Injun Scouts? Why don't you go ask some other Injun? I dunno."

"Maybe so you find out pronto. Me Apache Devil. She my mother. You tellum damn pronto or Apache Devil cut your damn fool throat. Sabe?"

The woman felt the edge of a knife against the flesh at her throat. "She's in the next tent," she whispered hastily.

"You lie me come back and kill," he said, then he bound her hands and feet and tied a gag in her mouth, using strips torn from her own clothing for these purposes.

In the next tent they found Sons-ee-ah-ray, and a few minutes later five bushes crossed the post that four had previously crossed.

In the new camp south of Casa Grande the renegades found peace but for a few days, and then came Mexican troops one morning and attacked them. The skirmishing lasted all day. A few Mexican soldiers were killed; and at night the Apaches, having sustained no loss, moved eastward into the foothills of the Sierra Madres.

A few more days of rest and once again the Mexican troops, following them, attacked; but the Apaches had not been caught unawares. Their women and children were sent deeper into the mountains, while the warriors remained to hold the soldiers in check.

During a lull in the fighting Geronimo gathered several of his followers about him. "The Mexicans now have a large army against us," he said. "If we stand and fight them many of us will be killed. We cannot hope to win. It is senseless to fight under such circumstances. Let us wait until our chance of victory is greater."

The others agreed with the War Chief, and the renegades withdrew. Shoz-Dijiji and Gian-nah-tah were sent to ascertain the strength of the troops against them and their location, while the main body of the renegades followed the squaws to the new camp.

It was very late when Shoz-Dijiji and Gian-nah-tah rejoined their fellows. They came silently into camp after having been challenged and passed by savage sentries. They wore grave faces as they approached Geronimo. The War Chief had been sleeping; but he arose when he learned that his scouts had returned, and when he had had their report he summoned all the warriors to a council.

"Shoz-Dijiji and Gian-nah-tah, with the speed of the deer, the cunning of the fox, and the vision of the eagle, have gone among the enemy and seen much. Let Shoz-Dijiji tell you what he told Geronimo."

"For many days," said Shoz-Dijiji, "we have been pressed

closely by the enemy. First by the Scouts of the pindah-lickoyee, then by the warriors of the Mexicans. Wherever we go, they follow. We have had no time to hunt or raid. We are almost without food. Usen has put many things in the mountains and upon the plains for Apaches to eat. We can go on thus for a long time, but I do not think we can win.

"These things you should know. We are but a few warriors, and against us are the armies of two powerful nations. Shoz-Dijiji thinks that it would be wise to wait a little until they forget. In the past they have forgotten. They will forget again. Then the Apaches may take up the war trail once more or remain in peaceful ways, hunting and trading.

"Today Gian-nah-tah and Shoz-Dijiji saw soldiers in many places all through the mountains. There were soldiers of the Mexicans, there were soldiers of the pindah-lickoyee, there were the Apache Scouts of Crawford. They are all waiting to kill us. Perhaps we can escape them, perhaps we cannot. It would be foolish to attack them. We are too few, and our brothers have turned against us."

"How many soldiers did you see?" asked Nachita.

"Perhaps two thousand, perhaps more," replied Shoz-Dijiji. "There are infantry and cavalry, and cannon mounted on the backs of mules."

"Chihuahua thought Shoz-Dijiji wished only to fight against the pindah-lickoyee," said Chihuahua. "He made big talk before we went on the war trail after we left San Carlos. Has Shoz-Dijiji's heart turned to water?"

"I do not know," said Shoz-Dijiji. "I think it has not turned to water, but it is very sad. Shoz-Dijiji learned at his mother's breast to love nothing better than fighting the enemies of the Shis-Inday, but he did not learn to love to fight his own people. I think it made his heart sick that day that he saw White Mountain firing upon White Mountain, Cho-kon-en upon Cho-kon-en. That is not war, that is murder.

"Every man's hand is against us, but that Shoz-Dijiji did not mind. What he does mind is to know that our own hands are against us, too."

"Shoz-Dijiji has spoken true words," said Kut-le. "It sickens the heart in the breast of a warrior to see brother and cousin fighting against him at the side of his enemies.

"We know that we are surrounded by many soldiers. We cannot fight them. Perhaps we can escape them, but they will follow us. It will be hard to find food and water, for these things they will first try to deprive us of.

"I think that we should make peace with our enemies. I have spoken."

Thus spoke Kut-le, the bravest of the renegades. Savage heads nodded approval.

"Let us go to the camp of the white-eyed soldiers in the morning," suggested one, "and lay down our weapons."

"And be shot down like coyotes," growled Geronimo. "No! Geronimo does not surrender. He makes peace. He does not stick his head in a trap, either. We will send a messenger to Crawford to arrange a parley with Nan-tan-des-la-par-en. The heart of Crawford is good. He does not lie to the Shis-Inday. By the first light of chigo-na-ay Shoz-Dijiji shall go to the kunh-gan-hay of the scouts and carry the message of Geronimo to Crawford. If he promises to protect us from the soldiers of the pindah-lickoyee and the Mexicans, we will accompany him north and hold a peace parley with Nan-tan-des-la-par-en." He turned toward Shoz-Dijiji. "You have heard the words of Geronimo. When dawn comes go to Crawford. You will know what to say to him."

Chapter Eight

GERONIMO AND CROOK

CRAWFORD'S scouts were preparing to ride with the coming of the new day when there appeared upon a little eminence near their camp the figure of an Indian. Silent and erect it stood—a bronze statue touched by the light of the rising sun. Slowly, to and fro, it waved a white rag that was attached to the muzzle of a rifle. A scout called Crawford's attention to the flag of truce; and the cavalry officer, bearing a similar emblem, went out alone and on foot toward the messenger, who now came slowly forward until the two met a couple of hundred yards from the camp.

Crawford recognized the Black Bear and nodded, waiting for him to speak.

"Shoz-Dijiji brings a message from Geronimio," said the Apache.

"What message does Geronimo send me?" asked the officer. Both men spoke in the language of the Shis-Inday.

"Geronimo has heard that Nan-tan-des-la-par-en wishes to hold a parley with him," replied Shoz-Dijiji.

"Nan-tan-des-la-par-en wishes only that Geronimo surrenders with all his warriors, women, and children," said Crawford. "There is no need for a parley. Tell Geronimo that if he will come to my camp with all his people, bringing also all his horses and mules, and lay down his arms, I will take him to Nan-tan-des-la-par-en in safety."

"That is surrender," replied Shoz-Dijiji. "Geronimo will not surrender. He will make peace with Nan-tan-des-la-par-en, but he will not surrender."

"Black Bear," said Crawford, "you are a great warrior among your people, you are an intelligent man, you know that we have you surrounded by a greatly superior force, you are worn by much fighting and marching, you are short of food, you cannot escape us this time. I know these things; you know them; Geronimo knows them.

"It will be better for you and your people if you come in peaceably now and return with me. Nan-tan-des-la-par-en will not be hard on you if you surrender now, but if you cause us any more trouble it may go very hard indeed with you. Think it over."

"We have thought it over," replied the Black Bear. "We know that a handful of braves cannot be victorious over the armies of two great nations, but we also know that we can keep on fighting for a long time before we are all killed and that in the meantime we shall kill many more of our enemies than we lose. You know that these are true words. Therefore it would be better for you to arrange for a parley with Nan-tan-des-la-par-en than to force us back upon the war trail.

"Geronimo is a proud man. The thing that you demand he will never consent to, but a peace parley with Nan-tan-des-la-par-en might bring the same results without so greatly injuring the pride of Geronimo.

"These things I may say to you because it is well known that your heart is not bad against the Apaches. Of all the pindah-lickoyee you are best fitted to understand. That is why Geronimo sent me to you. He would not have sent this message to any white-eyed man but you or Lieutenant Gatewood. Him we trust also. We do not trust Nan-tan-des-la-par-en any more; but if we have your promise that no harm shall befall us we will go with you and talk with him, but we must be allowed to keep our weapons and our livestock. I have spoken."

"I get your point," said Crawford after a moment of thought. "If Geronimo and the warriors in his party will give me their word that they will accompany us peaceably I will take them to General Crook and guarantee them safe escort, but I cannot promise what General Crook will do. Geronimo knows that I have no authority to do that."

"We shall come in and make camp near you this afternoon," said Shoz-Dijiji. "Tell your scouts not to fire upon us."

"When you come stop here, and I will tell you where to camp," replied Crawford. "Geronimo and two others may come into my camp to talk with me, but if at any time more of you enter my camp armed I shall consider it a hostile demonstration. Do you understand?"

Shoz-Dijiji nodded and without more words turned and retraced his steps toward the camp of the renegades, while Crawford stood watching him until he had disappeared beyond a rise of ground. Not once did the Apache glance back. The cavalry officer shook his head. "It is difficult," he mused, "not to trust a man who has such implicit confidence in one's honor."

That afternoon, January 11, 1886, promised to witness the termination of more than three hundred years of virtually constant warfare between the Apaches and the whites. Captain Crawford and Lieutenant Maus were jubilant—they were about to succeed where so many others had failed. The days of heat and thirst and gruelling work were over.

"Geronimo is through," said Crawford. "He is ready to give up and come in and be a good Indian. If he wasn't he'd never have sent the Black Bear with that message."

"I don't trust any of them," replied Maus, "and as for being a good Indian—there's only one thing that'll ever make Geronimo that"—he touched the butt of his pistol.

"That doctrine is responsible to a greater extent than any other one thing for many of the atrocities and the seeming treachery of the Apaches," replied Crawford. "They haved heard that so often that they do not really trust any of us, for they believe that we all hold the same view. It makes them nervous when any of us are near them, and as they are always suspicious of us the least suggestion of an overt act on our part frightens them onto the war trail and goads them to reprisals.

"It has taken months of the hardest kind of work to reach the point where Geronimo is ready to make peace—a thoughtless word or gesture now may easily undo all that we have accomplished. Constantly impress upon the scouts by word and example the fact that every precaution must be taken to convince the renegades that we intend to fulfill every promise that I have made them."

Shoz-Dijiji came and stood before Geronimo. "What did the white-eyed chief say to you?" demanded the old war chief.

"He said that if we lay down our arms and surrender he will take us to Nan-tan-des-la-par-en," replied Shoz-Dijiji.

"What did Shoz-Dijiji reply?"

"Shoz-Dijiji told the white-eyed man that Geronimo would not surrender, but that he would hold a parley with Nan-tan-des-la-par-en. At last the white-eyed chief agreed. We may retain our arms, and he promises that we shall not be attacked if we accompany him peaceably to the parley with Nan-tan-des-la-par-en."

"What did you reply?"

"That we would come and make camp near him this afternoon. He has promised that his scouts will not fire upon us."

"Good!" exclaimed Geronimo. "Let us make ready to move our camp, and let it be understood that if the word made between Shoz-Dijiji and the white-eyed chief be broken and shots fired in anger the first shot shall not be fired by a member of my band. I have spoken!"

As the renegades broke camp and moved slowly in the direction of Crawford's outfit a swart Mexican cavalryman, concealed behind the summit of a low hill, watched them, and as he watched a grim smile of satisfaction played for an instant about the corners of his eyes. Ten minutes later he was reporting to Captain Santa Anna Perez.

"They shall not escape me this time," said Perez, as he gave the command to resume the march in pursuit of the illusive enemy.

A short distance from Crawford's camp Geronimo halted his band and sent Shoz-Dijiji ahead to arrange a meeting between Geronimo and Crawford for the purpose of ratifying the understanding that Shoz-Dijiji and the officer had arrived at earlier in the day.

With a white rag fastened to the muzzle of his rifle the Black Bear approached the camp of the scouts and, following the instructions of Crawford to his men, was permitted to enter. Every man of Crawford's command Shoz-Dijiji knew personally. With many of them he had played as a boy, and with most of them he had gone upon the war trail, fighting shoulder to shoulder with them against both Mexicans and pindah-lickoyee; but today he passed among them with his head high, as one might pass among strangers and enemies.

Crawford, waiting to receive him, could not but admire the silent contempt of the tall young war chief for those of his own race whom he must consider nothing short of traitors; and in his heart the courageous cavalry officer found respect and understanding for this other courageous soldier of an alien race.

"I am glad that you have come, Shoz-Dijiji," he said. "You bring word from Geronimo? He will go with me to General Crook?"

"Geronimo wishes to come and make talk with you," replied the Black Bear. "He wishes his own ears to hear the words you spoke to Shoz-Dijiji this morning."

"Good!" said Crawford. "Let Geronimo—" His words were cut short by a fusilade of shots from the direction of the renegades' position. Crawford snatched his pistol from its holster and covered Shoz-Dijiji.

"So that is the word Geronimo sends?" he exclaimed. "Treachery!"

The Apache wheeled about and looked in the direction of

his people. The scouts were hastily preparing to meet an attack. Every eye was on the renegades—in every mind was the same thought that Crawford had voiced—treachery!

Shoz-Dijiji pointed. "No!" he cried. "Look! It is not the warriors of Geronimo. Their backs are toward us. They are firing in the other direction. They are being attacked from the south. There! See! Mexican soldiers!"

The renegades, firing as they came, were falling back upon the scouts' camp; and, following them, there now came into full view a company of Mexican regulars.

"For God's sake, stop firing!" cried Crawford. "These are United States troops."

Captain Santa Anna Perez saw before him only Apaches. It is true that some of them wore portions of the uniform of the soldiers of a sister republic; but Captain Santa Anna Perez had fought Apaches for years, and he well knew that they were shrewd enough to take advantage of any form of deception of which they could avail themselves, and he thought this but a ruse.

Two of his officers lay dead and two privates, while several others were wounded, and now the Apaches in uniform, as well as those who were not, were firing upon him. How was he to know the truth? What was he to do? One of his subordinates ran to his side. "There has been a terrible mistake!" he cried. "Those are Crawford's scouts—I recognize the captain. In the name of God, give the command to cease firing!"

Perez acted immediately upon the advice of his lieutenant, but the tragic blunder had not as yet taken its full toll of life. In the front line, a young Mexican soldier knelt with his carbine. Perhaps he was excited. Perhaps he did not hear the loudly shouted command of his captain. No one will ever know why he did the thing he did.

The others on both sides had ceased firing when this youth raised his carbine to his shoulder, took careful aim, and fired. Uttering no sound, dead on his feet, Captain Emmet Crawford fell with a bullet in his brain.

Shoz-Dijiji, who had been standing beside him, had witnessed the whole occurrence. He threw his own rifle to his shoulder and pressed the trigger. When he lowered the smoking muzzle Crawford had been avenged, and that is why no one will ever know why the Mexican soldier did the thing he did.

With difficulty Perez and Maus quieted their men, and it was with equal difficulty that Geronimo held his renegades in check. They were gathered in a little knot to one side, and Shoz-Dijiji had joined them.

"It was a ruse to trap us!" cried a brave. "They intended to get us between them and kill us all."

"Do not talk like a child," exclaimed Shoz-Dijiji. "Not one of us has been killed or wounded, while they have lost several on each side. The Mexicans made a mistake. They did not know Crawford's scouts were near, nor did Crawford know that the Mexican soldiers were approaching."

The brave grunted. "Look," he said, pointing; "the war chiefs of the Mexicans and the pindah-lickoyee are holding a council. If they are not plotting against us why do they not invite our chiefs to the council? It is not I who am a child but Shoz-Dijiji, if he trusts the pindah-lickoyee or the Mexicans."

"Perhaps they make bad talk about us," said Geronimo, suspiciously. "Maus does not like me; and, with Crawford dead, there is no friend among them that I may trust. The Mexicans I have never trusted."

"Nor does Shoz-Djiji trust them," said the Black Bear. "The battle they just fought was a mistake. That, I say again; but it does not mean that I trust them. Perhaps they are plotting against us now; for Crawford is dead."

"Maus and the Mexican could combine forces against us," suggested Geronimo, nervously. "Both the Mexicans and pindah-lickoyee have tricked us before. They would not hesitate to do it again. We are few, they are many—they could wipe us out, and there would be none left to say that it happened through treachery."

"Let us attack them first," suggested a warrior. "They are off their guard. We could kill many of them and the rest would run away. Come!"

"No!" cried Geronimo. "Our women are with us. We are very few. All would be killed. Let us withdraw and wait. Perhaps we shall have a better chance later. Only fools attack when they know they cannot win. Perhaps Nan-tan-des-la-

par-en will come and we shall make peace. That will be better.
I am tired of fighting."

"Let us go away for a while, at least until the Mexicans have
left," counseled Shoz-Dijiji. "Then, perhaps, we can make
terms with Maus. If not we can pick our own time and place to
fight."

"That is good talk," said Geronimo. "Come! We shall
move away slowly."

Maus and Perez, engaged in arranging terms for the removal
of Crawford's body and exchanging notes that would relieve
one another of responsibility for the tragic incident of the
battle between the troops of friendly nations, paid little attention to the renegades; and once again Geronimo slipped
through the fingers of his would-be captors, and as Maus' and
Perez' commands marched away together toward Nacori the
scouts of the old war chief watched them depart and carried
the word to Geronimo.

"They have marched away together—the Mexicans and the
pindah-lickoyee?" demanded Geronimo. "That is bad. They
are planning to join forces against us. They will return, but
they will not find us here."

Again the renegades changed camp; this time to a still
more remote and inaccessible position. The days ran into
weeks, the weeks to months. The band scattered, scouting and
hunting. At all times Geronimo knew the location of Maus'
command; and when he became reasonably convinced that
Maus was waiting for the arrival of Crook and was not planning a hostile move against the renegades he made no further
attempt to conceal his location from the white officer,
but he did not relax his vigilance.

It was late in March. Geronimo, Shoz-Dijiji, Gian-nah-tah,
and several others were squatting in the shade of a sycamore,
smoking and chatting, when two Apaches entered the camp
and approached them. One was one of Geronimo's own scouts,
the other wore the red headband of a government scout.
When the two halted before Geronimo the war chief arose.

"What do you want in the camp of Geronimo?" he asked,
addressing the government scout as though he had been a
total stranger.

"I bring a message from Maus," replied the other. "Nan-tan-des-la-par-en has come. He is ready to hold a parley with you. What answer shall I take back?"

"Tell Nan-tan-des-la-par-en that Geronimo will meet him to-morrow in the Canyon of Los Embudos."

When the morning came Geronimo set out with a party of chiefs and warriors for the meeting place. Mangas was with him and Na-chi-ta, and there were Shoz-Dijiji, Gian-nah-tah, Chihuahua, Nanáy, and Kut-le in the party. General Crook was awaiting them in the Canyon of Los Embudos. The two parties exchanged salutations and then seated themselves in a rough circle under the shade of large sycamore and cotton-wood trees.

General Crook addressed Geronimo almost immediately. "Why did you leave the reservation?" he demanded.

"You told me that I might live in the reservation the same as white people live," replied Geronimo, "but that was not true. You sent soldiers to take my horses and cattle from me. I had a crop of oats almost ready to harvest, but I could not live in the reservation after the way you had treated me. I went away with my wife and children to live in peace as my own people have always lived. I did not go upon the war trail, but you told your soldiers to find me and put me in prison and if I resisted to kill me."

"I never gave any such orders," snapped Crook.

Geronimo glanced at Shoz-Dijiji but did not reply.

"But," continued Crook, "if you left the reservation for that reason, why did you kill innocent people, sneaking all over the country to do it? What did those innocent people do to you that you should kill them, steal their horses, and slip around in the rocks like coyotes?

"You promised me in the Sierra Madre that *that* peace should last, but you have lied about it. When a man has lied to me once I want some better proof than his own word before I can believe him again."

"So does Geronimo," interrupted the war chief.

"You must make up your mind," continued Crook, "whether you will stay out on the warpath or surrender unconditionally. If you stay out I'll keep after you and kill the last one if it takes fifty years."

"I do not want to fight the white man," replied Geronimo;

"but I do not want to return to the reservation and be hanged, as many of the white people have said that I should be. People tell bad stories about me. I do not want that any more. When a man tries to do right, people should not tell bad stories about him. I have tried to do right. Does the white man try to do right? I am the same man. I have the same feet, legs, and hands; and the sun looks down upon me, a complete man.

"The Sun and the Darkness and the Winds are all listening to what we say now. They know that Geronimo is telling the truth. To prove to you that I am telling the truth, remember that I sent you word that I would come from a place far away to speak to you here, and you see me now. If I were thinking bad, or if I had done bad, I would never have come here."

He paused, waiting for Crook to reply.

"I have said all that I have to say," said the General; "you had better think it over tonight and let me know in the morning."

For two more days the parley progressed; and at last it was agreed that Geronimo and his band should accompany Lieutenant Maus and his battalion of scouts to Fort Bowie, Arizona. The northward march commenced on the morning of March 28th and by the night of the 29th the party had reached the border between Mexico and Arizona.

Chapter Nine

RED FOOLS AND WHITE SCOUNDRELS

IN the camp of the Apaches, which lay at a little distance from that of the troops, there was an atmosphere of nervousness and suspicion.

"I do not like the way in which Nan-tan-des-la-par-en spoke to me," said Geronimo. "I know that he did not speak the truth when he said that he had not ordered the soldiers to catch me and to kill me if I resisted. Perhaps he is not telling me the truth now."

"They have lied to us always before," said Na-chi-ta. "Now,

if we go back with them to Fort Bowie, how do we know that they will not put us in prison. We are chiefs. If they wish to frighten our people they may kill us. The white-eyed men are crying for the blood of Geronimo."

"If they kill Geronimo they will kill Na-chi-ta also," said Shoz-Dijiji.

"I have thought of that," replied Na-chi-ta.

"They will not kill us," said Chihuahua. "They will be content to know that we are no longer on the war trail. We have taught them a lesson this time. Now, maybe, they will let us alone."

"Chihuahua thinks only of the little farm the white-eyes let him work—like a woman," scoffed Shoz-Dijiji. "I hate them. I shall not go back to live upon a reservation. I shall not go back to be laughed at by white-eyed men, to hear them call me a damn Siwash, to listen while they make fun of my gods and insult my mother and my sisters."

"Shoz-Dijiji will go upon the war trail alone and do battle with all the soldiers of two great nations?" sneered Chihuahua.

"Then Shoz-Dijiji will at least die like a man and a warrior," replied the Black Bear.

"Have we not troubles enough without quarrelling among ourselves?" demanded Geronimo.

"And now Gian-nah-tah is bringing more trouble into our camp," said Chihuahua. "Look!" and he pointed toward the young warrior, who was walking toward them.

In each hand Gian-nah-tah carried a bottle of whiskey, and his slightly unsteady gait was fair evidence that he had been drinking. He approached the group of men, women, and children and extended one of the bottles toward Geronimo. The old chief took a long drink and passed the bottle to Na-chi-ta.

Shoz-Dijiji stood eyeing them silently. By no changed expression did he show either disapproval or its opposite; but when Na-chi-ta passed the whiskey on to him, after having drunk deeply, he shook his head and grinned.

"Why do you smile?" demanded Na-chi-ta.

"Because now I shall not turn back into Mexico alone," replied the Black Bear.

"Why do you say that?" asked Geronimo.

The bottle went the rounds, though all did not drink. Chihuahua was one who did not.

"Where did you get this, Gian-nah-tah?" asked Geronimo.

"A white-eyed man is selling it just across the border in Mexico. He is selling it to the soldiers too. He says that they are boasting about what they are going to do to Geronimo and his band. They make much bad talk against you."

"What do they say they are going to do to us?" demanded Geronimo, taking another drink.

"They are going to shoot us all as soon as we are across the border."

Chihuahua laughed. "The foolish talk of drunken men," he said.

"Many of the white-eyed soldiers are drunk," continued Gian-nah-tah. "When they are drunk they may kill us. Let us turn back. If we must be killed let us be killed in battle and not shot down from behind by drunken white-eyes."

"Now would be a good time to attack them," said Na-chi-ta, "while they are drunk."

"If we do not kill them they will kill us," urged Gian-nah-tah. "Come!"

"Shut up, Gian-nah-tah!" commanded Shoz-Dijiji. "The strong water of the white-eyed men does not make you a war chief to lead the braves of the Shis-Inday into battle—it only makes you a fool."

"Shoz-Dijiji calls Gian-nah-tah a fool?" demanded the young warrior angrily. "Shoz-Dijiji does not want to fight the pindah-lickoyee because Shoz-Dijiji is a coward and himself a pindah-lickoyee."

Shoz-Dijiji's eyes narrowed as he took a step toward Gian-nah-tah. The latter drew his great butcher knife, but he retreated. Then it was that Geronimo stepped between them. "If you want to kill," he said, "there is always the enemy."

"I do not want to kill Gian-nah-tah, my best friend," said Shoz-Dijiji. "Perhaps it was the strong water of the pindah-lickoyee that spoke through the mouth of Gian-nah-tah. Tomorrow, when he is sober, Shoz-Dijiji will ask him; but no man may call Shoz-Dijiji a white-eyes and live. Juh learned that when Shoz-Dijiji killed him."

"Shut up, Gian-nah-tah," advised Na-chi-ta; "and go to the

white-eyed fool who sold you this strong water and buy more. Here!" He handed Gian-nah-tah several pieces of silver money. "Get plenty."

Many of the braves already felt the effects of the adulterated, raw spirits that Tribollet was selling them at ten dollars a gallon, and most of those that had been drinking were daubing their faces with war paint and boasting of what they would do to the soldiers of the pindah-lickoyee.

They greeted Gian-nah-tah with shouts of savage welcome when he returned with more whiskey, and as they drank they talked loudly of killing all the white soldiers first and then taking the war trail in a final campaign that would wipe out the last vestige of the white race from the land of the Shis-Inday.

Shoz-Dijiji looked on in sorrow—not because they were drunk or because they talked of killing the white-eyed people; but because he knew that if they were not stopped they would soon be so drunk that they could not even defend themselves in the event that the soldiers of the pindah-lickoyee set upon them, as persistent rumors from Tribollet's ranch suggested might occur before dawn.

He went to Geronimo and urged him to make some effort to stop the drinking; but Geronimo, himself inflamed by drink, would do nothing. As a matter of fact there was really nothing that he could do since the Apache is a confirmed individualist who resents receiving orders from anyone.

Shoz-Dijiji considered the advisability of taking a few of the warriors who had not drunk to excess and leading them in a raid upon Tribollet's ranch, but he had to abandon the idea because he knew that it would lead to killing and that that would bring the soldiers down upon their camp.

In the end he hit upon another plan, and, shortly after, he was in the camp of the Apache scouts where he aroused Alchise and Ka-e-ten-na.

"Listen," said Shoz-Dijiji, "to the sounds you can hear coming from the camp of Geronimo."

"We hear them," said Alchise. "Are you fools that you do not sleep when tomorrow you must march all day in the hot sun?"

"They are all drunk upon the tizwin of the white-eyes,"

said Shoz-Dijiji. "If more of it is brought into the camp of Geronimo there will be trouble. Already many of the braves have put on the war paint. Shoz-Dijiji has come to you to ask that you go to Nan-tan-des-la-par-en and tell him that he must send soldiers to prevent the white-eyed fool from selling more firewater to the Apaches and to stop the stories that are being told to our people. Otherwise there will be trouble."

"When did Shoz-Dijiji begin to fear trouble with the white-eyed men?" demanded Ka-e-ten-na.

"When he saw the warriors of his people getting so drunk that soon they will be unable to defend themselves, though not so drunk but that some one of them, who may be a bigger fool than the others, will certainly fire upon the first pindah-lickoyee he sees when dawn comes. That is when Shoz-Dijiji began to fear—not war but certain defeat."

"Did Na-chi-ta send you with this message?" asked Alchise.

"Na-chi-ta is so drunk that he cannot stand upon his feet," replied Shoz-Dijiji.

"We will go to Nan-tan-des-la-par-en," said Ka-e-ten-na, "and ask him to let us take some scouts and stop the sale of this stuff to all Apaches."

"Shoz-Dijiji will wait here until you return," said the Black Bear.

As Shoz-Dijiji waited, the sounds that came to his ears indicated restlessness and activity in the camp of the white soldiers that lay at no great distance from that of the scouts; and these sounds aroused his suspicions, for at this hour of the night the camp should have been quiet. He read in them preparation for attack—treachery. He could not know that they were caused by a few drunken soldiers and portended nothing more serious than a few days in the guardhouse for the culprits when they reached the Post.

The false rumors that Tribollet and his men had spread among the renegades were working in the mind of Shoz-Dijiji, and he was already upon the point of returning to his own camp when Ka-e-ten-na and Alchise came back from their interview with Crook.

"Has Nan-tan-des-la-par-en told you to take warriors and stop the sale of firewater to the Apaches?" demanded Shoz-Dijiji.

"No," replied Alchise.

"He is going to send white-eyed soldiers instead?" asked the Black Bear.

"He will send no one," said Ka-e-ten-na.

"Why not?"

"We do not know."

Shoz-Dijiji was worried when he came again to the camp of the renegades. Na-chi-ta was lying helpelss upon the ground. Geronimo was drunk, though he still could walk. Most of the braves were asleep. Shoz-Dijiji went at once to Geronimo.

"I have just come from the camp of the scouts," he said. "I could hear the white-eyed soldiers preparing for battle. Perhaps they will attack us before dawn. Look at your warriors, Geronimo. They are all drunk. They cannot fight. All will be killed. You would not listen to Shoz-Dijiji then, but now you must. I am war chief of the Be-don-ko-he. You are war chief of all the Apaches, but you are too drunk to lead them in battle or to counsel them with wisdom. Therefore you shall listen to Shoz-Dijiji and do what he says. Only thus may we save our people from being wiped out by the soldiers of the pindah-lickoyee before chigo-na-ay has risen above the tree tops."

The words of Shoz-Dijiji had a slightly sobering effect upon Geronimo. He looked about him. By the flickering light of dying fires he saw the flower of his fighting force lying in drunken stupor, prone upon the ground, like beasts.

Shoz-Dijiji stood with a sneer upon his lip. "The pindah-lickoyee wants the Shis-Inday to come out of the mountains and live as they live," he said. "They want the poor Apache to be like them. Here is the result. We have come out of the mountains, and already we are like the pindah-lickoyee. If we live among them long our women will be like their women; and then you will not see an Apache woman whose nose has not been cut off or an Apache man who is not always lying in the dirt, drunk.

"But that will not be for those of us who are here, Geronimo, if we stay here until after Tapida brings the new day, for we shall all be dead. The soldiers of the white-eyes are already preparing to attack us. How may drunken men defend their families and themselves? We shall all be killed if we do not go at once. I have spoken."

Slowly Geronimo gathered his muddled wits. The words of Shoz-Dijiji took form within his brain. He saw the condition of his warriors, and he recalled not only the rumors that had come from Tribollet's but also the treacherous attacks that had been made upon his people by the white-eyed soldiers in the past.

"There is yet time," said Shoz-Dijiji. "The night is dark. If we leave at once and in silence we can be far away before they know that we have left. Another day, when our warriors are sober, we can fight them but not today."

"Awake them all," said Geronimo. "Gather the women and children. Tell them that we are going back into the mountains of Mexico. Tell them that we are not going to remain here to be murdered by our enemies or taken back to Bowie to be hanged."

They did not all answer the summons of Geronimo. Nachi-ta went but he did not know that he was going or where. They threw him across the back of a mule, and Shoz-Dijiji loaded Gian-nah-tah upon another, and Geronimo rode silently out through the night with these and eighteen other warriors, fourteen women, and two boys, down into the mountains of Mexico; and the results of months of the hardest campaign that, possibly, any troops in the history of warfare ever experienced were entirely nullified by one cheap white man with a barrel of cheap whiskey.

Chapter Ten

TWO THOUSAND DOLLARS FOR A HEAD

DOWN into the rugged mountain fastnesses of Sonora the remnants of Geronimo's band of renegades hurried from the menace of the white man's justice. Suffering from the after effects of Tribollet's whiskey they marched in sullen silence, thinking only of escape, for the fighting spirit of a sick man is not wont to rise to any great heights.

For sixteen hours they marched with but a single brief rest, and it was again dark when they went into camp.

Water and a little food revived their spirits. There was even laughter, low pitched lest it reach across the night to the ears of an enemy.

Shoz-Dijiji squatted upon his haunches chewing upon a strip of jerked venison that was both dirty and "high" and that not only pleased his palate but gave him strength, renewing the iron tissue of his iron frame. Less fastidious, perhaps, than a civilized epicure in the preparation and serving of his food, yet, savage though he was, he appreciated the same delicate flavor of partial decay.

As he ate, a tall warrior came and stood before him. It was Gian-nah-tah. Shoz-Dijiji continued eating, in silence.

"At the kunh-gan-hay beside the soldiers of Nan-tan-des-la-par-en," commenced Gian-nah-tah, presently, "the poisoned water of the pindah-lickoyee spoke through the mouth of Gian-nah-tah, saying words that Gian-nah-tah would not have said." He stopped, waiting.

"Shoz-Dijiji knew that Gian-nah-tah, his best friend, did not speak those words," replied Shoz-Dijiji. "It was the bad spirits that the white man puts into his strong water to make trouble between men. Gian-nah-tah is a fool to be tricked thus by the pindah-lickoyee."

"Yes," agreed Gian-nah-tah, "I am a fool."

Shoz-Dijiji scratched some criss-cross lines upon the ground where he squatted. With a bit of stick he scratched them. "These," he said, "are the troubles that have come between Shoz-Dijiji and Gian-nah-tah—the bad talk—the bad thoughts." With his palm he smoothed the ground. "Now they are gone," he said. "Let us forget them." He offered Gian-nah-tah a piece of venison, and his friend squatted beside him.

"Do you think the soldiers of the white-eyed men will follow us?" asked Gian-nah-tah.

Shoz-Dijiji shook his head. "I do not know," he replied. "I offered hoddentin to the winds and to the night, and I prayed that Usen would make the hearts of the pindah-lickoyee good that they might return to their own country and leave us in peace.

"I asked the tzi-daltai that Nan-ta-do-tash blessed for me if the white-eyed soldiers were pursuing us, but I have received no answer."

"Nan-tan-des-la-par-en said that if we did not come with him he would follow us and kill us all if it took fifty years," reminded Gian-nah-tah.

Shoz-Dijiji laughed. "That is just talk," he said. "Anyone can make big talk. For over three hundred years we have been fighting the pindah-lickoyee; and they have not killed us all, yet. Some day they will, but it will take more than fifty years. You and I shall have plenty of fighting before the last of the Shis-Inday is killed."

"I do not know," said Gian-nah-tah. "A spirit came to me while I slept the first night that we camped near the soldiers of Nan-tan-des-la-par-en. It was the spirit of my father. He said that he had waited a long time for me. He said that pretty soon I would come. I asked him when, but just then I awoke, and that frightened him away. Perhaps it will be tomorrow—who knows?"

"Do not say that, Gian-nah-tah," said Shoz-Dijiji. "Already have I seen too many of my friends go. One hundred and thirty-four we were when we went out from San Carlos less than twelve moons ago. Today we are thirty-eight. The others are dead, or prisoners of the pindah-lickoyee. The heart of Shoz-Dijiji is sad, as are the hearts of all Apaches. The hand of every man is against us—even the hands of our brothers. We must not think of death. Gian-nah-tah and Shoz-Dijiji must live for one another. Surely Usen will not take everything that we love from us!"

"Usen has forgotten the Apache," said Gian-nah-tah, sadly.

For a month the renegades rested and recuperated in the high sierras, and then one day a scout brought word to Geronimo that he had sighted three troops of United States Cavalry as they were going into camp a day's march to the north.

Geronimo shook his head. "They are always talking of peace," he said, "and always making war upon us. They will not leave us alone." He turned to Shoz-Dijiji. "Go to the camp of the pindah-lickoyee and try to talk with some of their scouts. Take Gian-nah-tah with you. Do not trust too much in the honor of the scouts, but learn all that you can without telling them anything."

Shoz-Dijiji and Gian-nah-tah arose. "That is all?" asked the young war chief of the Be-don-ko-he.

"That is all," replied Geronimo.

The soft rustle of their war moccasins faded into silence. The night swallowed them. Geronimo sat with bowed head, his eyes upon the ground. A girl looked after them and sighed. Then she cast hoddentin in the direction they had gone and whispered prayers for the safety of one of them. Also she prayed that some day she would be the mother of warriors and that Gian-nah-tah would be their father.

In four hours the two warriors covered the distance that it would take a troop of cavalry all of the following day to cover; but they traveled where no horse might travel, over trails that no cavalryman knew. They trod in places where only mountain sheep and Apaches had trod before.

Quiet lay upon the camp of —th Cavalry. Three weary sentries, softly cursing because they must walk their posts to save their horses, circled the lonely bivouac. At a little distance lay the camp of the Apache scouts. The dismal voice of an owl broke the silence. It came from the summit of a low bluff south of the camp. At intervals it was repeated twice.

One of the sentries was a rookie. "Gosh," he soliloquized, "but that's a lonesome sound!"

Once more came the eerie cry—this time, apparently, from the camp of the scouts.

Number One sentry was a veteran. He stepped quickly from his post to the side of his top sergeant, who lay wrapped in a sweaty saddle blanket with his head on a McClellan.

"H-s-st! McGuire!" he whispered.

"Wot the 'ell?" demanded the sergeant, sitting up.

"Hos-tiles! I just heard 'em signaling to our Siwashes— three owl calls and an answer."

The sergeant came to his feet, strapping his belt about his hips. He picked up his carbine. "Git back on your post an' keep your ears unbuttoned," he directed. "I'll mosey out that way a bit an' listen. Maybe it *was* a owl."

Shoz-Dijiji and Gian-nah-tah crept silently down the face of the bluff and approached the camp of the scouts. There was no moon, and light clouds obscured the stars. It was very dark. A figure loomed suddenly before them. "Who are you?" it demanded in a whisper that could not have been heard ten feet away.

"We are Be-don-ko-he," replied Shoz-Dijiji. "We bring a message from Geronimo."

"What is it?"

"He wants the soldiers to go back to their own country and leave him alone. He is not fighting the pindah-lickoyee. If they will go away he will not again raid in Arizona or New Mexico."

"You are Shoz-Dijiji," said the scout. "I am glad you came. We have word for Geronimo and all that are with h'.n. His fight is hopeless. He had better come in. If he does, perhaps they will not kill him. If he stays out he is sure to be killed. Every one of his warriors will be killed. Tell him to come in."

"Why do you think we will be killed? They have not killed us yet, and they have been trying to ever since we were born."

"Now they will," insisted the scout, "for they have offered to pay fifty dollars for the head of every warrior that is brought in and two thousand dollars for the head of Geronimo. There are Apaches who would kill their own fathers for fifty dollars."

"You do not kill us," said Shoz-Dijiji, "and our heads are worth one hundred dollars."

"Give thanks to Usen, then, that he sent me to meet you and not another," replied the scout.

"What are the plans of the pindah-lickoyee?" asked Shoz-Dijiji.

"Their orders are to get Geronimo and all his band. The Mexicans are helping them. It was the Mexicans who invited them down here to catch you."

"They shall pay," growled Shoz-Dijiji.

"So old Nan-tan-des-la-par-en will pay fifty dollars for my head, eh?" said Gian-nah-tah. "Very well, I shall go and get his head for nothing."

"It was not Nan-tan-des-la-par-en," said the scout. "He is no longer war chief of the pindah-lickoyee. They have taken him away and sent another. His name is Miles. It is he who has offered the money for your heads. He has ordered out many soldiers to follow you and catch you. Here there are three troops of the —th Cavalry; Lawton is coming with Apache scouts, cavalry, and infantry. As fast as men and horses are tired they will send fresh ones to replace them. A few men cannot fight against so many and win. That is why so many of us have joined the scouts. It is not that we love the white-eyed ones any better than you do. We know when we are beaten—that is all. We would live in peace. By going out you make trouble for us all. We want to put an end to all this trouble."

"I, too, like peace," said Shoz-Dijiji; "but better even than peace I like freedom. If you are content to be the slave of the pindah-lickoyee that is your own affair. Shoz-Dijiji would rather be forever on the war trail than be a slave. If you are men you will leave the service of the white-eyes and join Geronimo."

"Yes," said Gian-nah-tah, "take that message to our brothers who have turned against us."

"Come!" said Shoz-Dijiji, and the two warriors turned back toward the camp of Geronimo.

1st Sergeant McGuire, "K" Troop, —th Cavalry, strolled back to his blankets. On the way he paused to speak to Number One. "The next time you hear a owl," he said, "you just telegraph President Cleveland and let me sleep."

Chigo-na-ay was an hour high when Shoz-Dijiji and Gian-nah-tah stood again before the rude hogan of Geronimo deep hid upon the rough breast of the Mother of Mountains. The old war chief listened in silence while they narrated with primitive fidelity every detail of their interview with the scout.

"Fifty dollars for the head of a warrior, two thousand dollars for the head of Geronimo!" he exclaimed. "It is thus that they offer a bounty for the heads of wolves and coyotes. They treat us as beasts and expect us to treat them as men. When they war among themselves do they offer money for the head of an enemy? No! They reserve that insult for the Apache.

"They will win because Usen has deserted us. And when they have killed us all there will be none to stop them from stealing the rest of our land. That is what they want.

That is why they make treaties with us and then break them, to drive us upon the war trail that they may have an excuse to kill us faster. That is why they offer money for our heads.

"Oh, Usen! what have the Shis-Inday done that you should be angry with them and let their enemies destroy them?"

"Do not waste your breath praying to Usen," said Gian-nah-tah. "Pray to the God of the pindah-lickoyee. He is stronger than Usen."

"Perhaps you are right," said Geronimo, sadly. "He is a wicked God, but his medicine is stronger than the medicine of Usen."

"I," said Shoz-Dijiji, "shall pray always to the god of my fathers. I want nothing of the pindah-lickoyee or their god. I hate them all."

A brave, moving at an easy run, approached the camp and stopped before Geronimo.

"Soldiers are coming," he said. "Their scouts have followed the tracks of Shoz-Dijiji and Gian-nah-tah."

"Only Apaches could trail us," said Geronimo. "If our brothers had remained loyal and taken the war trail with us the pindah-lickoyee could not conquer us in a thousand rains."

"There is a place where we can meet them," said the brave who had brought the word, "and stop them."

"I know," replied Geronimo. He called four warriors to him. "Take the women and the boys," he said, "and cross over the summit to the burned pine by the first water. Those of us who live will join you there after the battle."

Stripped to breech-cloth and moccasins, eighteen painted savages filed silently through the rough mountains. A scout preceded them. Behind Geronimo walked the Apache Devil, his blue face banded with white. Stern, grim, terrible men these—hunted as beasts are hunted, retaliating as only a cornered beast retaliates—asking no quarter and giving none.

Equipped by civilization with the best of weapons and plenty of ammunition and by nature with high intelligence, courage, and shrewdness, they had every advantage except that of numbers over any enemy that might take the field against them.

They stopped the —th Cavalry that day as they had stopped other troops before and without the loss of a man, and with the coming of night had vanished among the rocks of their beloved mountains and rejoined their women in the new camp by the burned pine at the first water beyond the summit.

Stern, grim, relentless, the cavalry pursued. Cooperating with them were the troops of Governor Torres of Sonora. The renegades were hard pressed. Skirmishes were of almost daily occurrence now. And then Lawton came with his hand picked force of seasoned veterans.

It was May again. For a year this handful of savage warriors and women and children had defied, eluded, and ofttimes defeated the forces of two civilized nations. The military strategy of their leader had been pitted against that of a great American general and proved superior. A score of West Pointers had exhausted their every resource and failed, but they were at last nearing their goal—victory seemed imminent. Miles and Lawton would receive the plaudits of their countrymen; and yet, if the truth were known, Miles and Lawton might have continued to pursue Geronimo and his band to the day of their deaths, and without success, had it not been that Apache turned against Apache.

The Shis-Inday may date the beginning of the end from the day that the first Indian Scouts were organized.

Hunted relentlessly, given no opportunity to rest because their every haunt, their every trail, their every hiding place was as well known to the scouts who pursued them as it was to themselves, they found themselves at last practically surrounded.

With no opportunity to hunt they were compelled to kill their ponies for sustenance until at last only Nejeunee was left.

Geronimo sat in council after a day of running battle.

"The warriors of the pindah-lickoyee and the Mexicans are all about us," he said. "If we can break through and cross the mountains into Chihuahua perhaps we can escape them. Then we must separate and go in different directions. They will hear of us here today and there tomorrow. They will hurry from one place to another. Their horses will become tired and their soldiers footsore. Their force will be broken up into small parties. It will be easier for us to elude them. Tonight we shall move east. A camp of the enemy lies directly in our path, but if we can pass it before dawn we shall be in mountains where no cavalry can follow and tomorrow we shall be in Chihuahua.

"There is one pony left. Its meat will carry us through until we can find cattle in Chihuahua."

There was silence. Every warrior, every woman knew that Shoz-Dijiji had repeatedly refused to permit the killing of the little pinto stallion for food.

"Nejeunee is more than a war pony," Shoz-Dijiji had once said to Geronimo. "He is my friend. I will not eat my friend. I will not permit anyone to eat my friend."

Glances stole around the circle in search of Shoz-Dijiji. He was not there.

Up toward the camp of the enemy—the camp that stood between the renegades and Chihuahua—a painted warrior rode a pinto stallion. A gentle May wind blew down to the nostrils of the man and his mount. To Nejeunee it carried the scent of his kind from the picket line of the —th Cavalry. He pricked up his ears and nickered. Shoz-Dijiji slid from his back, slipped the primitive bridle from about his lower jaw and slapped him on the rump.

"Goodbye, Nejeunee," he whispered; "the pindah-lickoyee may kill you, but they will not eat you."

Slowly the Apache walked back toward the camp of his people. Like the stones upon the grave of Ish-kay-nay, many and heavy, his sorrows lay upon his heart.

"Perhaps, after all," he mused, "Gian-nah-tah is right and Usen has forgotten the Apaches. I have prayed to him in the high places; I have offered hoddentin to him upon the winds of the morning and the evening; I have turned a deaf ear to the enemies who bring us a new god. Yet one by one the friends that I love are taken from me. Oh, Usen, before they are all gone take Shoz-Dijiji! Do not leave him alone without friends in a world filled with enemies!"

"Where is Shoz-Dijiji?" demanded Geronimo, his blue eyes sweeping the circle before him. "Gian-nah-tah, where is Shoz-Dijiji?"

"Here is Shoz-Dijiji!" said a voice from the darkness; and

as they looked up, the war chief of the Be-don-ko-he stepped into the dim, flickering light of their tiny fire.

"Shoz-Dijiji," said Geronimo, "there is but one pony left. It is Nejeunee. He must be killed for food. The others are all gone."

"Nejeunee is gone, also," said Shoz-Dijiji.

"Gone?"

"I have told you many times that no one would ever eat Nejeunee while Shoz-Dijiji lived. I have taken him away. What are you going to do about it?"

Geronimo bowed his head. "Even my son has turned against me," he said, sadly.

"Those are not true words, Geronimo," replied Shoz-Dijiji. "Nejeunee was more to me than a great war pony. When Shoz-Dijiji was a youth and Nejeunee a colt, Shoz-Dijiji broke him. Little Ish-kay-nay rode upon his back. It was Nejeunee that was tied before the hogan of her father. It was Nejeunee that Ish-kay-nay led to water and fed the next morning. Nejeunee has carried me through many battles. His fleet feet have borne me from the clutches of many an enemy. He has been the friend of Shoz-Dijiji as well as his war pony. Now he is old and yet there is not a fleeter or braver pony in the land of the Shis-Inday. He deserves better of me than to be killed and eaten.

"Geronimo says that Shoz-Dijiji has turned against him. Every day Shoz-Dijiji offers his life for Geronimo, and all that he has asked in return is the life of his friend."

"Say no more," said Na-chi-ta, the son of Cochise. "Let Shoz-Dijiji have the life of his friend. We have been hungry before—we can be hungry again. It does not kill an Apache to be hungry. We are not pindah-lickoyee."

Chapter Eleven

A RED HERO

DAWN was breaking as the last of the renegades crept past the camp of the enemy, where the troopers, already astir an hour, stood to horse. It was known that the camp of the renegades lay just below them, surrounded. A sudden surprise ortie at dawn would either overwhelm them or send them scattering into the arms of other troops stationed to cut off their retreat in any direction. It began to look as though Geronimo and his band were to be wiped out or captured at last. Two scouts had gone down toward the camp of the Apaches to investigate. The commanding officer was impatiently awaiting their return. Presently it would be too light for a surprise attack.

The officers were congratulating their commander and themselves upon the nice work that had brought old Geronimo into a trap at last—a trap from which he could not conceivably escape. They were also talking about the pinto stallion that had wandered up to their picket line during the night.

"I know that pony, sir," said Lieutenant King to the commanding officer, "and I know the Indian who owns him—he saved my life once. If it is possible, sir, I should like very much to take the pony back to Arizona with me. There is a rancher there whom I believe would be very glad to have him and take care of him."

"Well, it's not exactly regular, Mr. King, but perhaps the pony was stolen from this rancher—eh?" the C. O. grinned.

"Perhaps," agreed King.

"Very well, you may return it to its owner."

"Thank you, sir!"

"Here are the scouts," said the C. O. "Return to your troops, and be ready to move out at once!"

Two Apaches approached the commanding officer. They wore the red headbands of government scouts.

"Well?" demanded the officer. Did you find Geronimo?"

"Him gone," said one of the scouts.

"Gone! Where in hell has he gone?"

"Mebby so there," he pointed to the canyon behind them.

"Hell! He couldn't have gone there. What do you suppose we been doing here?"

"Me no sabe," replied the Apache. "Him gone—there!"

"How do know?"

"Me follow tracks."

"You sure?"

"Sure!"

"How long?"

"Mebby so half hour."

The officer turned to his chief of scouts. "Did you hear that? Slipped through our fingers again. The old devil! Get after him at once. Pick up the trail. Keep after him. We'll follow. If you get in touch with him don't attack. Just keep in touch with him until we come up."

"Yes, sir!"

Two scouts preceded Geronimo's little band up the canyon that would take them to the summit and over into Chihuahua. Precipitous walls hemmed them in on both sides, effectually keeping them to the bottom of the canyon. Here the going was good; but, also, it would be good going for horses and no escape for the fleeing renegades should they be overtaken. They were marching rapidly, needing no urging, for each of them knew the life and death necessity for speed.

Behind the two scouts came the women and the two boys. All the fighting men except the two scouts were in the rear. A little behind the others came Gian-nah-tah and three fellows. These would be the first to sight the enemy and give the word that would permit the main body to take a position from which they might best offer a defense.

But half a mile remained of level going; then the canyon proper terminated in tumbled, terraced ledges leading upward among great boulders and tortured strata toward the summit that was their goal. Once they reached these ledges no cavalry could pursue.

The commanding officer of the pursuing —th knew this and sent one troop ahead with orders to overtake the renegades at all costs before they reached the sanctuary of those rock-strewn ledges. With clanking accouterments and the clash of iron shod hoofs on rocky ground "B" Troop galloped up the canyon, close upon the heels of the Apache scouts.

Just beyond a turn the canyon narrowed, the beetling cliffs approaching close and the rubble at their base leaving a level path scarce ten feet wide. It was at this point that Gian-nah-tah sighted the leading scout. A half mile more and the renegades would have been safe—just a few minutes and the women and the main body could all be hidden among the boulders at the top of the first terrace, where a thousand cavalrymen could not dislodge them.

Gian-nah-tah turned and fired at the first red-banded scout. Beyond the scout Gian-nah-tah now saw the leading horsemen of "B" Troop rounding the turn in the canyon.

He called to one of his fellows. "Go to Geronimo," he said. "Tell him to hurry. Gian-nah-tah can hold them off until all are among the rocks."

He knelt upon the red blanket he had thrown off when battle seemed imminent and took careful aim. His shot brought down the horse of a cavalryman. With loud yells "B" Troop came tearing on. Those who rode in front fired as they charged. A bullet passed through Gian-nah-tah's shoulder. The Apache fired rapidly, but he could not stem that avalanche of plunging horses and yelling men.

Another bullet passed through his chest; but still he knelt there, firing; holding the pass while his people fled to safety. The leading troopers were almost upon him. In an instant he would be ridden down! But he had not held them yet! If they passed him now they would overtake the little band before it won to safety.

He dropped his rifle and seizing the red blanket in both hands arose and waved it in the faces of the oncoming horses. They swerved—they turned, stumbling and plunging among the loose rock of the rubble heaps. Two fell and others piled upon them. For minutes—precious minutes—all was confusion; then they came on again. And again Gian-nah-tah flourished the red blanket in the faces of the horses, almost from beneath their feet. Again the frightened animals wheeled and fought to escape. Once again there was delay.

Another bullet pierced Gian-nah-tah's body. Weak from loss of blood and from the shock of wounds he could no longer stand, kneeling, he held the pass against fifty men. A fourth bullet passed through him—through his right lung—and, coughing blood, he turned them back again.

Through the yelling and the chaos of the fight the troop commander had been trying to extricate himself from the mêlée and call his men back. Finally he succeeded. The troop was drawn off a few yards.

"Sergeant," said the captain, "dismount and use your carbine on that fellow. Don't miss!"

Gian-nah-tah, kneeling, saw what they were doing; but he did not care. He had held them. His people were safe!

The sergeant knelt and took careful aim.

"Usen has remembered his people at last," whispered Gian-nah-tah.

The sergeant pressed his trigger, and Gian-nah-tah fell forward on his face, a bullet through his brain.

When Captain Cullis led his troop through that narrow pass a moment later he saluted as he passed the dead body of a courageous enemy.

That night Geronimo camped beyond the summit, in the State of Chihuahua. Shoz-Dijiji sat in silence, his head bowed. No one mentioned the name of Gian-nah-tah. None of them had seen him die, but they knew that he was dead. He alone was missing. A girl, lying upon her blanket, sobbed quietly through the night.

In the morning the band separated into small parties and, scattering, led the pursuing troops upon many wild and fruitless chases. Geronimo, with six men and four women, started north toward the United States. Shoz-Dijiji, silent, morose, was one of the party.

Even these small bands often broke up for a day or two into other, smaller parties. Often the men hunted alone, but always there were meeting places designated ahead. Thus Geronimo and his companions ranged slowly northward through Chihuahua.

Cutting wood in the mountains near Casa Grande in Sonora had become too hazardous an occupation since Geronimo had been ranging the country; and so Luis Mariel, the son of Pedro Mariel, the woodchopper of Casa Grande, had come over into Chihuahua to look for other work.

He had never cared to be a woodchopper but longed, as a youth will, for the picturesque and romantic life of a vaquero; and at last, here in Chihuahua, his ambition had been gratified and today, with three other vaqueros, he was helping guard a grazing herd upon the lower slopes of the Sierra Madre.

The four were youths, starting their careers with the prosaic duties of day herding and whiling away the hours with cigarettes and stories. Luis was quite a hero to the others, for he alone had participated in a real battle with Apaches. Chihuahua seemed a very dull and humdrum country after listening to the tales that Luis told of Apache raids and battles in wild Sonora. He told them of the Apache Devil and boasted that he was an old friend of the family.

Above the edge of a nearby arroyo unblinking eyes watched them. The eyes appraised the four cow ponies and sized up the grazing herd. They were stern eyes, narrowed by much exposure to the pitiless sunlight of the southwest. They were set in a band of white that crossed a blue face from temple to temple. They scrutinized Luis Mariel and recognized him, but their expression did not change.

The Apache saw before him horses that he and his friends needed; he saw food on the hoof, and Usen knew that they needed food; he saw the enemies of his people, any one of whom would shoot him down on sight, had they the opportunity. But it was he who had the opportunity!

He leveled his rifle and fired. A vaquero cried out and fell from his saddle. The others looked about, drawing their pistols. Shoz-Dijiji fired again and another vaquero fell. Now the two remaining had located the smoke of his rifle and returned his fire.

Shoz-Dijiji dropped below the edge of the arroyo and ran quickly to a new position. When his eyes again peered above the edge of his defense he saw the two galloping toward his former position. He appreciated their bravery and realized their foolhardiness as he dropped his rifle quickly on one of them and pressed the trigger; then he quickly tied a white rag to the muzzle of his smoking rifle and waved it above the edge of the arroyo, though he was careful not to expose any more of his person than was necessary.

Luis Mariel looked in astonishment. What could it mean? A voice called him by name.

"Who are you?" demanded Luis, whose better judgment prompted him to put spurs to his horse and leave the victors in possession of the field.

"I am a friend," replied Shoz-Dijiji. "We shall not harm you if you will throw down your pistol. If you do not we can shoot you before you can get away."

Luis appreciated the truth of this statement. Further, he thought that his enemies must number several men; also— he did not know that he who addressed him was not a Mexican, for the Spanish was quite as good as Luis' own. So he threw down his pistol, being assured by this time that they had been attacked by bandits who wished only to steal the herd. Perhaps they would invite him to join the band, and when was there ever a red-blooded youth who did not at some time in his career aspire to be a brigand or a pirate?

A painted face appeared above the arroyo's edge. "Mother of God!" cried Luis, "protect me."

The Apache sprang quickly to level ground and came toward the youth.

"The Apache Devil!" exclaimed Luis.

"Yes," said Shoz-Dijiji, stooping and picking up Luis' pistol. "I shall not harm you, if you will do as I tell you."

"Won't the others kill me?" asked the youth.

"There are no others," replied Shoz-Dijiji.

"But you said 'we,' " explained Luis.

"I am alone."

"What do you want me to do?"

"Round up those three horses and then help me drive this herd to my camp."

"You will not harm me, nor let your friends harm me?"

"Have I harmed you or your father in the past?"

"No."

"Do as I tell you then," said Shoz-Dijiji, "and you will not be killed."

Luis rode after the three horses which were now grazing with the herd that had been but momentarily disturbed by the shots. When he returned with them the two men, each leading one of the riderless animals, started the cattle slowly toward the north in the direction of the next meeting place of Geronimo's party after Shoz-Dijiji had collected the arms and ammunition that had belonged to Luis and his three companions and secured them to the saddle of the horse led by the Apache.

Shoz-Dijiji rode in silence. If he felt any elation because of the success of his adventure it was not apparent in his demeanor. Grim, morose, he herded the cattle onward. His eyes patrolled the world bounded by the horizon, searching for enemies.

Luis Mariel, partly frightened, wholly thrilled, glanced often at his companion. To ride with the Apache Devil—ah, what an adventure! From earliest childhood Luis' ears had been filled with the stories of Apache ferocity, treachery, cruelty, yet against these were set the knowledge that the Apache Devil had twice befriended his father and had once before befriended him. Perhaps the Apache Devil would not harm him, then; but what of the others?

He had heard hideous stories of the tortures inflicted by the Apaches upon their prisoners. It might be that the Apache Devil could not protect him from the ferocity of his fellows. This thought worried Luis and to such effect that he commenced to formulate plans for escape. If they did not come to the camp of the Indians before dark his chances would be better than to risk making a break for liberty in the face of the menace of the Apache Devil's marksmanship, which he had reason to know constituted a very real menace.

The afternoon wore on. Angry clouds, gathering in the sky, portended early darkness and a black night. The patient herd plodded slowly on. The hopes of Luis Mariel rose high. Two hours more and escape would be assured if, in the meantime, they did not reach the camp of the Apaches.

"B" Troop of the —th had been dispatched into Chihuahua in the search for the scattered bands of the marauding renegades. Lieutenant Samuel Adams King, with four troopers, was scouting far afield. He had been following what appeared to be a fresh, though faint, Indian track that led toward the north; but now, with night coming down and a storm threatening, he had lost it. While one of the troopers held the horses of the others, King and his remaining men searched on foot for the elusive spoor. Proceeding in different directions the four walked slowly, scrutinizing every inch of ground, searching for a turned pebble, a down-pressed spear of vegetation.

King's path took him through a deep arroyo and out upon the opposite bank. Absorbed in his search he took no note of the growing menace of the gathering storm nor of the distance, constantly increasing, between himself and his men. He knew that when the rain came it would wipe out all trace of the tracks they sought, and this knowledge constituted the urge that kept him oblivious to all other considerations.

The dusk of evening had fallen. Heavy clouds rolled angrily and low above the scene as a herd of cattle slowly topped a gentle rise to the south. Two men drove them, but only one of these saw the soldiers a couple of miles ahead—saw, and knew them for what they were. This one glanced quickly at the landscape ahead and at the gathering storm above. He knew that it was about to break. He knew, too, that the arroyo would soon be filled with muddy, raging water—a barrier impassable by man or beast. All but one of the soldiers would be upon the opposite side of the arroyo from the herd and him.

Knowing these things, Shoz-Dijiji urged the cattle onward in the general direction of the enemy, for even though he passed close to them they would be unable to see him after the rain came—the rain and night.

Luis Mariel viewed the prospect of the impending storm hopefully. Soon it would be dark, but even before that the blinding rain would obliterate all objects within a few yards of him. They had not yet come to the camp of the renegades, and Luis had a horse under him.

The storm was in their rear. The cattle, doubtless, would move on before it; but Luis would turn back into it, and when it had passed he would be safely beyond the ken of the Apache Devil.

A great cloud, black and ominous, bellied low above them, sagging as though to a great weight of water; jagged lightning shot through it, followed by a deafening crash of thunder; the rent cloud spewed its contents upon the earth. It was not rain; it did not fall in drops nor sheets but in a great mass of solid water.

With the bursting of the cloud King found himself in water a foot deep on the level, and afterward the rain fell in torrents that shut everything from view beyond a few yards. Lightning flashed and thunder roared, and the pounding of the rain between drowned all other sounds. The man floundered through the new made mud back in the direction of his men. All was water—above, below, around him. Suddenly there appeared before him, almost at his feet, a depression. Here the water swirled and eddied, running in a mighty current across his path.

At its very edge he stopped and, realizing what it was, staggered back a few steps—back from the brink of eternity. So close had he been to the shelving bank of the arroyo that another step might have hurled him into the racing, yellow flood that filled it now from brim to brim.

Disconcerted by the first great mass of water that fell upon them, the cattle stopped. The leaders turned back upon the herd. Shoz-Dijiji, in the rear, urged the stragglers forward until, presently, the herd was milling in a muddy circle; but with the coming of the steady torrent and beneath the heavy quirt of the Apache they gradually strung out again in the direction they had been traveling, the storm at their backs.

Shoz-Dijiji, seeing that he was handling the herd alone, looked about for his companion; but the blinding torrent hid everything but the nearer cattle, and Shoz-Dijiji did not know that Luis was driving his unwilling pony into the teeth of the storm in an effort to escape.

An hour later the storm was over. A full moon shone out of a clear sky. Directly ahead of him Shoz-Dijiji saw something that was frightening the leaders of the herd, causing them to stop and then turn aside. A moment later the Apache recognized the cause of the distraction. It was a man on foot. At first Shoz-Dijiji thought that it was Luis, but when he had ridden nearer he discovered that the man was a soldier. Shoz-Dijiji drew a revolver from the holster at his hip. He would ride close enough to make sure of his aim before firing. He was not afraid that the other would fire first, since the soldier, before he fired, would wish to make sure that Shoz-Dijiji was an enemy. In this Shoz-Diji had a great advantage. Being an Apache he knew that all men were his enemies. He could make no mistake on that score.

The soldier hailed him in rather lame Spanish, but there was something in the voice that sounded familiar to the Apache Devil who never forgot anything. So he rode yet closer.

And then, in perfectly understandable English, he said: "Put up your hands, King, or I'll kill you."

Lieutenant King put his hands above his head. As yet he had not recognized the other as an Indian. The English, the use of his own name, mystified him.

"Who the hell are you?" he inquired.

"Turn your back," commanded Shoz-Dijiji.

King did as he was bid, and the Apache rode up and disarmed him.

"All right," said Shoz-Dijiji, and King lowered his arms and turned about.

"Shoz-Dijiji!" exclaimed King.

"Shoz-Dijiji, war chief of the Be-don-ko-he Apaches," replied the Apache Devil.

"And you're on the warpath. That doesn't look so good for me, does it, Shoz-Dijiji?"

"Shoz-Dijiji not on war trail now. Shoz-Dijiji good Indian now. Go in cattle business."

In the moonlight King saw the grim half-smile that accompanied the words of the Indian, but he made no reply. Apache humor was something that he did not pretend to understand. All he knew about it was that upon occasion it might be hideous.

"Mebbe so you like go in cattle business with Shoz-Dijiji?" suggested the Apache.

"I guess that whatever you say goes," replied the officer.

"All right. Take this horse." The Indian indicated the lead horse at his side. "Now you help drive *our* cattle. Sabe?"

King grinned. "Perfectly," he said.

Slowly the two men urged the cattle onward until at dawn they came to a patch of meadow land well within the mountain range they had entered shortly after meeting. There was water there and good grazing and little likelihood that the tired animals would wander far from either.

Taking King with him, Shoz-Dijiji rode to the top of a high hill that commanded the broad valley to the south and west, across which they had come. For half an hour the Apache scanned the country below them, using field glasses that King recognized as having once belonged to him, glasses that had been taken from him several years before during an engagement with hostiles.

In the far distance the Indian saw a tiny speck and recognized it as Luis. Beyond Luis and approaching him from the southeast were horsemen. This was doubtless the company of soldiers to which King belonged. Shoz-Dijiji did not call the officer's attention to either Luis or the soldiers. In his mind he figured quickly just how long it would take the soldiers to reach this point should Luis put them upon the trail of the herd, which he knew that they could easily pick up and follow from the point at which the storm had overtaken them.

"Come," he said to King, and the two rode down from the hill and turned into a small canyon where they would be hidden from the view of anyone who might enter the meadow where the cattle grazed. In the canyon was a small spring and here they drank. Shoz-Dijiji proffered King a piece of jerked venison that stunk to high heaven, but the officer assured the Apache that he was not hungry.

Having eaten, Shoz-Dijiji bound King's wrists and ankles. "Now sleep," he said. He stretched himself nearby and was soon asleep, but it was some time before King fell into a fitful doze. When awoke, the Indian was removing the bonds from his wrists.

"Now we drive our cattle," said Shoz-Dijiji.

The balance of that day and all the following night they drove the weary beasts through the mountains. There was no pursuit. After their sleep Shoz-Dijiji had again taken King to the hill top and scanned the back trail. The dust of a cavalry troop could be faintly seen in the distance, but it was moving north parallel to the range they had entered and was not upon their trail.

Twice they had stopped for brief rests, not for themselves but for the cattle; and now, at dawn, the trail debouched into an open canyon where there was water and good feed.

At the edge of the pasture land Shoz-Dijiji drew rein and pointed up the canyon.

"There," he said to King, "is the camp of Geronimo. If you go there you will be killed. Mebbe so you like sell your half of the cattle business?"

King grinned. "What do you mean?" he asked.

"Shoz-Dijiji buy," replied the Apache. "He give you a horse and—your life. You sell?"

"You've bought some cattle, Shoz-Dijiji," exclaimed King; "but I can't understand you. You are not like any other Indian I ever heard of. Why have you done this?"

"Two men drive cattle easier than one," replied the Apache.

"Yes, I know that; but why are you giving me a chance to escape when you know that I'll go right back to chasing you and fighting you again? Is it because of Wichita Billings?"

"Shoz-Dijiji no sabe English," grunted the Indian. "Now you go!" and he pointed back down the canyon along the trail they had just come over.

King wheeled his horse around. "Good-bye, Shoz-Dijiji," he said. "Perhaps some day I can repay you."

"Wait!" said the Indian and handed the white man his pistol. Then he sat his horse watching until a turn in the canyon took the other from his sight.

Far away Luis Mariel rode with "B" Troop of the —th. He had not led the soldiers upon the trail of his friend, the Apache Devil.

Chapter Twelve

"SHOZ-DIJIJI KNOWS!"

LUIS MARIEL had attached himself to "B" Troop. He rode with it, made himself generally useful around camp; and, in return, they fed him. Incidentally he picked up a smattering of English that was much more effective than the original brand formerly purveyed by Mr. Webster, and learned to ask for either bacon or potatoes through the medium of set phrases that contained at least ten obscene or blasphemous words and did not mention either bacon or potatoes by their right names. He also discovered that one may call an American *anything*, provided that one smiles.

Much to his surprise he discovered that he liked the Gringoes, and because he was young and bright and good-natured the soldiers liked Luis.

He had been with them four or five days when Lieutenant Samuel Adams King, half starved and rather the worse for wear, rode into camp upon an equally starved pony that Luis immediately recognized as having formerly belonged to one of his fellow vaqueros who had been killed by the Apache Devil.

Being a privileged character Luis was present when King reported to his troop commander; and when, through the medium of much profanity, a great deal of Spanish, and a few words of remote English origin he had indicated that he knew something about the pony King was riding, an interpreter was summoned and Luis told his story to Captain Cullis and the officers accompanying him.

"Well, King," commented Cullis, "you have achieved all the distinction of a museum piece. You should have a place in the Smithsonian Institution."

"How so, sir?"

"As the only white man who ever fell into the hands of the

118

Apache Devil and lived to tell about it. I can't account for it. Can you?"

For a moment King hesitated before he replied, and then: "No, sir," he said, "I cannot."

During that instant of hesitation King had weighed his duty as an officer against the demands of gratitude. He knew that there was a price upon the head of the Apache Devil that might spell his death at the hands of any white man, as an outlaw, even after peace was restored and the renegades returned to the reservation. He was confident that he alone knew that Shoz-Dijiji and the Apache Devil were one and the same, provided of course that the young Mexican was correct in his assumption that the Apache who had captured him actually was the Apache Devil. Perhaps the lad was mistaken. King determined to give Shoz-Dijiji the benefit of the doubt. Gratitude would not permit him to do less.

It being evident that some of the renegades were returning to the United States, "B" Troop was ordered above the border; and with it went Luis Mariel, seeking new adventures. He attached himself to Lieutenant King and crossed the border as the officer's civilian servant.

King, who had taken a liking to the lad, helped him with his English, learned to trust him, and eventually dispatched him to the Billings' ranch with Nejeunee and a note to Wichita Billings asking her to take care of the little pinto war pony until King returned from the campaign.

And so Luis Mariel, the son of the woodchopper of Casa Grande, rode away; and with him went Nejeunee.

Up into New Mexico, making their way toward the range of mountains near Hot Springs, rode Geronimo and Shoz-Dijiji with five other warriors and four women. They had found it necessary to abandon the herd that Shoz-Dijiji had captured because of the impossibility of moving it through hostile country where every trail was patrolled by soldiers and every water hole guarded.

Keeping to the mountains by day, crossing the valleys under cover of night, the eleven rode north. On several occasions they were forced to pass cattle ranches, but they committed no depredations other than the killing of an occasional cow for food.

Their greatest hardship was shortage of water as they could not approach the well-guarded water holes and wells, and there was a time during which they had no water for two days. They suffered greatly, and their horses all but died from thirst.

Any but Apaches would have been forced to surrender under like conditions; but, being Apaches, they knew *every* place where water might be found, and so they came at last to one such place, which was not guarded because the white men did not know of its existence. It was hidden in the depths of a remote, parched canyon far beneath the hard baked surface of the ground; but it was there for the digging, and in such an unlikely spot that there was scarcely a remote possibility that soldiers would interfere with the digging.

From hill tops that commanded a view of the country in all directions three keen-eyed warriors watched while others dug for the precious water that would give them all, and their jaded mounts as well, a new lease on life.

And when they had drunk and their crude water bottles had been refilled, they replaced the sand and the rocks in the hole they had made, and so nicely did they erase every sign of their presence that only an Apache might have known that they had stopped there.

Into their old stamping grounds they came at last, and so cleverly had they eluded the soldiers that they ranged there in peace for weeks, while the troops searched for them in Arizona and Mexico.

Geronimo, handicapped by the paucity of his following, nevertheless kept scouts afield who watched the movements of the troops and kept fairly well in touch with the progress of the campaign through the medium of friendly reservation Indians.

Shoz-Dijiji was often engaged in some enterprise of this nature, and upon one occasion he went into the heart of the reservation at San Carlos. Returning, he rode through familiar mountains along an unmarked trail that recalled many memories of other days.

Shoz-Dijiji rode out of his way and against his better judgment. He was an Apache, iron willed and schooled to self-denial; but he was human, and so he would torture his poor heart by riding a trail that he had once ridden with *her*.

He would ride near the ranch. Perhaps he might see her, but she would never know that he was near.

The war chief of the Be-don-ko-he dreamed and, dreaming, relaxed his vigilance. Love, sorrow, reminiscence dulled his faculties for the moment. Otherwise he would never have been so easily surprised.

The way he had chosen led here down the steep declivity of a canyon side and along the canyon's bottom for a few hundred yards to a point where a nimble pony might clamber up the opposite side. It was very hot in the sun scorched cleft and very quiet. The only sound was the crunching of gravelly soil beneath unshod hoofs—the hoofs of the pony Shoz-Dijiji rode down the canyon and the hoofs of another pony bearing a rider up the canyon.

Perhaps chance so synchronized the gaits of the two animals that the footfalls of each hid those of the other from the ears of their riders. Perchance fate—but why speculate?

The fact remains that as Shoz-Dijiji rounded an abrupt turn he came face to face with the other pony and its rider. Surprise was instantly reflected upon the face of the latter; but the Apache, though equally surprised, let no indication of it disturb the imperturbability of his countenance.

Each reined in instantly and, for a moment, sat eyeing the other in silence. Shoz-Dijiji was the first to speak.

"You are alone?" he demanded.

"Yes."

"Why you ride alone when the Apaches are on the war trail?" he asked, sternly.

"The Apaches are my friends. They will not harm me."

"Some of the Be-don-ko-he Apaches are your friends, white girl; but there are others on the war trail who are not your friends," replied Shoz-Dijiji. "There are Cho-kon-en and Ned-ni with Geronimo."

"Shoz-Dijiji and Geronimo would not let them harm me."

"Shoz-Dijiji and Geronimo are not like the God of the white-eyed men—they cannot be here, there, and everywhere at the same time."

Wichita Billings smiled. "But perhaps He guides them to

the right place at the right time," she suggested. "Are you not here now, Shoz-Dijiji, instead of a Cho-kon-en or a Ned-ni?"

"You have strong medicine, white girl, but so did the great izze-nantan, Nakay-do-klunni. He made strong medicine that turned away the bullets of the white-eyed soldiers, but at Cibicu Creek they killed him. The best medicine is to stay out of danger."

"Well, to tell you the truth, Shoz-Dijiji," admitted the girl, "I did not dream that there was a renegade within a hundred miles of here."

"When the Shis-Inday are on the war trail they are like your God—they are here, there, and everywhere."

"Are there others with you, Shoz-Dijiji?"

"No, I am alone."

"What are you doing here? Were you—were you coming to the ranch, Shoz-Dijiji?" she asked, hesitatingly. "Were you coming to see me?" There was potential gladness in her voice.

"Shoz-Dijiji has been scouting," replied the Apache. "He is returning to the camp of Geronimo."

"But you were going to stop and see me, Shoz-Dijiji," she insisted.

"No. It would have made trouble. Your father does not like Shoz-Dijiji, and he would like to kill a renegade. Shoz-Dijiji does not wish to be killed. Therefore there would be trouble."

"My father is sorry for the things he said to you, Shoz-Dijiji. Come to the ranch, and he will tell you so. He was angry because he was very fond of Mason; and you know that they had just found Mason murdered—and scalped."

"Shoz-Dijiji knows. He knows more about that than your father. Shoz-Dijiji knows that it was not an Apache that killed Mason."

"How do you know? Do you know who did kill him? He was scalped."

"Are the white-eyed men such fools that they think that only an Apache can scalp? If they were not such fools they would know that it is only occasionally that Apaches do take the scalps of their enemies. They do know this, but they do not want to admit it. They know that whenever a white-eyed man wishes to kill an enemy he need only scalp him to convince every one that Apaches did it, because everyone wishes to believe that every murder is done by Apaches.

"Yes, I know who killed Mason and why. He was robbed in Cheetim's Hog Ranch, and he had sworn to get Cheetim. He was looking for him with a gun. Cheetim hired a man to ride out with Mason and shoot him in the back. That is all.

"Now come. Shoz-Dijiji ride back with you until you are near the ranch. You must not ride alone again even if you are not afraid of the Apaches, for there are bad men among the white-eyes—men who would harm you even more surely than an Apache."

He motioned her to precede him up the steep canyonside; and when the two ponies had scrambled to the summit he rode at her side, where the ground permitted, as they walked their ponies in the direction of the Billings ranch.

For a while they rode in silence, the Apache constantly on the alert against another and more dangerous surprise, the girl thoughtful, her face reflecting the cast of sadness in which her thoughts were molded.

Wichita Billings knew that the man at her side loved her. She knew that she was drawn to him more than to any other man that she had ever known, but she did not know that this attraction constituted love.

Raised as she had been in an atmosphere of racial hatred, schooled in ignorance and bigotry by people who looked upon every race and nation, other than their own race and nation, as inferior, she could scarce believe it possible that she could give her love to an Indian; and so her mind argued against her heart that it was not love that she felt for him but some other emotion which should be suppressed.

Shoz-Dijiji, on his part, realized the barrier that prejudice had erected between them and the difficulty that the white girl might have to surmount it in the event that she loved him. He, too, had faced a similar barrier in his hatred of the white race; but that his love had long since leveled. A greater obstacle, one which he could not again face, was the hurt that his pride had suffered when she had recoiled from his embrace.

Thoughts such as these kept them silent for some time until Wichita chanced to recall Nejeunee.

"Shoz-Dijiji," she exclaimed, "where is your pinto war pony?"

The Apache shrugged. "Who knows?"

"What became of him? Is he dead, or did you lose him in battle?"

"We were starving," said the Apache. "We had eaten all the ponies except Nejeunee. It was in Sonora. Your soldiers were pressing us on one side, the Mexicans upon the other. At night I led Nejeunee close to the picket line of the white-eyed soldiers. I have not seen him since."

"You were very fond of Nejeunee, Shoz-Dijiji."

"In Apache Nejeunee means friend," said the man. "One by one all of my friends are being taken from me. Nejeunee was just one more. Usen has forgotten Shoz-Dijiji."

"Perhaps not," replied Wichita. "What would you say if I told you that Nejeunee is alive and that I know where he is?"

"I should say that after all Usen has at last been good to me in giving me you as a friend. Tell me where he is."

"He's on our ranch—in the back pasture."

"On your ranch? How did Nejeunee get there?"

"You left him near the picket line of Lieutenant King's troop, and when they got back across the border he sent him up to me."

"King did not tell me."

"You have seen the lieutenant?"

"We met in Chihuahua," said Shoz-Dijiji.

"And you talked with him?"

"Yes."

"But you were on the warpath, and he was after you. How could you have met and talked?"

"King and Shoz-Dijiji went into the cattle business together."

"What do you mean?" demanded Wichita.

"When you see King ask him. He will tell you."

"Were you two alone together?"

"Yes, for a day and a night."

"And you did not kill him?"

"No. Shoz-Dijiji does not kill anyone that you love."

"Oh, Shoz-Dijiji," exclaimed the girl, "I can't tell you how much I appreciate that; but really you are mistaken in thinking that I love Lieutenant King."

"All right, next time I kill him."

"No, oh, no, you mustn't do that."

"Why not? He is on the war trail against me. He kill me all right, if he get the chance. If you no love him, I kill him."

"But he is my friend, my very good friend," insisted the girl. "He is your friend, too, Shoz-Dijiji. If I ask you not to kill him will you promise me that you won't?"

"Shoz-Dijiji promise you he no try to kill King. Mebbe so, in battle, Shoz-Dijiji have to kill him. That he cannot help."

"Oh, Shoz-Dijiji, why don't you come in and stop fighting us? It is so useless. You can never win; and you are such a good man, Shoz-Dijiji, that it seems a shame that you should sacrifice your life uselessly."

"No, we can never win. We know that, but what else is there for us? The white-eyed men make war upon us even in peace. They treat us like enemies and prisoners. We are men, the same as they. Why do they not treat us like men? They say that we are bad men and that we torture our prisoners and that that is bad. Do they not torture us? We torture the bodies of our enemies, but the white men torture our hearts. Perhaps all the feelings of the white-eyed men are in their bodies, but that is not so with the Shis-Inday. Bad words and bad looks make wounds in our hearts that hurt us more than a knife thrust in the body. The body wounds may heal but the heart wounds never—they go on hurting forever. No, I shall not come in. I am a war chief among the Be-don-ko-he. Shall I come in to be a 'dirty Siwash' among the white-eyes?"

For a while the girl was silent after the Apache had ceased speaking. Their patient ponies stepped daintily along the rough trail. The descending sun cast their shadows, grotesquely, far ahead. The stifling heat of midday was gradually giving place to the promise of the coming cool of evening.

"We are almost home," said the girl, presently. "I wish you would come and talk with my father. He is not a bad man. Perhaps he can find some way to help you."

"No," said Shoz-Dijiji. "His people and my people are at

war. His heart is not friendly toward Apaches. It is better that I do not come."

"But you want to get Nejeunee," insisted the girl.

"You have told me where Nejeunee is. I will get him."

She did not insist, and again they rode in silence until the warrior reined in his pony just below the summit of a low hill. Beyond the hill, but hidden from their sight, stood the Billings' ranch house.

"Good-bye," said Shoz-Dijiji. "I think perhaps we never see each other again. When the soldiers come back from Mexico we go back there and do not come to this country any more."

"Oh, Shoz-Dijiji," cried the girl, "I do not want you to go."

"Shoz-Dijiji does not want to go," he replied. "Your people have driven Shoz-Dijiji from his own country."

"I should think that you would hate me, Shoz-Dijiji."

"No, I do not hate you. I love you," he said simply.

"You must not say that, Shoz-Dijiji," she answered, sadly.

"If Shoz-Dijiji was a white-eyed man, you would listen," he said.

She was silent.

"Tell me," he demanded, "is that not true?"

"Oh, God! I don't know, I don't know," she cried.

"Shoz-Dijiji knows," said the Bedonkohe. "Good-bye!"

He wheeled his pony and rode away.

The sun was setting as Wichita Billings dismounted wearily at the corral back of the ranch house. Luke Jensen came from the bunk house to take her pony.

"Where's Dad?" she asked.

"One of the boys found a beef killed this mornin'. He said it looked like Injuns hed done it. Yore Dad rid over to hev a look at it. He ought to be back right smart soon now." Luke glanced over across the back pasture toward the east. Wichita knitted her brows.

"Did he go that way?" she asked. "Alone?"

"Yep," assented Luke.

"Get one of the other boys to go with you, and ride out and meet him. If Apaches killed the beef there may be some of them around." Wichita turned toward the ranch house, hesitated, and then walked back to Luke.

"Luke," she said, "you don't hate all Indians do you?"

"You know I don't, Miss. I'd a bin dead now ef it hedn't a-bin fer one of 'em. Why?"

"Well, if you ever meet an Apache, Luke, remember that, and don't shoot until you're plumb sure he's hostile."

Jensen scratched his head. "Yes, Miss," he said, "but what's the idee?"

"There may be friendly Indians around, and if you should shoot one of them," she explained, "the rest might turn hostile."

As Wichita walked toward the house Luke stood looking after her.

"I don't reckon she's gone loco," he soliloquized, "but she shore better watch herself."

It was ten o'clock before Luke Jensen returned to the ranch. He went immediately to the house and knocked on the door, entering at Wichita's invitation.

"Your Dad back?" he demanded.

"No. Didn't you see anything of him?"

"Nary hide nor hair."

"Where do you suppose he can be?"

"I dunno. They's Indians around, though. I bumped plumb into one tother side of the willows in the draw outside the fer pasture gate, an' who do you reckon it was? Why none other than that Shoz-Dijiji fellow what give me a lift that time. He must-a thought some o' the hosses in the pasture were comin' through them willows, fer he never tried to hide hisself at all. I jest rid plumb on top o' him. He knew me, too. I couldn't help but think o' wot you told me just before I left about bein' sure not to shoot up any friendly. . . Say, did you know he was around?"

"How could I know that?" demanded Wichita.

"I dunno," admitted Luke, scratching his head; "but it did seem dern funny to me."

"It's funny the man with you didn't take a shot at him," commented Wichita. "Most all of the boys believe in shooting an Apache first and inquiring about his past later."

"There wasn't no one with me," explained Luke. "There wasn't no one around but me when I left, and I didn't want to waste time waiting fer someone to show up. Anyways,

I kin see alone jest as fer as I kin with help."

"Well, I reckon he'll be coming along pretty soon, Luke," said Wichita. "Good night."

"Good night, Miss," replied Jensen.

Chapter Thirteen

BACK TO SONORA

DAWN broke and Wichita Billings still sat fully dressed waiting for her father. It was the first time that she had ever worried greatly over his absence, and she could not explain why she worried now. She had always thought of her father as absolutely able to take care of himself in any emergency. He was a masterful man, utterly fearless, and yet not prone to take unnecessary chances.

A dozen times she had been upon the point of going to the bunk house and sending the entire outfit out to search for him, but each time she had shrunk from the ridicule that she well knew would be slyly heaped upon both her father and herself if she did so without good warrant; but now with a new day come and no word from him, she determined to swallow her pride and carry out her plan, however foolish it might appear.

Persistent knocking on the bunk house door finally elicited a profane request for information as to what was "eating" her.

"Dad's not back yet," she shouted.

"Oh, hell, is that you Miss? I didn't know it was you."

"Never mind. Roll out and get busy. We're goin' to find him if we have to ride to Boston," she cried.

Luke Jensen, being the youngest man in the outfit, both in years and point of service, was first from the bunk house, it being his duty to bring the saddle horses in from pasture. At the barn, he found that Wichita had already bridled the horse that was kept up for the purpose of bringing the others in and was on the point of swinging the heavy saddle to its back.

He greeted her cheerily, took the saddle from her, and completed its adjustment.

"You worried about your Paw, Miss?" he asked as he drew the latigo through the cinch ring.

"Something might have happened to him," she replied. "It won't hurt to look for him."

"No, it won't do no hurt, though I reckon he kin take keer o' hisself about as good as the next man. I wouldn't worry none, Miss," he concluded, reassuringly, as he stepped into the stirrup and swung his leg over the horse's rump.

Wichita stood by the corral gate watching Luke riding down into the east pasture at an easy lope. She saw him disappear among the willows that grow along the draw a mile from the corrals and two-thirds of the way across the pasture; and then "Smooth" Kreff, her father's foreman, joined her.

"Mornin', Miss," he greeted her. He looked at her sharply. "You-all been up all night, ain't you?"

"Yes," she admitted.

"Pshaw! Why didn't you rout us out? We'd a-gone lookin' fer him any time."

"There wouldn't have been much use looking for him at night."

"No, and there ain't much use lookin' fer him now; but it would a-made you-all feel easier," replied the man.

"Why isn't there any use looking for him now?" she demanded.

"Because the Boss kin take keer of himself. He ain't a-goin' to thank us none, I'm figgerin'."

"No, if he's all right, he won't; but if he isn't all right we'll be glad we did."

"Them hosses must a-gone plumb to the fer end of the pasture," remarked Kreff.

"They always do, if we're in a particular hurry to get them up," said Wichita.

The other men had come from the bunk house by now and were standing around waiting.

"Thet dog-gone 'cavvy' must a-knowed we wanted 'em bad," said one.

"Like as not they seed Luke comin' an' hid out in the willows," suggested another.

"They shore are an ornery bunch," admitted a third.

"I could of ridden down there backward on a bicycle an' rounded 'em up before this," boasted a fourth.

"Here they come now," exclaimed Wichita, as several horses broke from the willows and trotted toward the corrals.

In twos and threes they emerged from the dense foliage until some forty or fifty horses were strung out on the trail to the corrals, and then Luke Jensen rode into sight from out of the willows.

"What's thet critter he's leadin'?" demanded one of the men.

"It's saddled," volunteered another.

"It's Scar Foot," said Kreff.

After that there was silence. Some of the men glanced at Wichita, but most of them stood looking away, embarrassed. Scar Foot was Billings' favorite horse—the animal he had ridden out on the previous day.

The men walked out of the corral into the pasture to head the horses through the bars that had been let down to receive them. No one said anything. Kreff walked forward toward Luke; and the latter reined in and, leaning down, spoke to the foreman in a low voice. Wichita approached them.

"Where did you find Scar Foot?" she asked. "Where is Dad?"

"Scar Foot was jest outside the east gate, Miss," explained Jensen. "The other hosses was all up there by him, jest inside the fence."

"Did you see anything of Dad?" she demanded again.

"We-all's goin' to ride right out an' look fer him, Miss," said Kreff.

Inside the corral two men were roping, and the others were busy saddling their horses as they were caught.

Wichita climbed to the top of the corral. "I'll ride Two Spot," she called to one of the ropers.

Finally all the horses they needed had been caught and the others turned back into the pasture. One of the men who had been among the first to saddle was saddling Two Spot for Wichita. Luke Jensen, who had transferred his outfit to one of his own string, kept as far from Wichita as he could, but as she was about to mount, Kreff approached her, leading his own horse.

"I wouldn't come along, Miss, ef I was you," he advised. "We may have some hard ridin'."

"When did I get so I couldn't ride with any of you?" she asked, quietly.

"There may be some fightin'," he insisted, "an' I wouldn't want you-all to get hurted."

The girl smiled, ever so slightly. "It's good of you, 'Smooth,'" she said; "but I understand, I think." She swung into the saddle, and Kreff said no more.

Luke Jensen leading, they rode at a run down through the pasture, scattering the "cavvy," and into the dense willows, emerging upon the opposite side, climbing the steep bank of the draw, and away again at top speed toward the east gate. In silence they rode, with grim faces.

There, just beyond the fence, they found Billings—where Luke Jensen had found him. Wichita knelt beside her father and felt of his hands and face. She did not cry. Dry-eyed she arose and for the first time she saw that one of the men who had brought up the rear had led Scar Foot back with them; but even had she known it when they started she would not have been surprised, for almost from the moment that she had seen Luke Jensen leading the horse back toward the corrals and had seen him whisper to Kreff she had expected to find just what she had found.

Tenderly the rough men lifted all that was mortal of Jefferson Billings across the saddle in which he had ridden to his death, and many were the muttered curses that would have been vented vehemently and aloud had it not been for the presence of the girl, for Billings had been shot in the back and—scalped.

On walking horses the cortege filed slowly toward the ranch house, the men deferentially falling in behind the lead horse that bore the body of the "Boss" directly in rear of the girl who could not cry.

"He never had a chanct," growled one of the men. "Plugged right in the back between the shoulders!"

"God damned dirty Siwashes!" muttered another.

"I scen an Injun here yestiddy evenin'," said Luke.

"Why the Hell didn't you say so before?" demanded Kreff.

"I told Miss Chita," replied the young man; "but, Lor', it warn't him did it."

"Wot makes you-all think it warn't?" asked Kreff.

"He's a friend of hern. He wouldn't have hurted her old man."

"What Injun was it?"

"Thet Shoz-Dijiji fellow what saved me thet time I was hurted an' lost. I know he wouldn't hev done it. They must hev been some others around, too."

Kreff snorted. "Fer a bloke vot's supposed to hail from Texas you-all shore are simple about Injuns. Thet Siwash is a Cheeracow Apache an' a Cheeracow Apache'd kill his grandmother fer a lead nickel."

"I don't believe thet Injun would. Why didn't he plug me when he had the chanct?" demanded Jensen.

"Say!" exclaimed Kreff. "Thet there pinto stallion thet thet there greaser brung up from Chihuahua fer King warn't with the 'cavvy' this mornin'. By gum! There's the answer. Thet there pony belonged to Shoz-Dijiji. He was a-gettin' it when the Boss rid up."

"They had words last time the Siwash was around here," volunteered another.

"Sure! The Boss said he'd plug him if he ever seen him hangin' around here again," recalled one of the men.

At the ranch house they laid Jefferson Billings on his bed and covered him with a sheet, and then "Smooth" Kreff went to Wichita and told her of his deductions and the premises upon which they were based.

"I don't believe it," said the girl. "Shoz-Dijiji has always been friendly to us. I ran across him by accident in the hills yesterday, and he rode home with me because, he said, there were other renegades around and it might not be safe for me to ride alone. It must have been some other Indian who did it."

"But his cayuse is gone," insisted Kreff.

"He may have taken his pony," admitted the girl. "I don't say that he didn't do that. It was his, and he had a right to take it, but I don't believe that he killed Dad."

"Your Paw didn't have no use fer Injuns," Kreff reminded her. "He might have taken a shot at this Siwash."

"No; his guns were both in their holsters, and his rifle was in its boot. He never saw the man that shot him."

Kreff scratched his head. "I reckon thet's right," he admitted. "It shore was a dirty trick. Thet's what makes me know it was a Siwash."

The girl turned away sadly.

"Don't you worry none, Miss," said Kreff; "I'll look after things fer you, jes' like your Paw was here."

"Thanks, 'Smooth,'" replied Wichita. "You boys have been wonderful."

After the man had left the room the girl sat staring fixedly at the opposite wall. A calendar hung there and a colored print in a cheap frame, but these she did not see. What she saw was the tall, straight figure of a bronzed man, an almost naked savage. He sat upon his war pony and looked into her eyes.

"Shoz-Dijiji does not kill anyone that you love," he said to her.

The girl dropped her face into her hands, stifling a dry sob. "Oh, Shoz-Dijiji, how could you?" she cried.

Suddenly she sprang to her feet. Her lips were set in a straight, hard line; her eyes flashed in anger.

"Oh, God!" she cried. "You gave me love; and I threw it away upon an Indian, upon an enemy of my people; and now, in your anger, you have punished me. I was blind, but you have made me to see again. Forgive me, God, and you will see that I have learned my lesson well."

Stepping through the doorway onto the porch, Wichita seized a short piece of iron pipe and struck a triangle of iron that hung suspended from a roof joist. Three times she struck it, and in answer to the signal the men came from bunk house and corrals until all that had been within hearing of the summons were gathered before her.

Dry-eyed, she faced them, and upon her countenance was an expression that none ever had seen there before. It awed them into silence as they waited for her to speak. They were rough, uncouth men, little able to put their innermost thoughts into words, and none of them ever had looked upon

an avenging angel; otherwise they would have found a fitting
description for the daughter of their dead boss as she faced
them now.

"I have something to say to you," she commenced in a
level voice. "My father lies in here, murdered. He was shot
in the back. He never had a chance. As far as we know no
one saw him killed, but I guess we all know who did it.
There doesn't seem to be any chance for a doubt—it was the
Be-don-ko-he war chief, Shoz-Dijiji, Black Bear.

"If it takes all the rest of my life and every acre and
every critter that I own, I'm going to get the man that killed
my father; and I'm starting now by offering a thousand dollars to the man who brings in Shoz-Dijiji—*dead!*"

When she had ceased speaking she turned and walked back
into the house, closing the door after her.

The men, moving slowly toward the bunk house, talked
together in low tones, discussing the girl's offer.

Inside the house, Wichita Billings threw herself face down
upon a sofa and burst into tears.

* * *

Shoz-Dijiji slid from the back of the pinto war pony, Nejeunee, in the camp of Geronimo and stood before the great
war chief of the Apaches.

"Seven times, my son," said the old chief, "have I cast
hoddentin to the four winds at evening since you rode away;
seven times have I cast hoddentin to the four winds at dawn;
twice seven times have I prayed to the spirits whose especial
duty it is to watch over you to bring you back in safety. My
prayers have been answered. What word do you bring?"

"Shoz-Dijiji went to the reservation at San Carlos," replied
the young man. "None of our friends or relatives who went
out upon the war trail with us is there. I heard many stories,
but I do not speak of anything that I did not see with
my own eyes or hear with my own ears.

"There are many soldiers scouting everywhere. There are
so many that I think all the soldiers that were sent to Mexico
after us must have been called back to hunt for us here.

"The reservation Indians say that now that Miles is after
us we shall all be killed. They advise us to lay down our arms

and surrender. I think that very soon the soldiers will find our camp here."

"You are a war chief, my son," said Geronimo. "Already you are very wise. At the councils even the old men listen to you with respect. What would you advise?"

"We are very few," replied Shoz-Dijiji, thoughtfully. "We cannot take the war trail successfully against the pindah-lickoyee in this country where we are. Sooner or later they will kill us or capture us. This is no longer a good country for the Apache. It is our country that Usen made for us, but we cannot be happy in it any longer because of the pindah-lickoyee. Shoz-Dijiji does not wish to live here any more. Let us go to Mexico. Perhaps the soldiers of the pindah-lickoyee will not again follow us into Mexico. There we may live as we would wish to live and not as the pindah-lickoyee want us to live."

"And we can punish the Mexicans for inviting the soldiers of the pindah-lickoyee to come down to their country and kill us," added Geronimo. "I think you have spoken true words. I think we should go to Mexico. Perhaps there we shall find all of our friends and relatives from whom we became separated when the soldiers were hunting us in Sonora and Chihuahua. Perhaps we can even be happy again. Who knows?"

And so it was that when the troopers of "B" Troop rode into the camp of Geronimo a week later they found nothing but cold ashes where the cooking fires had been and the debris of a deserted Indian village that the Apaches had not taken their usual precautions to hide, since they expected never again to return to their beloved mountains.

Far to the south, below the line, frightened peons burned many candles and said many prayers, for they had heard stories. A man had found the bodies of three vaqueros, and he had seen the print of an Apache moccasin in the camp where they had been killed. They had not been tortured nor mutilated.

"The Apache Devil again!" whispered the peons.

A terrified freighter, a bullet through his shoulder, galloped an exhausted mule into a little hamlet. The wagon train that he had been with had been attacked by Apaches and all had been slain save he, and with his own eyes he had recognized Geronimo.

"Holy Mother, preserve us! Geronimo and the Apache Devil, both!"

Leaving a trail of blood and ashes behind them the renegades headed for the mountains near Casa Grande. Having committed no depredations north of the line they felt confident that the United States soldiers would not follow them into Sonora. Why should they? There was nothing for the soldiers of the pindah-lickoyee to avenge.

Thus the Apaches reasoned, since, in common with white men, they possessed the very human trait of easily forgetting the wrongs that they committed against others, even though they might always harbor those that were committed against them.

So now they either forgot or ignored what the whites still considered just causes for righteous anger—burnt ranches, stolen stock, tortured men, women, and children, mutilated corpses that had emblazoned their trail through Arizona from San Carlos to the border over a year before; but the whites had no intention of permitting these occurrences to go brown in their memories.

From one end of the country to the other Geronimo and his bloody deeds occupied more front-page newspaper space than any other topic, and to the readers of the newspapers of all the civilized world his name was a household word. For over a year the armies of two nations had been futilely engaged in an attempt to capture or kill a handful of men, women, and children. Geronimo and his renegades had outwitted, outgeneraled, and outfought them; and now, after again outwitting the army of the United States, they had come back to Mexico and were meting out punishment to those whom they mistakenly believed were responsible for bringing United States troops below the border to fight them; and in carrying out this policy they attacked every Mexican they saw after they crossed the border, all the way to Casa Grande. Nor did they desist then.

South of Casa Grande, near a place which the Apaches called Gosoda, a road wound out of the town through a mountain pass. Many were the freight trains that lumbered through the dust along this road, and near here hid Geronimo, the Apache Devil, and their followers.

Here the renegades remained for some time, killing freighters, taking what supplies they desired, and destroying the remainder; but the reputation that this road achieved was such as to discourage freighting for the nonce, though it attracted Mexican soldiers in embarrassing numbers.

Geronimo then led his followers into the Sierra de Antunez Mountains where they found all that now remained of their depleted tribe and learned that the United States soldiers had not left the mountains of Mexico but, on the contrary, were becoming more active than ever.

Geronimo was disheartened when he learned of this, for he had banked wholly on the belief that he would be rid of the menace of United States troops if he returned to Mexico without committing more depredations in the United States.

"What are we to do?" he demanded at the council fire. "Every man's hand is against us. If we return to the reservation we shall be put in prison and killed; if we stay in Mexico they will continue to send more and more soldiers to fight us."

"There is but one thing to do," replied Shoz-Dijiji when Geronimo had finished. "We must continue fighting until we are all killed. Already we are reckless of our lives; let us be more so; let us give no quarter to anyone and ask no favors. It is better to die on the war trail than to be put in prison and choked to death with a rope about the neck. I, Shoz-Dijiji, shall continue to fight the enemies of my people until I am killed. I have spoken."

"You are a young man," said Geronimo. "Your words are the words of a young man. When I was young I wanted nothing better than to fight, but now that I am getting old I should like a little peace and quiet; although I should not object to fighting to obtain them if I thought that I might win them thus.

"But now," he continued, sadly, "I cannot see any hope of winning anything but death by fighting longer against the pindah-lickoyee. There are too many of them, and they will not let us rest. I would make a peace treaty with them, if I could."

"They do not want to make a peace treaty with us," said
Shoz-Dijiji. "They want only to kill us all that there may
be no more Apaches left to dispute the ownership of the land
they have stolen from us. Let the old men and the women
and the children make a peace treaty with the pindah-
lickoyee. Shoz-Dijiji will never make peace if it means that
he must return to San Carlos and be a reservation Indian."

"I think that we should make peace with them," said Na-
chi-ta, "if they will promise that we shall not be killed."

"The promises of the pindah-lickoyee are valueless,"
growled a warrior.

Thus they spoke around their council fires at night, and
though most of them wanted peace and none of them saw any
other alternative than death, they clung doggedly to the war
trail. During three months they had many skirmishes with
the white soldiers; and five times their camps were surprised,
yet in no instance were the troops of the pindah-lickoyee able
either to capture or defeat them; never was there a decisive
victory for the trained soldiers who so greatly outnumbered
them.

In July 1886 Geronimo's force numbered some twenty-five
fighting men, a few women, and a couple of boys. Outside of
their weapons and the clothing that they wore they possessed
a few hundred pounds of dried meat and nineteen ponies—
the sole physical resources at their command to wage a campaign against a great nation that already had expended a
million dollars during the preceding fourteen months in futile
efforts to subjugate them and had enlisted as allies the armed
forces of another civilized power.

Moving farther and farther into Old Mexico as the troops
pressed them, the renegades were camped on the Yongi
River, nearly three hundred miles south of the boundary,
late in July. They believed that they had temporarily thrown
their pursuers off the track and, war weary, were taking advantage of the brief respite they had earned to rest.

Peace and quiet lay upon the camp beside the Yongi. The
braves squatted, smoking, or lay stretched in sleep. The
squaws patched war worn moccasins. There was little conversation and no laughter. The remnant of a once powerful

nation was making its last stand, bravely, without even the sustaining influence of hope.

A rifle cracked. War whoops burst upon their ears. Leaping to their feet, seizing the weapons that lay always ready at hand, the renegades fell back as the soldiers and scouts of Lawton's command charged their camp. The surprise had been complete, and in their swift retreat the Apaches lost three men, whom they carried off with them, as they abandoned their supply of dried meat and their nineteen ponies to the enemy. Now they had nothing left but their weapons and their indomitable courage.

Clambering to inaccessible places among the rocks, where mounted men could not follow, they waited until the soldiers withdrew. Shoz-Dijiji arose and started down toward the camp.

"Where are you going?" demanded Geronimo.

"The white-eyes have taken Nejeunee," replied the war chief. "Shoz-Dijiji goes to take his war pony from them."

"Good!" exclaimed Geronimo. "I go with you." He turned and looked inquiringly at the other warriors before he followed Shoz-Dijiji down the steep declivity. After the two came the balance of the grim warriors.

Keeping to the hills, unseen, they followed Lawton's command in the rear of which they saw their ponies being driven. As the hours passed, Geronimo saw that the distance between the main body of troopers and the pony herd was increasing.

A few miles ahead was a small meadow just beyond which the trail made a sharp turn around the shoulder of a hill. Geronimo whispered to Shoz-Dijiji who nodded understanding and assent. The word was passed among the other warriors; and at the same time Shoz-Dijiji turned to the left to make a detour through the hills, while a single warrior remained upon the trail of the troops.

At a smart trot the Be-don-ko-he war chief led his fellows through the rough mountains. For an hour they pushed rapidly on until Shoz-Dijiji dropped to his belly near the summit of a low hill and commenced to worm his way slowly upward. Behind him came twenty painted savages. In the rear of concealing shrubbery at the hill top the Apache Devil stopped, and behind him stopped the twenty.

Below Shoz-Dijiji was a little meadow. It lay very quiet and peaceful in the afternoon sun, deserted; but Shoz-Dijiji knew that it would not be deserted long. Already he could hear the approach of armed men. Presently they came into sight. Captain Lawton rode in advance. At his side was Lieutenant Gatewood. Behind them were the scouts and the soldiers. The formation was careless, because they all knew that the renegades, surprised and defeated, were far behind them.

Shoz-Dijiji watched them pass. In the rear of the column he saw Lieutenant King who had been temporarily detached from his own troop to serve with this emergency command of Lawton's. The length of the meadow they rode. The head of the column disappeared where the trail turned the shoulder of a hill, and still Shoz-Dijiji and the twenty lay quietly waiting.

Now half the column was out of sight. Presently Shoz-Dijiji watched King disappear from view, and once again the little meadow was deserted, but not for long.

A little pinto stallion trotted into view, stopped, pricked dainty ears and looked about. Behind him came other ponies —nineteen of them—and behind the ponies three sun-parched troopers in dusty, faded blue.

Silently Shoz-Dijiji arose, and behind him arose twenty other painted warriors. They uttered no war whoops as they raced silently down into the meadow in front of the ponies. There would be noise enough in a moment; but they wished to delay the inevitable as long as possible lest the main body of the command, warned by the sounds of combat, should return to the meadow before the mission of the Apaches was completed.

The first trooper to see them vented his surprise in lurid profanity and spurred forward in an attempt to stampede the ponies across the meadow before the renegades could turn them. His companions joined him in the effort.

Shoz-Dijiji and six other warriors raced swiftly to intercept the ponies, while the other renegades moved down to the turn in the trail where they could hold up the troop should it return too soon.

The Apache Devil whistled sharply as he ran and the pinto

stallion stopped, wheeled, and ran toward him. Three ponies, frightened by the shouts of the soldiers, raced swiftly ahead, passing Shoz-Dijiji and his six, passing the balance of the twenty who had not yet reached their position, and disappeared around the turn.

Shoz-Dijiji leaped to Nejeunee's back and headed the remaining ponies in a circle, back in the direction from which they had come and toward the six who had accompanied him.

It was then that one of the three soldiers opened fire, but the Apaches did not reply. They were too busy catching mounts from the frightened herd, and they had not come primarily to fight. When they had recaptured their ponies there would be time enough for that, perhaps, but it was certain that there was no time for it now. They had their hands full for a few seconds, but eventually seven warriors were mounted; and Geronimo and the remainder of the renegades were coming down the meadow at a run as Shoz-Dijiji and his six drove the herd along the back trail.

Hopelessly outnumbered, cut off from their fellows, the three troopers looked for some avenue of escape and fell back in front of the herd, firing. It was then that the Apaches opened fire; and at the first volley one of the soldiers fell and the other two turned and raced for safety, rounding the side of the herd, they spurred their mounts along the flank of the renegades.

A few hasty shots were sent after them; but the Apaches wasted no time upon them, and they won through in safety while Shoz-Dijiji and the six urged the ponies at a run along the back trail toward camp, as those on foot took to the hills and disappeared just as Lawton's command came charging to the rescue, too late.

Lawton followed the Apaches; but, being fearful of ambush, he moved cautiously, and long before he could overtake them the renegades had made good their escape.

Chapter Fourteen

SKELETON CANYON

THE weeks dragged on—lean and hungry weeks of slinking through the mountains with an implacable enemy always on their heels. The renegades had little food and little rest. Their cause seemed hopeless even to the most warlike and the most sanguine of their number. Only Shoz-Dijiji held out for war. That was because he had nothing to live for. He courted death, but no bullet found him.

At last the others determined to give up and Geronimo sent a messenger to the commander of a body of Mexican troops that was camped near them, asking for a parley.

All that the Mexicans asked was that Geronimo should take his band out of Mexico; and this the old chieftain promised to do, both sides agreeing not to fight any more against the other.

Moving northward toward the border, Geronimo made no effort to elude the American troops, as he was really anxious to arrange for a parley with them; but by chance they did not come into contact with any, and at last the renegades went into camp near the big bend of the Bivaspe River, in Sonora.

"How can you remain here?" demanded Shoz-Dijiji. "You have promised the Mexicans that you will leave their country, and you cannot go into Arizona or New Mexico because the soldiers of the pindah-lickoyee will not let you. Where are you going? You should not have promised the Mexicans that you would leave. Now they will attack you, when they find that you have not left, for they know that you have had time enough to get out of Mexico."

"We cannot remain here," replied Geronimo, "and we cannot go elsewhere—as long as we are at war with the pindah-lickoyee. We are too few to fight them. There remains nothing but to make the best peace with them that we can."

"It is right that you should do so," said Shoz-Dijiji, "for that is to the best interests of the Be-don-ko-he for the welfare of the tribe, but for Shoz-Dijiji there can be no peace. I shall not go back to the reservation with you."

"That is the right of every Apache, to choose for himself," said Na-chi-ta; "but for the tribe it is better that we make peace and go back to the reservation. Na-chi-ta will vote for peace if the pindah-lickoyee will promise not to kill any of us."

"I shall send White Horse, my brother, to arrange for a parley with the white-eyed chiefs," said Geronimo.

The day after White Horse left upon his mission the renegades sent two squaws into Fronteras to purchase food and mescal, and as they returned to camp they were followed to the last hiding place of the great war chief of all the Apaches.

Scarcely had the squaws laid aside their burdens when one of Geronimo's scouts hurried into the camp and reported to the war chief that two government scouts had come, bringing a message to Geronimo.

"I will talk with them," said the old chief, and a few minutes later Ka-yi-tah, the Cho-kon-en, and Marteen, the Ned-ni, stood before him, the red headbands of their service alone differentiating them from the warriors who crowded about them.

"You bring a message from the white-eyed chiefs to Geronimo?" demanded the war chief.

"With Lieutenant Gatewood we have brought a message from General Miles, the new chief of the white-eyed soldiers," replied Ka-yi-tah.

"Speak!" commanded Geronimo.

"The message is that if you will surrender you will not be killed; but will be taken some place to the East, you and your families—all of you who are now upon the war trail and who will surrender."

"How many soldiers has Gatewood with him?" demanded Geronimo.

"There are no soldiers with Gatewood," replied Ka-yi-tah; "but Lawton's soldiers are not far away."

"Geronimo will talk with Gatewood," announced the old chief, "but with no one else. Gatewood does not tell lies to the Apache. Tell them not to let any soldiers come near my camp, and I shall talk with Gatewood. Go!"

And so it was that through the confidence that Geronimo felt in Lieutenant Charles B. Gatewood, Sixth United States Cavalry, arrangements were made for a parley with General Miles, and on September 4th 1886 Geronimo and Na-chi-ta surrendered at Skeleton Canyon, Arizona.

Shoz-Dijiji did not accompany the other chiefs to the parley. With only his own sad thoughts as company he remained in camp, and there Geronimo found him when the parley was over. Shoz-Dijiji arose and faced the old chieftain.

"I do not need to ask Geronimo what has happened," said the young chief. "I see sorrow in his eyes. It is the end of the Apaches."

"Yes," replied Geronimo, "it is the end."

"What talk passed between Geronimo and the white-eyed chief?" asked Shoz-Dijiji.

"We shook hands; and then we sat down, and the white-eyed war chief said to Geronimo: 'The President of the United States has sent me to speak to you. He has heard of your trouble with the white men, and says that if you will agree to a few words of treaty we need have no more trouble. Geronimo, if you will agree to a few words of treaty all will be satisfactorily arranged.'

"He told me how we could be brothers to each other. We raised our hands to heaven and said that the treaty was not to be broken. We took an oath not to do any wrong to each other or to scheme against each other."

"And you believed the pindah-lickoyee?" demanded Shoz-Dijiji. "Each time that we go upon the war trail they promise us many things to induce us to lay down our arms—and do they keep their promises? No! Nor will they keep this promise."

"I do not know. All that I can do is hope, for no longer can we fight against them," answered Geronimo, wearily.

"What else said the pindah-lickoyee?" asked the Apache Devil.

"He talked with me for a long time and told me what he would do for me in the future if I would agree to the treaty. I did not greatly believe him, but because the President of the United States had sent me word I agreed to make the treaty and to keep it.

"He said to me: 'I will take you under government protection; I will build you a house; I will fence you much land; I will give you cattle, horses, mules, and farming implements. You will be furnished with men to work the farm, for you yourself will not have to work. In the fall I will send you blankets and clothing so that you will not suffer from cold in the winter time.

" 'There is plenty of timber, water, and grass in the land to which I shall send you,' he told me. He said that I should live with my tribe and with my family and that if I agreed to the treaty I should be with my family within five days.

"Then I said to General Miles: 'All the officers that have been in charge of the Indians have talked that way, and it sounds like a story to me; I hardly believe you.'

" 'This time,' he said, 'it is the truth,' and he swept a spot of ground clear with his hand and said: "Your past deeds shall be wiped out like this, and you will start a new life.'

"All this talk was translated from English into Spanish and from Spanish into Apache. It took a long time. Perhaps the interpreters did not make any mistakes. I do not know."

"Are you going to live on the reservation at San Carlos?" asked Shoz-Dijiji.

"No. They are going to send us out of Arizona because they say that the white men whose families and friends we have killed would always be making a lot of trouble for us, that they would try to kill us."

"Where are they going to send you?"

"To Fort Marion in a country called Florida." The old man bowed his head. Could it be that there were tears in those cold blue eyes?

Shoz-Dijiji placed a hand on his father's shoulder. "I know now that I shall never see you again," he said. "The pindah-lickoyee, who have never kept a promise that they have made to the Shis-Inday, will not keep this one. When you have laid down your arms they will kill you, as they killed Mangas Colorado.

"It is not too late even now to turn back," continued the young man. "We have ponies, we have arms, we have ammunition; and there are places in the mountains of Sonora where a few men could elude the pindah-lickoyee forever. Do not let them take you to a strange country where they will either kill you or make a slave of you."

Geronimo shook his head. "No, my son," he said, "that cannot be. The war chief of the pindah-lickoyee and the war chief of all the Apaches stood between his troopers and my warriors. We placed a large stone on the blanket before us. Our treaty was made by this stone, and it was to last until the stone should crumble to dust. So we made the treaty and bound each other with an oath. Geronimo will keep that treaty."

Slowly Shoz-Dijiji turned and walked away. Far up among the rocks above the rocky camp site he went; and there he remained all night praying to Usen, praying to Intchi-Dijin, the black wind, asking for guidance, asking for wisdom; for Shoz-Dijiji, the Black Bear, did not know what to do.

When morning came he returned to the camp of the renegades; and there he found his people, sullen and morose, preparing to lay down their weapons and give themselves up as prisoners of war to the enemy that they feared, hated, and mistrusted.

He went to the pony herd and caught Nejeunee and brought him back to camp. Then he squatted beside a rock, and with a bronze forefinger laid the war paint of the Apache Devil across his face. Upon his head he placed his war bonnet of buckskin with its crest of feathers; about his neck he hung a single strand of turquoise and silver beads; in his ears were small silver rings, and covering his feet and legs were stout Apache war moccasins.

A belt of ammunition encircled his slim waist, and from it hung two pistols and a great butcher knife. He carried a rifle and bow and arrows.

The others saw his preparations, but they made no comment. When he was done he mounted Nejeunee—an Apache war chief tricked out in all the panoply of the war trail.

He rode to where Geronimo sat stolidly upon a pony waiting for the preparations for departure to be completed. The old war chief looked up as the younger man approached, but the expression upon his inscrutable face did not change as he saw the war paint and the weapons.

"My father," said Shoz-Dijiji, "all night I have prayed in the high places, prayed to Usen and to Intchi-Dijin, asking them to give me some sign if they wished me to give myself up to the enemy and go into bondage with Geronimo and our people. But they gave me no sign, and so I know that they do not wish me to do these things; and I am satisfied.

"Therefore I ride out alone, the last of the Apaches, upon

the war trail against the enemies of my people. While I live I shall devote my life to killing the pindah-lickoyee. I, Shoz-Dijiji, war chief of the Be-don-ko-he, have spoken."

"Wait," said Geronimo. "Wait until you have heard the words of Geronimo before you bind yourself to such an oath.

"We go into bondage. We shall never take the war trail again. Had it been otherwise I should never have told you what I am going to tell you now.

"All your life you have been as a son to me. I have loved you. I have been proud of you. It is because I love you, Shoz-Dijiji, that I am going to tell you this thing now. When I have told you you will know that you need not throw away your life fighting the pindah-lickoyee, fighting the battles of the Apaches.

"Shoz-Dijiji, you are not an Apache. You are not a Shis-Inday. You are a pindah-lickoyee."

The eyes of the Apache Devil narrowed. "You are my father," he said, "but not even you may call Shoz-Dijiji a pindah-lickoyee and live. That, Juh learned."

Geronimo shook his head sadly. "Juh knew," he said. "He was with me when we killed your father and mother in a pass in the Stein's Peak Range. It was Juh who dragged you from the wagon and would have killed you but for Geronimo."

"It is a lie!" growled Shoz-Dijiji.

"Has Geronimo ever lied to you?" asked the old war chief.

"Cochise swore before the council fire that I was as much an Apache as he," cried the young man.

"Cochise did not lie," said Geronimo. "You are as much an Apache as any of us in heart and spirit, but in your veins flows the blood of your white-eyed father.

"Twenty-three times have the rains come since the day that I killed him; and I have kept my lips sealed because I loved you and because you were as much my son to me as though you were flesh of my own flesh; but now the time has come that you should know, for as an Apache every man's hand will be turned against you, but as a pindah-lickoyee you will have a chance that no Apache ever may have."

For a few moments Shoz-Dijiji sat in brooding silence. Presently he spoke.

"Pindah-lickoyee! White-eyed man!" he cried contemptuously, almost spitting the words from his mouth. "Had you told me that I am a coyote I could have carried my shame and faced the world, but to be a white man!" He shuddered.

"My son," said Geronimo, "it is not the color of our skin or the blood that runs in our veins that makes us good men or bad men. There are bad Apaches and there are good white men. It is good to be a good Apache. It is not bad to be a good white man. Now, perhaps, it is better to be a good white man than even a good Apache. Times have changed. Usen does not look with favor upon the Shis-Inday. Time will heal your wound. Go and live among your own people, and some day you will thank Geronimo because he told you."

"Never!" cried the Black Bear. "Good-bye, Geronimo. You have been a good father to Shoz-Dijiji. Now Shoz-Dijiji has no father. Shoz-Dijiji has no mother. Shoz-Dijiji has no people, for he is not an Apache; and he will not be a pindah-lickoyee. But he is still a war chief of the Apaches. He is the only war chief that goes upon the war trail. Now, I think, he is the only Apache left in the world. All the rest of you are pindah-lickoyee, for do you not go to live with the pindah-lickoyee? Only Shoz-Dijiji lives like an Apache."

He wheeled Nejeunee about, and then turned on his blanket and faced Geronimo again.

"Good-bye! Shoz-Dijiji, last of the Apaches, war chief of all the Apaches, rides out upon the last war trail."

Down the rocky hill side toward the south the pinto war pony bore his gorgeous master, while an old man, seeing dimly through blue eyes that were clouded by unaccustomed tears, watched the last martial gesture of his once powerful people until pinto stallion and painted war chief disappeared into the blue haze that lay upon the early morning trail that wound southward toward Sonora.

Chapter Fifteen

THE LAST OF THE RENEGADES

GERONIMO had surrendered! For the first time in three hundred years the white invaders of Apacheland slept in peace. All of the renegades were prisoners of war in Florida.

Right, at last, had prevailed. Once more a Christian nation had exterminated a primitive people who had dared defend their homeland against a greedy and ruthless invader.

Imprisoned with the renegades, and equally prisoners of war, were Apaches who had long been loyal and faithful servants to the government; but what of that! Who was there to defend a friendless people?—friendless and voteless.

Transported from the hot, dry uplands of their native country to the low, damp, malarial surroundings of their prison, the Apaches sickened and died; others, unable to endure confinement, suffering pangs of homesickness, took their own lives.

And down in Sonora, in the inaccessible depths of the Mother of Mountains, Shoz-Dijiji and Nejeunee shared the hunting and the pasture with the cougar and the mountain sheep. They trod in the footsteps of God, where man and horse had never walked before. No man saw them and, for months on end, they saw no man.

Long since had Shoz-Dijiji washed the war paint from his face. He was a hunter now, and upon the rare occasions that he saw other human beings he experienced no urge to kill them.

He had thought it all out during the long, lonely days and nights. Geronimo had made treaties with the Mexicans and with the pindah-lickoyee. He had promised that the Apaches would fight no more against them. That treaty, Shoz-Dijiji felt, bound him, for there were no other Apaches than he. He could not, as yet, think of himself as a pindah-lickoyee. He was an Apache—the last of the Apaches.

He promised himself that he would not kill again except in self-defense. He would show them that it was not the Apaches who broke treaties, but experience warned him that the only way to keep peace was to keep hidden from the eyes of man. He knew that the first one who saw him would shoot at him, if he dared, and that thereafter he would be hunted like the coyote and the cougar.

"Only we shall know that we are keeping the treaty, Nejeunee," he said, and the pinto stallion nuzzled his shoulder in complete accord with this or any other view that his beloved master might hold.

Accustomed to being much alone though he was, yet the

man often longed for the companionship of his kind. He conjured pictures of camps beneath the pines and cedars of his beloved Arizona hills, of little fires before rude hogans of boughs and skins. He saw Geronimo and Sons-ee-ah-ray squatting there; and with them was Shoz-Dijiji, son of the war chief. These three were always laughing and happy.

Gian-nah-tah came to the fire, and Ish-kay-nay. Sometimes these were little children and again they were grown to young man- and womanhood. He saw many others. Squat, grim warriors, slender youths, lovely maidens whose great, dark eyes looked coquettishly at Shoz-Dijiji.

Most of these were dead. The others, bitter, sullen, had marched away into captivity.

Another figure came, but not to the camp fires of the Shis-Inday. This one came, always, riding a pony over sun-scorched hills. Shoz-Dijiji took her in his arms; but she drew away, striking at him. He saw in her eyes, then, a look that he called the snake look. It made him sad and yet this picture came most often to his mind.

He wondered if the snake look would come if she knew that he was a pindah-lickoyee like herself. Perhaps she would not believe it. It was difficult for him to believe it himself. Had any other than Geronimo told him he would not have believed it, but he knew that Geronimo would not lie to him.

Well, she would never know it. It was a shame and a disgrace that he would hide from the knowledge of all men as long as he lived. A white-eyes! Usen! What had Shoz-Dijiji done to deserve this?

But, after all, he *was* white, he mused. From that fact he could never escape, and it was very lonely living in the mountains forever with only Nejeunee. Perhaps the white girl would believe him; and if she did would it not be better to go and live among the white-eyes as one of them?

He recalled how he used to pity any who had been born white. It would not have been quite so bad had he been born a Mexican, for he knew that there was Indian blood in many of the Mexicans he had known. It would have comforted him had he known that the grandfather of his mother had been a full-blooded Cherokee, but he did not know that. He was never to know it, for he was never to know even the names of his father and mother.

He tried to argue with himself that it was no disgrace to be white. Wichita Billings was white, and he thought none the less of her; Lieutenant King was white, and he knew that he was a fine, brave warrior; and there had been Captain Crawford, and there was Lieutenant Gatewood. These men he admired and respected.

Yes, it was all right for them to be white; but still the thought that Shoz-Dijiji, war chief of the Be-don-ko-he, was white seemed all wrong. He could not forget the pride that had always filled his heart because of the fact that he was an Apache. He had been a great Apache warrior. As a white man he would be nothing. If he went to live among them he would have to wear their hideous clothing and live in their stuffy houses; and he would have to live like the poorest of them, for he would have no money. No, he could not do it.

He thought about the matter a great deal. The lonelier he became the more he thought about it. Wichita Billings was constantly the center of his thoughts. His mind also dwelled upon memories of happy camping places of the past, and it seemed that the sweetest memories hung about the home camps of Arizona.

His lonely heart yearned not only for human companionship but for the grim country that was home to him. Something was happening to Shoz-Dijiji. He thought that he was sick and that he was going to die. He was homesick.

"I could go back and die in my own mountains," he thought. The idea made him almost happy. He stroked Nejeunee's soft muzzle and his sleek, arched neck. "How would you like to go home, Nejeunee?" asked Shoz-Dijiji. Nejeunee, after the manner of stallions, nipped the bronze shoulder of his master; but whether it was to signify approbation of the suggestion or was merely in the nature of a caress, only Nejeunee knew.

Lieutenant Samuel Adams King sat beneath one of the cottonwood trees that stands in front of the ranch house of the Crazy B Ranch, his chair tilted back against the bole of the tree. Near him sat Wichita Billings, her fingers busily engaged in the work that was commanding their attention. She might have been embroidering her initials upon a pillowslip or fashioning some dainty bit of lingerie, but she was not. She was cleaning a six-shooter.

"It sure seems tame around these parts now," she remarked. "Do you know I almost miss being scared out of seven years' growth every once in a while since the 'bronchos' were rounded up and shipped to Florida."

"I suppose you are cleaning that pistol, then, just as a sentimental reminder of the happy days that are gone," laughed King.

"Not entirely," she replied. "There are still plenty of bad hombres left—all the bad ones weren't Indians, not by a jug full."

"I suppose not," agreed King. "As a matter of fact I doubt if the Apaches were responsible for half the killings that have been laid at their door; and, do you know, Chita, I can't bring myself to believe even yet that it was an Apache that killed your father. We got it pretty straight from some of the renegades themselves that at the time they were all with Geronimo in the mountains near Hot Springs, except those that were still in Sonora, and Shoz-Dijiji."

"Well, that narrows it down pretty close to one man, doesn't it?" demanded the girl, bitterly.

"Yes, Chita," replied King, "but I can't believe that he did it. He spared my life twice merely because I was your friend. If he could do that, how could he have killed your father?"

"I know, Ad. I've argued it out a hundred times," said the girl, wearily; "but—that thousand dollars reward still stands."

"The chances are that it will stand forever, then," said King. "Shoz-Dijiji didn't come in with the other renegades, and, of course, you can't get anything out of them; but it is better than an even bet that he was killed in Sonora during one of the last engagements. I know several bucks were killed, but they usually got them away and buried them, and they never like to talk about their dead."

"I hope to God that he is dead," said the girl.

King shook his head. He knew how bitterly she must feel—more bitterly, perhaps, because the man she suspected was one to whom she had given her friendship and her aid when he was bearing arms against her country.

He had not told her of his conviction that Shoz-Dijiji and the dread Apache Devil were one and the same; and he did not tell her, for he knew that it would but tend to further assure her of the guilt of the Apache. There were two reasons why he did not tell her. One was his loyalty to the savage enemy who had befriended him and who might still be living. The other was his belief that Wichita Billings had harbored a warmer feeling than friendship for the war chief of the Be-don-ko-he, and King was not the type of man who takes an unfair advantage of a rival.

Perhaps it galled this scion of an aristocratic Boston family to admit, even to himself, that an untutored savage might have been his rival in seeking the hand of a girl; but he did not permit the suspicion to lessen his sense of gratitude to Shoz-Dijiji or dim the genuine respect he felt for the courage and honor of that savage warrior.

For a time the two sat in silence, Wichita busy with her revolver, King feasting his eyes upon her regular profile.

"Everything on the ranch running smoothly?" he asked, presently.

Wichita shook her head. "Not like they did when Dad was here," she admitted. "The boys are good to me, but it's not like having a man at the head of things. Some of them don't like 'Smooth' and I've lost several of my best men on that account. A couple of them quit, and 'Smooth' fired some. I can't interfere. As long as he's foreman he's got to be foreman. The minute the boys think I've lost confidence in him he won't have any more authority over them than a jack rabbit."

"Are you satisfied with him?" asked King.

"Well—he sure knows his business," she replied; "you'd have to hunt a month of Sundays before you found a better cow man; but he can't get the work out of his men. They don't feel any loyalty for him. They used to cuss Dad; and I've seen more than one of them pull a gun on him, but they'd work their fool heads off for him. They'd get sore as pups and quit; but they always came back—if he'd take them— and when he died, Ad, I saw men crying that I bet hadn't cried before since they were babies."

"That is like the old man," said King, thinking of his troop commander. "Gosh! How I have hated that fellow—and while I'm hating him I can't help but love him. There are men like that, you know."

"They are the real men, I guess," mused Wichita; "they don't grow on every sage brush, not by a long shot."

"Why don't you sell out, Chita?" King asked her. "This is no job for a girl—it's a man's job, and you haven't the man for it."

"Lord, I wouldn't know what to do, Ad," she cried. "I'd be plumb lost. Why, this is my life—I don't know anything else. I belong here on a cow ranch in Arizona, and here I'm going to stay."

"But you don't belong here, Chita," he insisted. "You belong on a throne, with a retinue of slaves and retainers waiting on you."

She leaned back and laughed merrily. "And the first thing I'd know the king would catch me eating peas with my knife and pull the throne out from under me."

"I'm serious, Chita," urged King. "Come with me; let me take you away from this. The only throne I can offer you is in my heart, but it will be all yours—forever."

"I'd like to, Ad," she replied. "You don't know how great the temptation is, but——"

"Then why not?" he exclaimed, rising and coming toward her. "We could be married at the post; and I could get a leave, I'm sure, even though I haven't been in the service two years. All your worries about the ranch would be over. You wouldn't have anything to do, Chita, but be happy."

"It wouldn't be fair, Ad," she said.

"Fair? What do you mean?" he demanded.

"It wouldn't be fair to you."

"Why?"

"Because I don't know whether I love you enough or not."

"I'll take the chance," he told her. "I'll make you love me."

She shook her head. "If I was going to marry a man and face a life that I was sure was going to be worse than the one I was leaving, I'd know that I loved him, and I wouldn't hesitate a minute; but if I marry you it might just be because what you have to offer me looks like heaven compared to the life I've been leading since Dad died. I think too much of you and my self-respect to take the chance of waking up to the fact some day that I don't love you. That would be Hell for us both, Ad; and you don't deserve it—you're too white."

"I tell you that I'm perfectly willing to take the chance, Chita."

"Yes, but I won't let you. Wait a while. If I really love you I'll find it out somehow, and you'll know it—if you don't I'll tell you—but I'm not sure now."

"Is there someone else, Chita?"

"No!" she cried, and her vehemence startled him.

"I'll wait, then, because I have to wait," he said, "and in the meantime if there is any way in which I can help you, let me do it."

"Well," she said, laughing, "you might teach the cows how to drill. I can't think of anything else around a cow outfit, right offhand, that you could do. Sometimes it seems to me like they didn't have any cows back where you came from."

King laughed. "They used to. All the streets in Boston were laid out by cows, they say."

"Out here," said Chita, "we drive our cows—we don't follow them."

"Perhaps that's the difference between the East and the West," said King. "Out here you blaze your own trails. I guess that's where you get your self-confidence and initiative."

"And it may account for some of our shortcomings, too," she replied. "When you're just following cows you have lots of time to think of other things and improve yourself, but when you're driving them you haven't time to think of anything except just cows. That's the fix I'm in now."

"When you have discovered that you might learn to love me you will have time for other things," he reminded her.

"Time to improve myself?" she teased.

"Nothing could improve you in my eyes, Chita," he said, honestly. "To me you are perfect."

"If Margaret Cullis hadn't taught me that it was vulgar I should say 'Rats' to that."

"Please don't."

"I won't," she promised. "And now you must run along. You know your orders never said anything about spending two hours at the Billings' ranch this afternoon. What will your detachment think?"

"They'll think I'm a fool if I don't stay all afternoon and ride back to the post in the cool of the night."

"And get court-martialed when you get there. Boots and saddles for you, Lieutenant Samuel Adams King!"

"Yes, sir!" he cried, clicking his heels together and saluting. Then he seized her hand and kissed it.

"Don't!" she whispered, snatching it away. "Here comes Luke."

"I don't care if the World's coming."

"That's because you don't know what it is to be joshed by a bunch of cowpunchers," she told him. "Say, why when it comes to torture, Victorio and Geronimo and old Whoa could have gone to school to some of these red necks from the Pan Handle."

"All right, I won't embarrass you. Good-bye and good luck, and don't forget the message I brought from Mrs. Cullis. She wants you to come and spend a week or so with her."

"Tell her I thank her heaps and that I'll come the first chance I get. Good-bye!"

She watched him walk away, tall, erect, soldierly; trim in his blue blouse, his yellow-striped breeches, his cavalry boots, and campaign hat—a soldier, every inch of him and, though still a boy, a veteran already.

And she sighed—sighed because she did not love him, sighed because she was afraid that she would never love him. Lines of bitterness touched the corners of her mouth and her eyes as she thought of the beautiful and priceless thing that she had thrown away—wasted upon a murdering savage— and a flush of shame tinged her cheeks.

Her painful reveries were interrupted by the voice of Luke Jensen.

"I jest been ridin' the east range, Miss," he said.

"Yes? Everything all right?"

"I wouldn't say thet it was an' I wouldn't say thet it wasn't," he replied.

"What's wrong?"

"You recollect thet bunch thet always hung out near the head o' the coulee where them cedars grows out o' the rocks?"

"Yes, what about them?"

"They's about half of 'em gone. If they was all gone I'd think they might have drifted to some other part o' the range; but they was calves, yearlin's, and some two an' three year olds still follerin' their mothers in thet bunch, an' a bunch like thet don't scatter fer no good reason."

"No. What do you make of it, Luke?"

"If the renegades warn't all c'ralled I'd say Apaches."

" 'Kansas' reported another bunch broken up that ranges around the Little Mesa," said Wichita, thoughtfully. "Do you reckon it's rustlers, Luke?"

"I wouldn't say it was an' I wouldn't say it wasn't."

"What does 'Smooth' say?"

"He allows they just natch'rally drifted."

"Are you riding the east range every day, Luke?"

"Most days. Course it takes me nigh onto a week to cover it, an' oncet in a while 'Smooth' sends me som'ers else. Yistiddy, he sent me plumb down to the south ranch—me an' 'Kansas.' "

"Well, keep your eyes open for that bunch, Luke—they might have drifted."

"Well, I wouldn't say they would of and I wouldn't say they wouldn't of."

Chapter Sixteen

THE JACK OF SPADES

LUIS MARIEL, profiting by the example of the Americanos, stood up to "Dirty" Cheetim's bar and drank cheap whiskey.

"Wot you doin', Kid?" asked Cheetim.

"Nothing," replied Luis.

"Want a job, or hev you still got some dinero left?"

"I want a job," replied Luis. "I am broke."

"You got a hoss, ain't you?"

"Si, Señor."

"Come 'ere," he motioned Luis to follow him into the back room.

There Luis saw a tall man with sandy hair sitting at a table, drinking.

"Here's a good kid fer us," said Cheetim to the sandy-haired man. "He ain't been up here long; an' nobody don't know him, an' he don't know nobody."

"Does he savvy U.S.?" demanded the man.

"Si, Señor," spoke up Luis. "I understand pretty good. I speak it pretty good, too."

"Can you keep your mouth shut?"

"Si, Señor."

"If you don't, somebody'll shut it for you," said the man, drawing his forefinger across his throat meaningly. "You savvy?"

"What is this job?" demanded Luis.

"You ain't got nothin' to do but herd a little bunch o' cattle an' keep your trap closed. If anyone asks you any questions in United States you don't savvy; and if they talk Greaser to you, why you don't know nothin' about the cattle except that a kind old gentleman hired you to ride herd on 'em."

"Si, Señor."

"You get thirty-five a month an' your grub—twenty-five fer ridin' herd an' the rest fer not knowin' nothin'. How about it?"

"Sure, Señor, I do it."

"All right, you come along with me. We'll ride out, an' I'll show you where the bunch is," and the sandy-haired man gulped down another drink and arose.

He led Luis north into the reservation, and at last they came to a bunch of about fifty head grazing contentedly on rather good pasture.

"They ain't so hard to hold," said the sandy-haired man, "but they got a hell of a itch to drift east sometimes. They's a c'ral up thet draw a ways. You puts 'em in there nights and lets 'em graze durin' the day. You won't hev to hold 'em long." He took a playing card from his pocket—the jack of spades—and tore it in two. One half he handed to Luis. "When a feller comes with tother half o' this card, Kid, you kin let him hev the cattle. Savvy?"

"Si, Señor."

"Oncet in a while they may a couple fellers come up with some more critters fer you. You jest let 'em drive in with your bunch. You don't hev to say nothin' nor ask no questions. Savvy?"

"Si, Señor."

"All right. Let 'em graze til sundown; then c'ral 'em and come down to the Hog Ranch fer the night. You kin make down your bed back o' the barn. The Chink'll feed you. So long, Kid."

"Adios, Señor."

Luis Mariel, watching the tall, sandy-haired man ride away, tucked his half of the jack of spades into the breast pocket of his shirt, rolled a cigarette, and then rode leisurely among the grazing cattle, inspecting his charges.

He noted the marks and brands, and discovering that several were represented concluded that Cheetim and the sandy-haired man were collecting a bunch for sale or shipment. Impressed by the injunction to silence laid upon him, and being no fool, Luis opined that the cattle had come into their possession through no lawful processes.

But that they had been stolen was no affair of his. He had not stolen them. He was merely employed to herd them. It interested him to note that fully 90 per cent of the animals bore the Crazy B brand on the left hip, a slit in the right ear, and a half crop off the left, the remainder being marked by various other brands, some of which he recognized and some of which he did not.

The Crazy B brand he knew quite well as it was one of the foremost brands in that section of Arizona. He had tried to get work with that outfit when he had brought the pinto stallion up from the border for El Teniente King.

At that time he had talked with Señor Billings, who had since been killed by Apaches; but he had been unable to secure employment with him. Later he had learned that the Billings' ranch never employed Mexicans, and while knowledge of this fact aroused no animosity within him neither did it impose upon him any sentiment of obligation to apprise the owners of the brand of his suspicion that someone was stealing their cattle.

Luis Mariel was far from being either a criminal or vicious young man. He would not have stolen cattle himself, but it was none of his business how his employers obtained the cattle that he was hired to herd for them. Since he had come up from Mexico he had found means of livelihood through many and various odd employments, sometimes as laborer, sometimes as chore boy, occasionally in riding for some small cow outfit, which was the thing of all others that he liked best to do. It was the thing that Luis Mariel loved best and did best.

More recently he had been reduced to the expedience of performing the duties of porter around the bar of "Dirty" Cheetim's Hog Ranch in order that he might eat to live and live to eat. Here, his estimate of the Gringoes had not been materially raised.

Pedro Mariel, the woodchopper of Casa Grande, was a poor man in worldly goods; but in qualities of heart and conscience he had been rich, and he had raised his children to fear God and do right.

Luis often thought of his father as he watched the Gringoes around "Dirty" Cheetim's place, and at night he would kneel down and thank God that he was a Mexican.

Many of the Gringoes that he saw were not bad, only fools; but there were many others who were very bad indeed. El Teniente King was the best Americano he had ever seen. Luis was sorry that El Teniente had no riding job for him. These were some of the thoughts that passed through the mind of the Mexican youth as he rode herd on the stolen cattle.

*　　*　　*

Up from the south rode Shoz-Dijiji. From the moment that he crossed the border into Arizona his spirits rose. The sight of familiar and beloved scenes, the scent of the cedars and the pines, the sunlight and the moonlight were like wine in his veins. The Black Bear was almost happy again.

Where there were no trails he went unseen. No longer were the old water holes guarded by the soldiers of the pindah-lickoyee. Peace lay upon the battle ground of three hundred years. He saw prospectors and cowboys occasionally, but they did not see Shoz-Dijiji. The war chief of the Be-don-ko-he knew that the safety of peace was for the white-eyed men only—he was still a renegade, an outlaw, a hunted beast, fair target for the rifle of the first white man who saw him.

He moved slowly, and often by night, drinking to the full the joys of homeland; but he moved toward a definite goal and with a well-defined purpose. It had taken days and weeks and months of meditation and introspection to lay the foundation for the decision he had finally reached; it had necessitated trampling under foot a lifetime of race consciousness and pride in caste; it had required the sacrifice of every cherished ideal, but the incentive was more powerful than any of these things, perhaps the greatest single moral force for good or evil that exists to govern and shape the destinies of man— love.

Love was driving this Apache war chief to the object of his devotion and to the public avowal that he was no Apache but, in reality, a member of the race that he had always looked upon with the arrogant contempt of a savage chieftain.

In his return through Arizona he found his loved friend, Nejeunee, an obstacle to safe or rapid progress. A pinto pony, while perhaps camouflaged by Nature, is not, at best, an easy thing to conceal, nor can it follow the trackless steeps of rugged mountains as can a lone Apache warrior; but, none the less, Shoz-Dijiji would not abandon this, his last remaining friend, the sole and final tie that bound him to the beloved past; and so the two came at last to an upland country, hallowed by sacred memories—memories that were sweet and memories that were bitter.

Luke Jensen was riding the east range. What does a lone cowboy think about? There is usually an old bull that younger bulls have run out of the herd. He is always wandering off, and if he be of any value it is necessary to hunt him up and explain to him the error of his ways in profane and uncomplimentary language while endeavoring to persuade him to return. He occupies the thoughts of the lone cowboy to some extent.

Then there is the question of the expenditure of accumulated wages, if any have accumulated. There are roulette and faro and stud at the Hog Ranch, but if one has recently emerged from any of these one is virtuous and has renounced them all for life, along with wine and women.

A hand made, silver-mounted bit would look well and arouse envy, as would sheepskin chaps and a heavy, silver hatband. A new and more brilliant bandanna is also in order.

Then there are the perennial plans for breaking into the cattle business on one's own hook, based on starting modestly with a few feeders to which second thoughts may add a maverick or two that nobody would miss and run from these all the way up to rustling an entire herd.

Thoughts of Apaches had formerly impinged persistently upon the minds of lone cowboys. Luke Jensen was mighty glad, as he rode the east range, that he didn't have to bother his head any more about renegades.

He was riding up a coulee flanked by low hills. Below the brow of one that lay ahead of him an Apache war chief watched his approach. Below and behind the warrior a pinto stallion lay stretched upon its side, obedient to the command of its master.

Shoz-Dijiji, endowed by Nature with keen eyes and a retentive memory, both of which had been elevated by constant lifelong exercise to approximate perfection, recognized Luke long before the cowboy came opposite his position —knew him even before he could discern his features.

"Hey, you!" called Shoz-Dijiji without exposing himself to the view of the youth.

Luke reined in and looked about. Mechanically his hand went to the butt of his six-shooter.

"No shoot!" said Shoz-Dijiji. "I am friend."

"How the hell do I know that?" demanded Jensen. "I can't see you, an' I ain't takin' no chances."

"I got you covered with rifle," announced Shoz-Dijiji. "You better be friend and put away gun. I no shoot. I am Shoz-Dijiji."

"Oh!" exclaimed Jensen. The one thousand dollars reward instantly dominated his thoughts.

"You no shoot?" demanded the Indian.

Luke returned his revolver to its holster. "Come on down," he said. "I remember you."

Shoz-Dijiji spoke to Nejeunee, who scrambled to his feet; and a moment later the pinto stallion and its rider were coming down the hillside.

"We thought you was dead," said Luke.

"No. Shoz-Dijiji been long time in Sonora."

"Still on the war path?" asked the cowboy.

"Geronimo make treaty with the Mexicans and with your General Miles," explained the Apache. "He promise we never fight again against the Mexicans or the Americans. Shoz-Dijiji keep the treaty Geronimo made. Shoz-Dijiji will not fight unless they make him. Even the coyote will fight for his life."

"What you come back here fer, Shoz-Dijiji?" asked Luke.

"I come to see Wichita Billings. Mebby so I get job here. What you think?"

Many thoughts crowded themselves rapidly through the mind of Luke Jensen in the instant before he replied and foremost among them was the conviction that this man could not be the murderer of Jefferson Billings. Had he been he would have known that suspicion would instantly attach to him from the fact that Wichita had seen him near the ranch the day her father was killed and that on that same day the pony he now rode had been stolen from the east pasture.

"Well, what do you think about it, Shoz-Dijiji?" parried Luke.

"I think mebby so she give me job, but Shoz-Dijiji not so damn sure about her father. He no like Shoz-Dijiji "

"Don't you know that her ol' man's dead?" demanded Luke.

"Dead? No, Shoz-Dijiji not know that. Shoz-Dijiji been down in Sonora long time. How he die?"

"He was murdered jest outside the east pasture and—scalped," said Luke.

"You mean by Apaches?"

"No one knows, but it looks damn suspicious."

"When this happen?" demanded Shoz-Dijiji.

"We found him the mornin' after you took thet there pony out of the east pasture."

Shoz-Dijiji sat in silence for a moment, his inscrutable face masking whatever emotions were stirring within his breast.

"You mean they think Shoz-Dijiji kill Billings? Does Chita think that, too?"

"Look here, Shoz-Dijiji," said Jensen, kindly, "you done me a good turn oncet thet I ain't a-never goin' to forgit. I don't mind tellin' you I ain't never thought you killed the ol' man, but everyone else thinks so."

"Even Chita?" asked Shoz-Dijiji.

"I wouldn't say she does and I wouldn't say she doesn't, but she ain't never took off the thousand dollar reward she offered to any hombre what would bring you in dead."

Not by the quiver of an eyelid did Shoz-Dijiji reveal the anguish of his tortured heart as he listened to the words that blasted forever the sole hope of happiness that had buoyed him through the long days and nights of his journey up through hostile Sonora and even more hostile Arizona.

"You get one thousand dollars, you kill me?" he asked.

"Yep."

"Why you no kill me, then?"

Jensen shrugged. "I reckon it must be for the same reason you didn't kill me when you had the chanc, Shoz-Dijiji," he replied. "There must be a streak of white in both of us."

"Good-bye," said Shoz-Dijiji, abruptly. "I go now."

"Say, before you go would you mind tellin' me fer sure thet it wasn't you killed the ol' man?" asked Luke.

Shoz-Dijiji looked the other squarely in the eyes. "If Wichita Billings offer one thousand dollars reward to have Shoz-Dijiji killed she must *know* Shoz-Dijiji kill her father. Good-bye. Shoz-Dijiji ride straight up coulee, slowly. Mebby so you want one thousand dollars, now you get it. Sabe?" He wheeled Nejeunee and walked the pony slowly away while Luke Jensen, slouching in his saddle, watched him until he had disappeared beyond a low ridge.

Not once did Jensen experience any urge to reach for the six-shooter at his hip or the rifle in its boot beneath his right leg.

"I could shore use a thousand dollars," he mused as he turned his pony's head back toward the Crazy B Ranch, "but I don't want it thet bad."

As he rode into the ranch yard later in the afternoon he saw Wichita Billings standing near the bunk house talking with "Kansas." Luke was of a mind to avoid her, feeling, as he did, that he should report his meeting with Shoz-Dijiji and dreading to do so because of the fear that a posse would be organized to go out and hunt the Apache down the moment that it was learned that he was in the vicinity.

But when Wichita saw him she called to him, and there was nothing less that he could do than go to her. She had finished her conversation with "Kansas," and the latter had gone into the bunk house when Luke reached her side.

"Walk up to the office with me, Luke," said the girl. "I want to talk with you," and he fell in beside her as she walked along. "I have just been talking with 'Kansas,'" she continued, "and he tells me that a few head are missing off the north range. Did you miss any today or see anything unusual?"

Had he seen anything unusual! There was a poser. Luke scratched his head.

"I wouldn't say that they was any more critters missin'," he replied, "an' I wouldn't say as they wasn't." He looked down at the ground in evident embarrassment.

Wichita Billings, who knew these boys better than they knew themselves, eyed him suspiciously. They walked on in silence for a few moments.

"Look here, Luke," said the girl, presently. "Someone is stealing my cattle. I don't know who to trust. I've always looked to 'Smooth' and you and 'Kansas' and Matt as being the ones I sure could tie to. If you boys don't shoot straight with me no one will."

"Who said I warnt shootin' straight with you, Miss?" demanded Luke.

"I say so," replied Wichita. "You're holding something out on me. Say, I can read you just like a mail order catalogue. If you don't come clean you're through—your pay check's waiting for you right now."

"I kin always git another job," parried Luke, lamely.

"Sure you can; but that isn't the question, Luke," replied the girl, sadly.

"I know it ain't, Miss," and Luke dug a toe into the loose earth beneath the cottonwood tree. "I did see somethin' onusual today," he blurted suddenly.

"I thought so. What was it?"

"An Apache—Shoz-Dijiji."

Wichita Billings' eyes went wide. Involuntarily her hand went to her breast, and she caught her breath in a little gasp before she spoke.

"You shot him?" The words were a barely audible whisper. "You shot him for the reward?"

"I shore did not," snapped Luke. "Look here, Miss, you kin have my job any time you want it, but you nor no one else kin make me doublecross a hombre what saved my life—I don't give a damn who he killed—I beg yore pardon, Miss—and anyway I hain't never believed he did kill your paw."

In his righteous indignation Luke Jensen had failed to note what appeared to be the relaxation of vast relief that claimed Wichita Billings the instant that he announced that he not shot Shoz-Dijiji. Could it be that Wichita, too, had her doubts?

"Did you ask him about the killing?" demanded the girl.

"Yep."

"What did he say? Did he deny it?"

"Well, I wouldn't say he did and I wouldn't say he didn't."

"Just what did he say?"

"He said that ef you was offerin' a thousand dollars fer him dead you must be plumb shore he done it."

"How did he know about the reward?"

"I told him."

"*You* told him?"

"Shore I did. I don't think he done it. Ef I hadn't told him he was a comin' here an' some of the fellers would have plugged him shore. You ain't mad, are you?"

"You are very sure he didn't kill Dad, aren't you, Luke?"

"Yep, plumb certain."

"But he didn't deny it, did he?"

"No, an' he didn't admit it, neither."

"There may be some doubt, Luke. I'm going to draw down that offer, because I can't take the chance of being mistaken, but as long as I live I shall believe in my heart that Shoz-Dijiji killed my father. If you ever see him again, tell him that the reward has been called off; and tell him, too, that if ever I see him I'll kill him, just like I think he killed my Dad, but I can't ask anyone else to. Send 'Smooth' here when you go back to the bunk house."

As Luke was walking away the girl called to him. "Wait a minute, Luke, there is something else," she said. "I have just been thinking," she continued, when the youth was near her again, "that the Indian you saw today might have had something to do with the cattle stealing. Had you thought of that?"

Luke scratched his head. "No, ma'am, I hedn't thought of that; but now that you mention it I reckon as how it ain't at all unlikely. I never seen one yet that wouldn't steal."

"I guess we're on the right trail now, Luke," said the girl. "Don't say anything to anyone about seeing him. Just keep your eyes open, and let me know the minute you see anything out of the way."

"All right, Miss, I'll keep a right smart look out," and Jensen turned and walked toward the bunk house.

As Wichita waited for her foreman her thoughts were overcast by clouds of sorrow and regret. The animosities that were directed upon Shoz-Dijiji were colored by the shame she felt for having permitted her heart to surrender itself to an Indian. That she had never openly admitted the love that she had once harbored for a savage did not reconcile her, nor did the fact that she had definitely and permanently up-rooted the last vestige of this love and nurtured hatred in its stead completely clear her conscience.

It angered her that even while she vehemently voiced her belief that Shoz-Dijiji had killed her father she still had doubts that refused to die. She was bitter in the knowledge that though she had suggested that he was stealing her cattle, deep in her heart she could not bring herself to believe it of him.

Her somber reveries were interrupted by the approach of Kreff.

"There are a couple of things I wanted to speak to you about, 'Smooth,' " said the girl.

"Fire away, Chita," said the man, with easy familiarity.

"In the first place I want you to pass the word around that the reward for bringing in that Apache is off."

"Why?" demanded the man.

"That's my business," replied the girl, shortly.

The words and her tone reminded Kreff of the dead Boss —she was her father all over—and he said no more.

"The other thing is this report about cattle stealing," she continued.

"Who said there was any cattle stealin' goin' on?" he asked.

"Luke has missed a few head off the east range."

"Oh, that kid's loco," said Kreff. "They've drifted, an' he's too plumb lazy to hunt 'em up."

" 'Kansas' has missed some, too, from up around the Little Mesa on the north range," she insisted. "I don't know so much about Luke, he hasn't been with us so long; but 'Kansas' is an old hand—he's not the kind to do much guessing."

"I'll look into it, Chita," said Kreff, "an' don't you worry your little head no more about it." There was something in his tone that made her glance up quickly, knitting her brows. His voice was low and soothing and protective. It didn't sound like "Smooth" Kreff in spite of his nickname, which, she happened to know, was indicative of the frictionless technique with which he separated other men from their belongings in the application of the art of draw and stud.

"You hadn't ought to hev nothin' to worry you," he continued. "This here business is a man's job. It ain't right an' fittin' thet a girl should hev to bother with sech things."

"Well, that's what I've got you and the other boys for, 'Smooth.' "

"Yes, but hired hands ain't the same. You ought to be married—to a good cowman," he added.

"Meaning?" she inquired.

"Me."

"Are you proposing to me, 'Smooth'?"

"I shore am. What do you say? You an' me could run this outfit together fine, an' you wouldn't never hev to worry no more about nothin'."

"But I don't love you, 'Smooth.' "

"Oh, shucks, that ain't nothin'. They's a heap o' women marry men they don't love. They git to lovin' 'em afterward, though."

"But you don't love me."

"I shore do, Chita. I've allus loved you."

"Well, you've managed to hide it first rate," she observed.

"They didn't never seem no chance, 'til now," he explained; "but you got a lot o' horse sense, an' I reckon you kin see as well as me thet it would be the sensible thing to do. You can't marry nothin' but a cowman, an' they ain't no other cowman thet I knows of thet would be much of a improvement over me. You'll larn to love me, all right. I ain't so plumb ugly, an' I won't never beat you up."

Wichita laughed. "You're sure tootin', 'Smooth,' " she said. "There isn't a man on earth that's ever going to try to beat me up, more than once."

Kreff grinned. "You don't hev to tell me that, Chita," he said. "I reckon that's one o' the reasons I'm so strong fer you —you shore would make one grand woman fer a man in this country."

"Well, 'Smooth,' as a business proposition there is something in what you say that it won't do any harm to think about, but as a proposal of marriage it hasn't got any more bite to it than a white pine dog with a poplar tail."

"But you'll think it over, Chita?" he asked, drawing a sack

of Durham and a package of brown papers from his shirt pocket.

"You dropped something, 'Smooth,' " she said, gesturing toward the ground at his feet. "You pulled it out of your pocket with the makings."

He looked down at a bit of paste board, at one half of a playing card that had been torn in two—one half of the jack of spades.

Chapter Seventeen

CHEETIM STRIKES

IT was night. The oil lamps were burning brightly in the barroom of the Hog Ranch. The games were being well patronized. The girls were circulating among the customers, registering thirst. It looked like a large night.

In the back room two men, seated at opposite sides of a table, were conversing in low tones. A bottle, two glasses, and a mutilated jack of spades lay between them. One of the men was Cheetim, the other was Kreff.

"How much longer does thet feller think we kin hold them critters without hevin' every galoot in the Territory ridin' onto 'em an' blowin' the whole business?" demanded Kreff.

"I been tellin' him to see you," said Cheetim.

Kreff pushed the jack of spades across the table to the other man. "You take this," he said. "You see him oftener than I do. Don't turn this over to him 'til you git the money, but tell him that ef he don't get a hump on hisself we'll drive the bunch north an' sell 'em up there. They can't stay around here much longer—the girl's wise now thet somethin's wrong. Two of the hands has told her they been missin' stock lately."

Cheetim sat in silence, thinking. Slowly he filled Kreff's glass and poured another drink for himself.

"Here's how!" he said and drank.

"How!" replied Kreff.

"I been thinkin'," said Cheetim.

"Don't strain yourself, 'Dirty,' " Kreff admonished him.

"It's this-a-way," continued the other, ignoring Kreff's

pleasantry. "Ef it warn't for the girl we could clean up big on thet herd. This here Agent'll buy anything an' not ask no questions."

"What do you want me to do," inquired Kreff, "kill her?"

"I want you to help me get her. If I kin get her fer a few days she'll be glad enough to marry me. Then I'll give you half what I get out of the cattle."

"Ride your own range, 'Dirty,' " said Kreff, rising, "and keep off o' mine."

"What do you mean?"

"Ef either one of us gets her it's me, that's what I mean." There was an ugly edge to his voice that Cheetim did not fail to note.

"Oh, hell," he said, "I didn't know you was sweet on her."

"You know it now—keep off the grass."

*   *   *

A pinto stallion, tied to a stunted cedar, dozed in the midday heat. His master, sprawled at the summit of a rocky knoll, looked down upon the other side at a bunch of cattle resting until it should be cooler, the while they pensively chewed their cuds. A youth lay upon his back beneath the shade of a tree. A saddled pony, with drooping head and ears, stood near by lazily switching its tail in mute remonstrance against the flies. Bridle reins, dragging on the ground, suggested to the pony that it was tethered and were all-sufficient.

Somnolence, silence, heat—Arizona at high noon.

Shoz-Dijiji surveyed the scene. With a reward of a thousand dollars on his head it behooved him to survey all scenes in advance. The reward, however, was but a secondary stimulus. Training and environment had long since fixed upon him the habit of reconnaissance.

Immediately he had recognized Luis Mariel. If he were surprised he gave no evidence of it, for his expression did not change. His eyes wandered over the herd. They noted the various brands, ear-marks, wattles, jug-handles; and though Shoz-Dijiji could not have been termed a cattle man he read them all and knew the ranch and range of every animal in the bunch, for there was no slightest thing from one end of Apache-land to the other that an Apache let pass as of too slight importance to concern him.

He saw that most of the cattle belonged to Wichita Billings, but he knew that it was not a Crazy B cowboy that was herding them, for the Crazy B outfit employed no Mexicans.

Long before Luis Mariel was aware of the fact Shoz-Dijiji knew that several horsemen were approaching; but he did not change his position since, if they continued in the direction they were going, they would pass without seeing him.

Presently four men rode into view. He recognized them all. Two of them were Navajoes, one a half-breed and the fourth a white man—the Indian Agent.

Shoz-Dijiji did not like any of them, especially the Indian Agent. He fingered his rifle and wished that Geronimo had not made that treaty with General Miles in Skeleton Canyon.

Presently Luis heard the footfalls of the approaching horses and sat up. Seeing the men, he arose. They rode up to him, and the Agent spoke. Shoz-Dijiji saw him take a bit of paper from his pocket and show it to Luis. Luis took another similar bit of paper from his own pocket and compared it with the one that the Agent now handed him. Shoz-Dijiji could not quite make out what the bits of paper were—from a distance they looked like two halves of a playing card.

Luis mounted his pony and helped the men round up the cattle, but after they had started them in the direction of the Agency Luis waved his *adios* and reined his pony southward toward the Hog Ranch.

Shoz-Dijiji remained motionless until all were well out of sight, then he wormed his way below the brow of the hill, rose and walked down to Nejeunee. He had spent the preceding night in the hogan of friends on the reservation. They had talked of many things, among them being the fact that the Agent was still buying stolen cattle at a low price and collecting a high price for them from the Government.

Shoz-Dijiji knew that he had seen stolen cattle delivered to the Agent, which would not, of itself, have given him any concern; but the fact that most of these cattle had evidently been stolen from Wichita Billings put an entirely different aspect on the matter.

The fact that she hated him, that she had offered a reward for him, dead, could not alter the fact that he loved her; and, loving her, he must find a way to inform her of what he had discovered. Naturally, the first means to that end which oc-

curred to him was Luke Jensen. He would ride back to where
Luke Jensen rode and find him.

It is a long way from where Cheetim and Kreff had hidden
the stolen herd to the Billings' east range, and when one is a
fair target for every rifle and six-shooter in the world it be-
hooves one to move warily; so Shoz-Dijiji lay up until night
and then rode slowly toward the east.

                    *   *   *

Luis Mariel had ridden directly to the Hog Ranch and reported to Cheetim, handing him both halves of the jack of
spades as evidence that the herd had been turned over to the
proper party in accordance with Luis' instructions.

"That's jest what I been waitin' fer," said Cheetim. "Now
I got some more work fer you, if you're game. They's fifty
dollars extra in it fer you."

"What is it?" asked Luis.

"It ain't none o' your business what it is," replied Cheetim.
"All you got to know is thet they may be some shootin' in it,
an' all you got to do is do what I tell you. If you're skeered
I don't want you."

"I am not afraid, Señor," replied Luis. The fifty dollars appeared a fortune.

"All right. You savvy the Crazy B Ranch?"

"Si, Señor."

"I want you to take a note to 'Smooth' Kreff, the foreman
o' thet outfit."

"Is that all?"

"No. After you deliver the note you hang around and see
what happens. They's a girl there. When I come I'll want to
know where she is and how many men there are left at the
ranch. There'll be four or five fellers with me. After that I'll
tell you what to do."

"When does the shooting happen?" asked Luis.

"Oh, maybe they won't be no shootin'," replied Cheetim.
"I was jest warnin' you in case they was. I'll write the letter
now an' then you hit the trail. Ef you ride hard you'll make it
before sun up. I want you there before the hands start out
fer the day. Savvy?"

Laboriously, with the stub of a pencil that he constantly
wet with his tongue, "Dirty," Cheetim wrote. It appeared to

Luis that Señor Cheetim was not accustomed to writing—he seemed to be suffering from mental constipation—but at last the agony was over and Cheetim handed Luis a sheet of soiled paper folded many times into a small wad.

"If Kreff asks you about the cattle you say that when you went up this mornin' the bars o' the c'rral was down an' the cattle gone, an' don't you tell him nothin' different. If you do you won't get no fifty dollars 'cause you won't need 'em where I'll send you." Cheetim slapped the six-shooter at his hip.

"I undestand," said Luis. He did not like Señor Cheetim, but fifty dollars are fifty dollars.

The sun was but a few minutes high when Luis Mariel reined into the Billings' ranch yard. From a slight eminence a mile or two away, beyond the east pasture fence, Shoz-Dijiji saw him come and wondered.

The Apache had taken his position just before dawn and at the first flush of the new day had fixed his field glasses upon the ranch yard. He wished to get in touch with Jensen as quickly as possible and saw in this plan the surest method of determining when and in what direction Luke rode that morning.

Luis went at once to the bunk house, where the men were already astir, and delivered the letter to Kreff, whom he at once recognized as the tall, sandy-haired man who had taken him to the herd and given him the torn playing card and his instructions. Kreff recognized Luis, too, but he only frowned.

Almost as laboriously as Cheetim had written it, Kreff deciphered the note.

"Frend Kref:" he read. "Sum fellers stole the herd bring al yore hands & help Me round them up they will think the fellers stol them & That will let us out doan fetch the greser i think he wus in on it dirty yours truely."

"Hell!" ejaculated Kreff.

"What's eatin' you?" inquired "Kansas."

" 'Dirty' Cheetim says a bunch of rustlers is runnin' off some of our stock. He seen 'em headin' past his place. Luke! Rustle up that 'cavvy,' pronto. You fellers feed while Luke's gone. We're all hittin' the trail after them lousy thieves."

"I reckon 'Dirty' is jest sore 'cause he didn't git to the bunch ahead o' them other fellers," drawled "Kansas."

Luke tucked his shirt tails into his trousers, grabbed his Stetson, and bolted for the corral. When Kreff had finished dressing he went to the cookhouse and told the Chinese cook to hurry breakfast. Then he walked over to the ranch house and stopping under Wichita's window called her name aloud.

A moment later, a Navajo blanket about her shoulders, the girl appeared at the window. "What is it, 'Smooth?'" she asked.

"You was right about the rustling," he said. "Cheetim jest sent a Greaser with a note sayin' he'd seen some fellers runnin' off a bunch of our stock. I'm takin' all the men an' ridin' after 'em. They can't git away."

"Good!" cried the girl. "I'll go with you."

"No, you better not. They's almost sure to be shootin'."

"I can shoot," she replied.

"I know thet; but please don't do it, Chita. We'd all be lookin' after you an' couldn't do like we would if they wasn't a woman along."

"Perhaps you are right," she admitted. "Gosh! Why wasn't I born a boy?"

"I'm shore glad you wasn't."

Shoz-Dijiji, seeing Luke riding early and alone straight in his direction, felt that once again, after long forgetfulness, Usen had remembered him. He knew that the youth would come only as far as the horses pastured in the east pasture, and so he rode down and came through the gate to meet the cowboy. The willows in the draw screened them from each other's sight until Luke spurred up the steep bank of the wash and came face to face with the Apache.

"Hello, there!" he exclaimed in surprise. "What you doin' here?"

"I want you take word to Wichita," said Shoz-Dijiji. "The Indian Agent is buying cattle that are stolen from her. I saw it yesterday, on the reservation. You tell her?"

"We just got word of the same bunch, I reckon," replied Luke. "We're all ridin' out after 'em now. Which way was they headin' when you saw them?"

"Toward the Agency."

"Thanks a lot, Shoz-Dijiji," said Luke. "I'll tell her any-way when I see her about your sendin' the word to her."

"No," said the Apache. "Do not tell her who sent the word."

"All right. I got to be movin'. The boys is waitin' fer these broncs. So long, Shoz-Dijiji!"

"Adios!" replied the Apache, and as Jensen herded the horses toward the corrals Shoz-Dijiji rode away, out through the pasture gate, onto the east range.

Something was troubling Shoz-Dijiji's mind. He had seen Luis Mariel guarding the stolen herd and yet it was he who brought word to the ranch concerning these same cattle. What did it mean?

Through his glasses the Apache watched the departure of the Crazy B cow hands. Apparently all had left the ranch with the exception of Luis Mariel. Why was Luis remaining? He had seen Wichita come into the yard and talk with some of the men as they were mounting, and he had seen her wave them godspeed. She had spoken to Luis, too, and then gone into the house. Luis was hanging around the corrals.

Shoz-Dijiji shook his head. Luis was a good boy. He would not harm anyone. There was something else to think about and that was breakfast. Shoz-Dijiji rode a short distance to the east, dismounted and with bow and arrows set forth in search of his breakfast. In half an hour he had a cottontail and a quail. Returning to Nejeunee he sought a secluded spot and cooked his breakfast.

Ten minutes after Luis Mariel had departed from the Hog Ranch the previous evening Cheetim with four others had ridden out along the same trail; and when Kreff and the other men of the Crazy B rode away in the morning in search of the rustlers, from the hills south of the ranch these five had watched them depart.

"We got lots of time," said Cheetim, "an' we'll wait until they are plenty far away before we ride down. You four'll hev to git the girl. Ef she seen me comin' she'd start shootin' be-fore we was inside the gate, but she don't know none of you. I was damn sure to pick fellers she didn't know. You ride in an' ask fer grub an' a job. The Greaser'll be there to tell you ef they is any men left around an' where the girl is. You won't have no trouble. Jes' grab her an' don't give her no

chance to draw thet gun o' hers, fer I'm here to state thet ol'
man Billings' girl wouldn't think no more o' perforatin' your
ornery hides then she would of spittin'."

The ride ahead of Kreff and his men was, the foremen
knew, a long and hard one. There was some slight chance of
borrowing a change of horses at a ranch near Cheetim's
place; but it was only a chance, and so Kreff conserved
his horse flesh and did not push on too rapidly.

As he rode he had time to think things out a little more
clearly than he had in the excitement and rush of preparation, and he wondered why it had been that Cheetim had not
organized a party to go after the rustlers and save the cattle
for themselves. He could easily have done it, as there were
always several tough gunmen hanging around his place who
would commit murder for a pint of whiskey. Yes, that did
seem peculiar. And if he had mistrusted the Mexican, why
had he intrusted the message to him? Kreff did not trust
Cheetim to any greater extent than a cottontail would trust a
rattler, and now that he had an opportunity to consider the
whole matter carefully he grew suspicious.

Suddenly it occurred to him that he had left Wichita alone
on the ranch with only the Chinese cook, and that the Mexican
had remained behind after they had left. The more he thought
about it the more it worried him. He called Luke to his side.

"Kid," he said, "we left thet Greaser there on the ranch. I
don't guess we should have. You ride back an' look after
things—an' don't let no grass grow under you while you're
doin' it."

Luke, though disappointed at the thought of missing the
excitement of a brush with the rustlers, reined in, wheeled
his pony, and spurred back toward the ranch.

Wichita, coming from the office door after breakfast, saw
four strange men ride into the ranch yard. She saw the Mexican youth who had brought word of the stolen cattle ride up to
them, but she could not hear what they said, nor was it apparent that the Mexican was acquainted with the newcomers.

The four rode toward her presently, and as they neared
her one of them removed his hat and asked if he could see the
boss.

"I'm the boss," she replied.

"We're lookin' fer work," said the man; and as he spoke he

dismounted and walked close to her, the others reining near as though to hear what her answer would be.

When the man was quite close he suddenly seized her, whirled her about and held her hands behind her. At the same instant another of his fellows dismounted and stepped quickly to her. She struggled and fought to free herself; but she was helpless, and in another moment they had bound her wrists behind her.

As they were lifting her to one of the horses the Chinese ran from the cook house, calling to them to stop; but one of the men drew his six-shooter, and a single, menacing shot was enough to send the unarmed domestic back into his kitchen.

Cheetim, watching from the hills south of the ranch, saw all that transpired within the yard and was highly elated at the ease with which his nefarious plan was being carried out; but, alas, things were running far too smoothly.

What was that? He bent an attentive ear toward the west and recognized the cadenced pounding of the hoofs of a rapidly galloping horse—the little rift within the lute.

In the ranch yard the men had stopped to argue. Cheetim could see them but he could not understand the delay. He could only curse silently, dividing his attention between them and the road to the west, along which he could hear the approaching hoofbeats.

"What's the use of packin' this girl double?" the man who had been assigned to carry Wichita demanded. "We got plenty time an' they's a hoss standin' right down there in the c'ral."

" 'Dirty' said not to waste no time," demurred another.

The mention of Cheetim's descriptive nickname was the first intimation Wichita had received of the origin and purpose of the plan to abduct her. Now she understood—it was all clear, horribly clear. For years the man had hounded and annoyed her. Twice before he had tried to take her forcibly. It looked now as though he might succeed. Who was there to succor her? Her father dead and every man in her employ gone; for how long she could not guess. There was no one. She wondered why it was that at that moment the figure of an almost naked, bronze savage filled her thoughts to the exclusion of every other source of salvation, and that while she nursed her hatred of him she involuntarily almost prayed that some miracle might bring him to her.

The man who had suggested a separate horse for Wichita insisted. "It won't take two minutes," he said, "an' if we are follered we kin make better time than if one of the hosses is packin' double."

"Hell, then," exclaimed one of his fellows, "instead of chawin' the fat let's git a hoss. Here, you!" he addressed Luis. "Fetch that hoss. Throw a saddle onto him an' a lead rope."

As Luis hastened to obey, Cheetim, seeing the further delay, became frantic. The horseman was approaching rapidly along the road from the west, and the men in the ranch yard were wasting valuable time.

Out on the east range Shoz-Dijiji, having finished his breakfast, mounted Nejeunee and turned the pony's head toward the east, toward the distant mountains where the Gila rises, toward the ancient stamping grounds of the Be-don-ko-he.

He had no plans for the future. He wanted only to get away. He had seen Wichita Billings through his field glasses, and the sight of her had but aggravated the old hurt. Sad and lonely, the war chief rode toward the deserted camp grounds of his vanished people, where now were only brooding memories.

Luke Jensen galloped into sight of the ranch. Cheetim, lying behind a boulder at the top of a hill, covered him with his rifle sights and fired. Luke heard the bullet scream past his ear. Forewarned of some danger, he knew not what, he was prepared. He took two flying shots at the puff of smoke at the hill top where his unknown assailant lay, dug the rowels into his pony's sides, and raced for the ranch gate that he saw was standing open.

Cheetim fired once more; but again he missed, and then Luke was inside the yard. Coming toward him from the corrals he saw five men and Wichita, and he knew that something was radically wrong even before one of the men drew his gun and opened fire on him. Unable to return the man's fire without endangering Wichita, Jensen spurred in the direction of an out-building that would give him shelter until he could get his rifle into action.

The five men spurred toward the gate, quirting Wichita's horse to equal speed. Three of them were firing at Luke; and just as he reached the out-building, just when he was within a second of safety, Wichita saw him lunge from his saddle, hit.

Then her captors raced through the gate and into the hills south of the ranch, whirling Wichita Billings away with them.

Chapter Eighteen

"THE APACHE DEVIL!"

OUT on the east range a horseman reined in his mount and listened as the rapid reports of rifle and pistol came faintly to his ears. There was something amiss at the Crazy B Ranch and Wichita was there, practically alone! Shoz-Dijiji wheeled Nejeunee so suddenly that the little pinto reared almost straight in air and then, at a touch of his master's heels and a word in his pointed ears, leaped off in the new direction at a swift run.

After sending Luke back to the ranch Kreff's suspicions, now thoroughly aroused, continued to increase. He began to realize that if they were well-founded, one man might not be sufficient. He wished that he had sent more. Presently he wished that he had gone himself; and soon he reined in, halting his companions.

"Fellers," he said, "the more I think about it the more I think that mebby Cheetim's givin' us a dirty deal. He may have jest wanted to git us all away from the ranch. He's tried to get Chita twicet before. I'm a-goin' back an' I'm a-goin' to take Jake an' Sam with me. 'Kansas,' you take Charlie an' Matt an' ride after them rustlers. Ef you kin pick up some fellers along the way, all right; ef you can't, do the best you kin alone. So long! Come on, fellers!"

*　　*　　*

As the five men entered the hills with Chita, Cheetim joined them. It was evident that he was much elated.

"Good work, boys!" he cried. "I reckon I didn't pull the wool over 'Smooth's' eyes nor nothin', eh?" He rode to Chita's side and grinned into her face. "Say, dearie," he exclaimed, "you don't hev to worry none. I've decided to do the right thing by you. We'll spend our honeymoon up in the hills 'til things blows over a bit an' then we'll mosey down to the Hog Ranch an' git married."

Wichita looked the man straight in the eyes for a moment and then turned away in disgust, but she did not speak. Luis Mariel, sober-eyed, serious, looked on. He had not bargained on a part in any such affair as this.

"Well, fellers," said Cheetim, "let's pull up a second an' licker. I reckon we've earned a drink."

They stopped their ponies and from five hip pockets came five pint bottles.

"Here's to the bride!" cried Cheetim, and they all laughed and drank, all except Luis, who had no bottle.

"Here, kid," said Cheetim, "hev a drink!" He proffered his flask to Luis.

"Thank you, Señor, I do not care to drink," replied the Mexican.

Deep into the hills they rode—five miles, ten miles. Wichita guessed where they were taking her—to an old two-room shack that prospectors had built years before beside a little spring far back in the mountains. Apaches had gotten the prospectors, and the shack had stood deserted and tenantless ever since.

She felt quite hopeless, for there seemed not the slightest foundation for belief that there could be any help for her. Luke, if he were not badly hurt, or possibly Chung, the cook, could get word to their nearest neighbor; but he lived miles and miles away; and any help to be effective must reach her within a few hours, for after that it would be too late. And even if men were found to come after her it might be a long time before they could locate Cheetim's hiding place.

Cheetim and his men had finished a flask apiece as they rode; but this was not the extent of their supply—each had another flask in his shirt—so that by the time they reached the shack they were more than content with themselves and all the world.

Once Luis had ridden close beside Wichita and spoken to her. "I am sorry, Señorita," he whispered. "I did not know what they were going to do. If I can help you, I will. Maybe, when they are drunk, I can help you get away."

"Thanks," replied the girl. As she spoke she turned and looked at the youth, noticing him more than casually for the first time, and realized that his face seemed familiar. "Where have I seen you before?" she asked.

"I brought the pinto pony from El Teniente King to your rancho a year ago," replied Luis.

"Oh, yes, I remember you now. You brought Shoz-Dijiji's pony up from Mexico."

"Shoz-Dijiji's pony? Was that Shoz-Dijiji's pony? You know Shoz-Dijiji, Señorita?"

"I know him," said the girl; "do you?"

"Yes, very well. He saved my father's life, and twice when he could have killed me he did not."

Their conversation was interrupted by Cheetim who rode back to Wichita's side.

"Well, here we are, dearie," he said, "but we ain't goin' to stay here long. Tomorrow morning we hit the trail fer a place I know where God himself couldn't find us."

The shack, before which the party had stopped and were dismounting, was a rough affair built of stone and mud and such timber as grew sparsely on the slopes of the canyon in the bottom of which is nestled. A tiny spring, now choked with dirt, made a mud hole a few yards to one side of the building. The men led their horses to the rear of the building where there were a few trees to which they could fasten them. Two of the men started to clean out the spring, and Cheetim escorted Wichita into the shack.

"We brung along some grub," he said. "It won't be much of a weddin' breakfast to brag on, but you wait 'til we git back to the Hog Ranch! We'll have a reg'lar spread then an' invite every son-of-a-gun in the territory. I'm goin' to treat you right, kid, even ef you haven't been any too damn nice to me."

Wichita did not speak.

"Say, you can jest start right now cuttin' out thet high-toned stuff with me," said Cheetim. "I'll be good to you ef you treat me right, but by God I ain't a-goin' to stand much more funny business. You kin start now by givin' me a little kiss."

"Cheetim," said the girl, "listen to me. You're half-drunk now, but maybe you've got sense enough left to understand what I am going to say to you. I'd a heap rather kiss a Gila monster than you. You may be able to kiss me because you're stronger than I am, and I guess even kissing a Gila monster wouldn't kill me; but I'm warning you that if you ever do kiss me you'd better kill me quick, for I'm going to kill myself if anything happens to me——"

"Ef you want to be a damn fool that's your own look out," interrupted Cheetim, with a snarl, "but it won't keep me from doin' what I'm goin' to do. Ef you're fool enough to kill yoreself afterward, you can."

"You didn't let me finish," said Wichita. "I'll kill myself, all right, but I'll kill you first."

The men were entering the room, and Cheetim stood, hesitating, knowing the girl meant what she said. He was a coward, and he had not had quite enough whiskey to bolster up his courage to the point of his desires.

"Oh, well," he said, "we won't quarrel this a-way on our honeymoon. You jest go in the other room there, dearie, an' make yourself to home, an' we'll talk things over later. Git me a piece of rope, one o' you fellers. I ain't goin' to take no chances of my bride vamoosin'."

In the small back room of the shack they tied Wichita's wrists and ankles securely and left her seated on an old bench, the only furniture that the room boasted.

Out in the front room the men were making preparations to cook some of the food they had brought with them, but most of their time was devoted to drinking and boasting. Cheetim drank with a purpose. He wanted to arrive, as quickly as possible, at a state of synthetic courage that would permit him to ignore the moral supremacy of the girl in the back room. He knew that he was physically more powerful, and so he could not understand why he feared her. Cheetim had never heard of such a thing as an inferiority complex, and so he did not know that that was what he suffered from in an aggravated form whenever he faced the level gaze and caustic tongue of Wichita Billings.

The more Cheetim drank the louder and more boastful he became. Wichita could hear him narrating the revolting details of numerous crimes that he had committed.

"Yo shua ah some bad hombre, 'Dirty'," eulogized one of his party.

"Oh, I don't claim to be no bad man," replied Cheetim,

modestly. "What I says is thet I has brains, an' I use 'em. Look how I fooled 'Smooth'—sent him off on a wild goose chase an' then swipes his girl while he's gone." They all laughed uproariously.

"An' he better not get funny about it neither, even ef he don't like it. I kin use my brains fer other things besides gettin' me my women. Ol' man Billings larnt thet. He kicked me out oncet; an' I suppose he thought I was afraid of him, but I was jest waitin'. I waited a long time, but I got him."

"You got him? You did not. He was kilt by Injuns," contradicted one.

"Injuns, Hell!" ejaculated Cheetim. "Thar's where I used my brains. I killed Billings, but I was cute enough to scalp him. I——"

Drunk as he was, he realized that he had gone too far, had admitted too much. He looked wickedly about the room. "What I've told you is among friends," he said. "Ef any of you fellers ever feels like you'd like to join Billings all you got to do is blab what I jest told you. Savvy?"

In the other room Wichita Billings, listening, heard every word that Cheetim spoke, and her soul was seared by shame and vain regret for the wrong she had done the friendless redman. She reproached herself for not listening to the counsel and the urging of her heart, for she knew—she had always known—that she had battled against her love for Shoz-Dijiji, had trampled it beneath her feet, that she might encourage her belief in his perfidy.

If she could only see him once more, if she could only tell him that she knew and ask his forgiveness; but now it was too late.

She heard Cheetim speaking again. "You fellers finish rustlin' the grub," he said. "I'm goin' in an' visit my wife." This sally was applauded with much laughter. "An' I don't want to be disturbed," he concluded. "Savvy?"

*　　*　　*

A pinto stallion, racing like the wind, bore its rider toward the Crazy B ranch house following thc shots that had attracted the attention of the Apache. Fences intervened, but though there were gates in them Shoz-Dijiji had no time to waste on gates. Straight for them he rode Nejeunee; and the

pinto took them in his stride, soaring over them like a bird
on the wing.

Chung, kneeling beside Luke in the ranch yard, voiced a
startled cry as he saw a pinto stallion, bearing a feared
Apache warrior, rise over the bars of the corral; but Chung
did not flee. He stood his post, though scarce knowing what
to do. Luke's six-shooter was close beside his hand; but Chung
was too surprised to think of it, and a second later the warrior
had reined in beside them, his pony sliding upon its haunches
for a dozen feet.

Throwing himself to the ground Shoz-Dijiji knelt beside
Luke.

"What has happened?" he demanded. "Where is Chita?"

Luke looked up. "Oh, it's you, Shoz-Dijiji? Thank God for
that. A bunch of skunks jest rid off into the south hills with
her. I ain't hurted bad, but I can't ride. You go!"

"Sure I go!" As he arose Shoz-Dijiji stripped his clothing
from him in an instant, and when he leaped to Nejeunee's
back again he wore only moccasins, his G-string, and a head
band.

"I get her!" he cried, reassuringly, waving his rifle above
his head, and an instant later he was racing for the gate.

Down the road from the west thundered Kreff and Jake and
Sam just as Shoz-Dijiji swept through the gate.

"There's the Siwash killed the Boss!" shouted Sam, who
was in the lead, and the words were scarce out of his mouth
before he had drawn his gun and opened fire on the Indian.
Jake joined in the fusillade of shots; and Shoz-Dijiji, turning
upon the back of his war pony, sent a half dozen bullets
among them before he vanished into the hills. It was only the
rapidity with which their mounts had been moving that pre-
vented any casualties.

"Even a coyote will fight for his life," soliloquized the
Apache Devil; but he did not feel like a coyote. Once more
he was an Apache war chief riding naked upon the war trail
against the hated pindah-lickoyee; and just as he rode from
the sight of the white men he could not restrain a single, ex-
ultant Apache war whoop.

Into the ranch yard thundered Kreff and his companions.
They saw Luke trying to drag himself to his feet and stag-
ger toward him.

"You lop-eared idiots!" he yelled. "Wot in Hell you shootin' at him fer? He's ridin' after the fellers that stole Chita."

"Stole Chita?" cried Kreff. "By God, I was right! Cheetim!"

"I didn't see Cheetim," said Luke. "Whoever it was rid south into the hills. Git the hell out of here and git after them, an' ef you see that Apache leave him be—he's the best friend Wichita Billings's got."

"Chung, you git Luke into the bunk house an' take keer o' him 'til we gets back," Kreff called over his shoulder as the three spurred away again, this time following the trail taken by Shoz-Dijiji.

Plain before the trained eyes of Shoz-Dijiji lay the spoor of his quarry. Swiftly he rode. The errand, the speed of his fleet pony, his own nakedness stirred every savage instinct within him. He had never expected to live again; but this, O, Usen, was life! He dipped into the pouch at his side and drew out a little silver box that he had never expected to use again, and dipping into it with a forefinger he banded his face with the blue and white war paint of the Apache Devil. He could not lay the colors on carefully at the speed Nejeunee was carrying him; but he wore them, as a ship of war runs up its battle flag as it goes into action.

* * *

As Cheetim left them and entered the rear room of the shack, the men in the front room nudged one another, chuckled, and took a drink. They were wiping their mouths with the backs of their hands when the outer door swung open, and a painted warrior stepped into the room.

Luis Mariel, who was standing in a corner, looked wide eyed at the newcomer. The other men reached for their six-shooters.

"The Apache Devil!" cried Luis.

Shoz-Dijiji looked quickly at him. "Lie down!" he said to him in Spanish. Already he had commenced to shoot. He asked no questions. A man fell.

In the back room Cheetim and Wichita heard the dread name as Luis cried it aloud. Cheetim had just entered and closed the door behind him. He was approaching Wichita as Luis spoke the name of the scourge of three states. At the first shot Cheetim crossed the room at a bound and leaped from the window. A half-dozen shots followed in quick succession. Four men lay dead in the outer room when Shoz-Dijiji sprang to the door of the smaller room and swung it open, just in time to see Cheetim mounting a horse in the rear of the building. He recognized him instantly; then he turned toward the girl.

"You hurt?" he deemanded.

"No. Oh, Shoz-Dijiji, thank God, you came!"

The Apache called to Luis who came running to the door. "You," he said, pointing at the youth. "You know the Apache Devil. You know what he do to his enemies. You take this girl home. If she don't get home safe the Apache Devil settle with you. Sabe?"

He crossed the room to the window.

"Where are you going?" cried Wichita.

"To kill my last pindah-lickoyee," replied Shoz-Dijiji, as he vaulted across the sill.

"Wait! Wait, Shoz-Dijiji," the girl called after him; but Shoz-Dijiji, war chief of the Be-don-ko-he, war chief of all the Apaches, had gone.

The little pinto stallion was scrambling up the steep canyon side as Luis Mariel cut the bonds that held Wichita Billings. The girl ran to the window.

Far above she saw war pony and warrior silhouetted against the darkening sky; and then Shoz-Dijiji, last of the war chiefs, and Nejeunee, last of his wild friends, dropped below the crest and disappeared.

For several minutes the girl stood at the window gazing out into the gathering night; then she turned back into the room where Luis stood just within the doorway.

"The Apache Devil!" There was a shudder in Wichita's voice. Her eyes discovered Luis. "Oh," she said, as though she had forgotten his presence, "you are here?"

"Si, Señorita."

Again there was a long silence.

"The Apache Devil!" Wichita squared her shoulders and lifted her chin. "I do not care," she cried, defiantly.

"No, Señorita."

The girl looked fixedly at the Mexican youth for a moment as though his presence suggested a new thought that was formulating in her mind.

"What is your name?" she asked.

"Luis, Señorita," he replied; "Luis Mariel."

"You said that you would help me, Luis, if you could. Do you remember?"

"I remember, Señorita."

"You can, Luis. Ride after the—the Apache Devil and tell him that I want him to come back."

"Gladly, Señorita."

"Go," she urged. "Hurry! Go now!"

Luis glanced behind him through the doorway into the other room and then back at Wichita.

"And leave you alone, at night, with all these dead men?" he exclaimed. "Santa Maria, Señorita! No, I cannot do that."

"I am not afraid, Luis," she said.

"S-s-st!" exclaimed Luis in a hoarse whisper. "What is that?"

They both listened.

"Someone is coming," said the girl. "Perhaps—perhaps it is he."

"There is more than one," said the youth. "I hear them talking now." He stepped quickly into the adjoining room and, stooping, took a six-shooter from the floor where it lay beside one of the dead men. Returning, he handed it to Wichita Billings. "Perhaps these are more of Señor Cheetim's friends," he suggested.

Together they stood waiting. The sounds of approaching horses ceased, and all was quiet. Wichita knew that whoever it was that came had reached a point where the shack was visible for the first time and were doubtless reconnoitering. Finally a voice broke the silence.

"Chita!" it called aloud, ringing and echoing through the canyon.

"They are my friends," she said to Luis and ran through the outer room to the front doorway. "Here, 'Smooth'!" she called. "It is all right. I am in the shack."

Luis came and stood just behind her shoulder. It was not yet so dark but that features might be recognized at short distances. The two saw Kreff riding forward with Sam and Jake. Luis layed a hand on Wichita's arm. "They are Cheetim's friends," he said. "I know that first one well." He brushed by her, his revolver in his hand.

"No!" she cried, seizing his arm. "They are my own men. The first one is my foreman."

"Here's one of 'em, boys!" cried Kreff as he recognized Luis. "Here's the damned Greaser that brought me thet lyin' letter from 'Dirty.' Git out o' the way, Chita!" and leaping from his horse he ran forward.

"Stop!" cried Luis. His weapon was leveled at Kreff's stomach.

"This boy is all right!" exclaimed Wichita. "Put your guns away, all of you."

Slowly and with no great alacrity Kreff and Mariel returned their revolvers to their holsters. The other two men followed their example.

"What's happened here?" demanded Kreff. "Has anyone hurted you, Chita?"

"No, I'm all right," she replied. "I'll tell you all about it later. Get your horse, Luis, and take the message that I gave you. I'll be starting back for the ranch now. I'll be waiting there. Tell him that I shall be waiting there for him."

Kreff looked on, puzzled, as Wichita gave her instructions to Luis. He saw the youth mount and ride up the canyon side. Then he turned to the girl. "Where's he goin'?" he demanded. "Who you goin' to wait fer?"

"For Shoz-Dijiji," she replied. "He did not kill Dad—it was Cheetim. Come along, now; I want to go home."

Chapter Nineteen

THE LAST WAR TRAIL

THROUGH the descending dark an Apache rode along the war trail, following the tracks of an enemy. He saw that the man ahead of him had been urging his mount at perilous speed down the rocky gorge, but the Apache did not hurry. He was a young man. Before him stretched a lifetime in which to bring the quarry to bay. To follow recklessly would be to put himself at a disadvantage, to court disaster, defeat, death. Such was not the way of an Apache. Doggedly, stealthily he would stalk the foe. If it took a lifetime, if he must follow him across a world, what matter? In the end he would get him.

What was that, just ahead? In the trail, looming strange through the dusk, lay something that did not harmonize with the surroundings. At first he could not be quite certain what it was, but that it did not belong there was apparent to his trained senses.

Cautiously he approached. It was a horse lying in the trail. It was alive. It tried to rise as he came nearer, but it stumbled and fell again—and it groaned. He saw that it was saddled and bridled. He waited in concealment, listening. There was no other sound. Creeping nearer he saw that the horse could not rise because one of its legs was broken. It suffered. Shoz-Dijiji drew his butcher knife and cut its throat, putting it out of its misery. Cheetim had ridden too fast down this rocky gorge.

On foot now, leading Nejeunee, Shoz-Dijiji followed the faint spoor of the dismounted man. He found the place where it turned up the precipitous side of the gorge where no horse could go, and here Shoz-Dijiji abandoned Nejeunee and followed on alone.

All night he followed. At dawn he knew that he was close upon the man he sought. Small particles of earth were still crumbling back into the depression of a footprint where Cheetim had stepped but a few moments before.

Did Shoz-Dijiji hasten forward? No. On the contrary he followed more cautiously, more slowly than before, for he gave the enemy credit for doing precisely what Shoz-Dijiji would have done had their positions been reversed—except that Shoz-Dijiji would have done it hours earlier.

With infinite patience and care he crept up each slope and from the summit surveyed the terrain ahead before he proceeded. He knew that Cheetim was just ahead of him and that he would soon stop to rest, for the spoor told him that the man was almost exhausted. For a long time Shoz-Dijiji had guessed that the other knew he was being followed—before that he had only feared it. The end must be near.

Shoz-Dijiji crept slowly up a hillside. Just below the summit he stopped and took a red bandanna from his pouch. This he wrapped loosely about the stock of his rifle; and then, holding the piece by the muzzle, raised it slowly just above the hill top. Instantly there came the report of a rifle from beyond the hill; and Shoz-Dijiji, almost smiling, jerked the bandanna from sight.

Quickly he hastened to the right, keeping well below the line of vision of his adversary; and when he crept upward again it was behind a low bush, through the branches of which he could see without being seen.

A hundred yards away Cheetim lay behind a boulder upon another hill top. He was peering out from behind his shelter. Shoz-Dijiji took careful aim—not at the head of his enemy, which was in plain sight, but at his shoulder. Shoz-Dijiji had plans.

He pressed his trigger, and with the report Cheetim jumped convulsively and slumped forward. Slowly the Apache arose and keeping his man covered with his rifle walked toward him. He found the white man, just as he had expected, stunned by the shock of the wound but not dead.

Shoz-Dijiji removed Cheetim's weapons from his reach and sat down and waited. With the patience that is an Apache's he waited. Presently Cheetim opened his eyes and looked into the painted face of the Apache Devil. He shuddered and closed them again, but Shoz-Dijiji knew that the man was conscious.

The Indian spoke no word as he bent and seized Cheetim by the hair. Again the man opened his eyes. He saw the butcher knife in the hand of the Indian and screamed.

"Fer God's sake don't!" he cried. "I'll give you whiskey, money—anything you want ef you'll let me go."

Shoz-Dijiji did not answer him. The keen blade sank into the flesh of the white man. Cheetim screamed and struggled. There was a quick, deft, circular motion of Shoz-Dijiji's hand, and a bloody scalp-lock dangled from the fingers of the war chief. It was then that Cheetim fainted.

Shoz-Dijiji sat down and waited. Five, ten, fifteen minutes he waited before Cheetim gave signs of returning consciousness. Still Shoz-Dijiji waited. At last the white man was fully cognizant of his surroundings. He began to weep— tears of self-pity. Shoz-Dijiji arose and bent over him.

"What are you going to do?" shrieked his victim, but the Apache did not answer him—in words. Instead he took some buckskin thongs from his pouch and making a running noose in one end of each he slipped one upon each wrist and ankle of the prostrate man. Then with his butcher knife he cut some stakes from stout shrubs that grew about them. Returning to Cheetim he turned the man upon his back and, stretching each arm and leg to its full extent, out spread, he staked the screaming coward to the ground.

Rising, he stood looking down at Cheetim for a long minute. Then, in silence he turned and walked away, back along the trail he had come.

"Don't leave me!" screamed Cheetim. "Fer God's sake come back! Come back and kill me. Don't leave me here to die alone—like this!"

Shoz-Dijiji, war chief of the Be-don-ko-he, walked on in silence. Not once did he turn to look back in the direction of the first enemy he had ever tortured. Had he he would have seen a vulture circling high against the blue on stationary wings above the last victim of the Apache Devil.

Where he had left Nejeunee Shoz-Dijiji found Luis Mariel waiting for him.

"I knew that you would come back to your pony," said Luis.

"Why did you follow me?" demanded the Apache.

"The Señorita sent me after you."

"Why?"

"She wished me to say to you that you are to come back to her."

* * *

It was dark when Luis Mariel and Shoz-Dijiji rode into the ranch yard of the Crazy B. Wichita Billings was standing beneath the cottonwood trees that grew in front of the ranch house as they rode up to her and dismounted.

"Luis," she said, "take his horse and yours and turn them into the east pasture; then go to the cook house. Chung will give you supper."

Shoz-Dijiji said nothing. He watched Luis leading Nejeunee away. He waited. Wichita came close to him and laid her hands upon his breast as she had once before, long ago. Again came the terrible urge to take her in his arms, but this time he did not surrender to it.

"You sent for me?" he asked.

"To ask you to forgive me."

"For what?"

"For everything," she replied.

"There is nothing to forgive. You did not understand—that is all."

"I understand now."

"I am glad," he said simply. "Is that all?"

"No. Kreff has left. I do not know why. He wouldn't even stop for supper. Just got his stuff and his check and rode away. I need another foreman. Will you take the job?"

"Do you want me?"

"Yes."

"Then I will take it. Now I go to the bunk house."

"Wait."

"Is there something more?"

"Yes. You know there is. Oh, Shoz-Dijiji, are you a man or a stone?" she cried.

"I am an Apache, Señorita," he said. "Do not forget that. I am an Apache, and you are a white girl."

"I do not care. I love you!" She came very close to him again.

"Are you very sure, Chita?" he asked. "You must make no mistake this time."

"I am very sure, Shoz-Dijiji."

"We shall see," he said, "for we must both be sure. Shoz-Dijiji will be very happy if he finds that you can love him even though he is an Indian—then he will tell you something that you will be glad to know, but not now."

"There is something that you could tell me now that I should like to hear, Shoz-Dijiji," she whispered.

"What is that?"

"You have not told me that you love me."

The war chief took his mate into his arms and looked down into her tear-filled eyes.

"Shoz-Dijiji no sabe," he said, smiling. Then he bent and covered her lips with his.

In the east pasture a filly nickered, and a pinto stallion arched his neck and answered her.